THE ACCIDENTAL VISCOUNTESS

Just a Touch of Scandal Book I

CARO KINKEAD

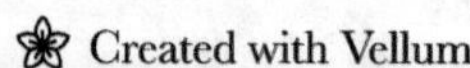 Created with Vellum

For Fred
Finally did it!

CHAPTER 1

"Mama! Lord Harrington's said the most dreadful things about the Duke of Stockwood, who I invited last evening. He'll be insulted if you asked them both!"

Dorothea Hindley shook her head at her cousin's petulant tone, pencil stuttering slightly along the surface of her notebook. No surprise Alyssa would throw a temper fit before the end of Lady Dilmore's assembly. Did she have to do it as Lady Wilmont spoke with one of the biggest gossips in the Ton?

"Excuse me a moment, sir." The good lady kept her smile fixed as she pulled her daughter away. A jerk of her head and Dorothea gladly followed. She had no desire to remain near Lord Manville or his predatory gaze any longer than necessary.

"You will be quiet," came the hissed command before they were out of earshot. "He is offering suggestions on guests I might find useful, so you are not to interrupt."

"But His Grace—"

"Is invited to my table when I say, not you. Your father told you he'll refuse a request for your hand from the duke, so you might as well stop making moon eyes at him." A glance at Dorothea. "Did you add Lord Harrington's name to the list?"

"Yes, Aunt Honoria, along with the others."

"If he offers up any more names, make certain you write them down." Turning her attention back to Alyssa, Lady Wilmont asked, "Are you ready to behave yourself?"

The response was a sullen expression and pouty lip. "Because if you aren't, I have no issues with going home."

"You wouldn't." Alyssa's voice sounded half defiant, half horrified.

"Dorothea, where is my husband?"

"In the card room, but I believe he's been caught by Lord Newlyn. They're likely discussing the king's illness." An easy guess. The topic dominated political conversation these days. "I can find him if you wish."

She ignored Alyssa's angry glare, focused on her aunt. "Well?" Lady Wilmont tapped her fan against her palm impatiently. "Will you behave yourself? The season hasn't truly begun -- do you want to test me so early?"

For a moment, Alyssa stared defiantly at her mother, then lowered her head. "I'll behave," she said in a resentful whisper.

Which most likely meant she'd stop interrupting for the next five minutes. Dorothea suspected Alyssa would act out in other ways. Two weeks in London showed her behavior here would be no different than in Buxdale. Lady Wilmont's frown hinted she believed the same, but accepted the declaration with a stern nod, then returned to where Lord Manville stood. "We were speaking of gentlemen who might add interest to my table."

Manville began his suggestions again. Given his sly smile, he had only pretended not to listen.

Certain there'd be more items to list, Dorothea tried to move closer to Lady Wilmont, but found herself cut off by Alyssa. "Don't step on my gown," she snapped

Any further complaint was stifled by her mother's warning glare. Dorothea used the moment to position herself on her aunt's opposite side. Manville noted the movement with a smile suggesting another juicy tidbit acquired for the gossip mill. More talk of dinner guests who might be the best fit, which allowed her to focus on her notes.

At last, Lady Wilmont turned to ask, "Did you catch everything?"

"I believe so." Dorothea held out the notebook for inspection. As she did, Alyssa also moved closer. Out the corner of her eye, she caught the movement of Alyssa's hand, narrowly avoiding being pinched by a quick sidestep. Another move which didn't go unnoticed by Manville, another piece of gossip for him. He had to be enjoying this, a young lady positioning herself as a diamond of the first water, only to behave as a petulant schoolgirl.

Lady Wilmont didn't notice—or chose not to acknowledge—the by-play as she handed the notebook back. "Well done," she said. "We'll make plans when we return home."

"You're fortunate in such a helpful companion as Miss Hindley," Manville commented.

"Dorothea is my ward, not a paid companion. But, yes, I am blessed in her. When the season is done …"

"Lord Manville! I thought you had abandoned me, you naughty boy!"

Lady Knowle's greeting caused them to turn as the woman approached Manville to give him a kiss on each cheek. Lady Wilmont received the same, with Alyssa given a nod. Dorothea was ignored completely, which didn't surprise her one bit. Then she recognized the others with Lady Knowle.

By now, she knew the Dowager Viscountess Abernathy, the bane of Lady Wilmont's existence, by sight, as well as her children, the current Viscount Abernathy and Miss Cecilia Drayton. For the last two weeks, the woman had kept a careful, wary distance. That distance had disappeared, Lady Knowle having steered Lady Abernathy close enough where etiquette required two women at least nod to one another.

Lady Abernathy acknowledged Manville's bow, but when Lady Wilmont made a polite semi-curtsey, she gave no acknowledgement save a touch to Lady Knowle's arm. "We should continue on. The Duke of Stockwood is here, who will, of course, want to claim Cecilia for a dance."

It was a cut, no other way to describe the action. Given their expressions, exactly what Manville and Lady Knowle hoped for. "Why does she think His Grace would be interested in someone like her?" Alyssa asked, focused on the only item important to her.

"Quiet." The word was deadly in its intensity. Even more worrying was the fury on Lady Wilmont's face as Lady Abernathy turned away. "The years haven't improved your manners," she spat out. "Or is your eyesight is failing with age?"

Wincing, Dorothea hoped Lady Abernathy wouldn't rise to the bait, but she stopped. Immediately, her children began to whisper furiously to her, likely to the same end Dorothea desire. *Walk on. Please walk on.*

Hope failed as Lady Abernathy turned backed slowly, cool, icy elegance. "My eyesight is fine, but I prefer to concentrate on important things."

Not an apology, and now Lord Abernathy winced. Dorothea couldn't resist throwing him a sympathetic glance. To her surprise, he acknowledged her with a look of shared suffering.

"I'm surprised at what you considered 'important'," Lady Wilmont said, pulling Dorothea's attention back to her. "Courtesy never seemed high on the list."

"As decorum was never one of your virtues."

"Mother." Lord Abernathy spoke the word firmly. Miss Drayton leaned in as well, though her words didn't carry.

Lady Wilmont tried to come up with a suitably witty riposte but Lady Abernathy was quicker. "Now you have been seen, so I hope this will satisfy your long-held desire for recognition."

Lady Wilmont sputtered, whatever withering reply she wanted to make not quite completing the journey from brain to mouth. Lady Abernathy gave off a smug air, an attitude clearly not shared by her children.

Lady Knowle threw more fuel on the fire by saying, "We should continue on. You did say you were certain the Duke of Stockwood wanted to dance with Miss Cecilia. Do you think perhaps he'll ask for more than two sets?"

Which meant some folk anticipated a proposal, including Lady Abernathy, given her smug expression. "Perhaps. We are expecting a wedding in the spring, after all."

Miss Drayton rolled her eyes, a hint she might not be as enamored of the idea as her mother. The words were enough to make Alyssa stir again. Dorothea tried to catch her as she stepped forward, but Alyssa jerked her arm away. "Mama, are you going to let her——"

"Enough." Lady Wilmont didn't move from where she faced Lady Wilmont.

"But, the Duke of Stockwood——"

"I said quiet."

This time, Lady Wilmont did turn, endowing the words with enough force both Dorothea and Alyssa stepped back.

"A pity the children are so unruly," Lady Abernathy said. "Perhaps they are not yet ready for London."

Lady Wilmont turned, face warning she was ready to commit mayhem. Before she could make new threats, Miss Drayton gave a weary sigh, "Can't we just be done with this, Mother? Why are you wasting your time on her?"

The horrified look on Miss Drayton's face showed she had not meant the comment to be said aloud. Worse, while two ladies near in age and rank might snipe at one another, for an unmarried girl to speak so about her elder was outside the pale.

For just a moment, Lady's Abernathy's cool exterior cracked, displaying anger mixed with embarrassment, before quickly hustling her daughter away. Lord Abernathy opened his mouth as if to say something, then bowed to Lady Wilmont before hurrying after his mother.

"I was wrong," Lady Wilmont said. "Her manners have changed. They're worse."

Manville and Lady Knowle offered sympathetic noises, then made their excuses, departing to spread news of what they'd witnessed.

When they departed, Lady Wilmont turned to Dorothea. "I shouldn't have lost my temper, but what's done is done."

"We do have suggestions for guests," Dorothea said.

"Most of which I won't be using, especially Lord Harrington. Not if I'm putting the Duke of Stockwood back on the guest list."

"Mama!" Alyssa preened. Why not? Nothing else had impacted her.

"This doesn't mean I've changed my mind about him as a suitor," Lady Wilmont sniffed. "But if That Woman is pursuing him for her daughter, why should I let her have an easy time?"

She fixed Alyssa with a stern gaze. "We will have a discussion about your behavior later. You gave the most appalling display."

Silently, Dorothea agreed, as she updated her notes. She was afraid there would be more as the season stretched on.

❦

"That was the most appalling display," Martin Drayton, Fourth Viscount Abernathy said when he caught up with his mother and sister.

They were almost to the ballroom door, Lady Abernathy leading Cecilia toward the retiring room. "I agree," she said. "That horrid woman nearly drove poor Cecilia to tears."

"Not her, Mother," Cecilia said. "Martin and I begged you to avoid Lady Wilmont, or at least be distantly civil. But, no. You had to engage on her level."

"So, I should let such an insult pass?"

"You're the one who gave insult first," Martin said. "If you'd simply nodded in acknowledgement, then continued on, there'd be no insult to worry about."

Lady Abernathy flicked open her fan, fluttering it briskly. "While she martyred herself to Lord Manville how I was rude? He'd enjoy such a tidbit."

Martin wished he was at his club, in the country, at a session of Parliament or on the Continent facing down a brigade of Napoleon's soldiers single-handedly. Anywhere but here. "Which you handed him. I don't understand why you care what the old meddler thinks. He and Lady Knowle live for gossip. I swear if they don't find a scandal, they'll invent one."

"Martin!" Lady Abernathy cast a furtive glance about them. "People might hear you," she said in a near whisper. "Cecilia's behavior was bad enough, but for you to speak so about a lady—"

Cecilia laughed derisively, which turned Lady Abernathy's disapproving glare from Martin to her. "Did you stop to consider what the Duke of Stockwood will think of this incident?"

"His Grace would have to actually think first. You want the match, Mother. Not me."

Not the most politic of answers, with their mother as tense as Cecilia appeared to be. "Go inside," Lady Abernathy ordered, indicating the ladies' retiring room. "Splash some water on your face, then try to compose yourself. I'll be in directly."

For a moment, Martin thought his sister might rebel, but with jaw firmly set, she marched away as instructed. Turning to Lady Abernathy, he said, "The Duke of Stockwood is a charming idiot who's unlikely to be affected by this one way or another. He finds Cecilia pleasant enough, but I seriously doubt he wants to marry her or anyone else. I wouldn't agree to a betrothal, either. Not unless Cecilia changed her opinion for some insane reason."

"Cecilia's son would be a duke. His Grace's family is an old and honorable one."

"His Grace's ancestress formed a liaison with Charles II and got her son a title for her pains. Cecilia can do better. Now, if you'll excuse me, I need to speak with some gentlemen about the upcoming sitting in Parliament."

He escaped before his mother could object. Yes, he did want to speak with some gentlemen regarding the bill, but he also didn't want to continue the argument any further tonight.

They weren't supposed to be here. The plan had been for the king to sign a proclamation proroguing Parliament until February. But George III lay mad in Windsor, unable to set his signature to anything. Which meant whispers had begun a regency bill would be needed, which wouldn't necessarily suit the prime minister's plans.

So, the pride of the English aristocracy gathered in London three months early, waiting, in desperate need of entertainment.

He just didn't want the entertainment to be his family.

Martin hadn't moved far into the ballroom before he found the gentlemen he sought. "Is everything well with Cecilia?" Sir Roger Phipps asked. "I saw the three of you hurrying out."

"We had an encounter with Lady Wilmont."

Lord Blair MacDonald winced. "I take it the feathers flew."

"Despite my urging, Mother insisted on engaging in the worst possible way. Sadly, Cecilia also said exactly what she was thinking." At Roger's groan, Martin added, "I think she's mostly annoyed at herself. And at Mother, who started worrying what the Duke of Stockwood would think when he heard."

"I think he'll choose discretion," Roger said. "He likes your sister, but he's a bit besotted with Miss Wilmont at this point."

Blair laughed. "I'll lay five pounds he's out of love with her within the month."

"Another five he lasts to the new year," Roger countered.

"As fascinating as this is," Martin said, "we've more important things to worry about. The Prime Minister will ask for another adjournment tomorrow."

Blair snorted. "Of course they will. Perceval's in no hurry to acknowledge a crisis. He worries the Prince of Wales will remove the Tories in the Cabinet, replacing them with Whigs at his first opportunity." He inspected his fingernails. "Care to wager they'll be singing praises about an 'improved' condition?"

Martin gave him a flat stare. "I don't take fool bets. Of course they will."

"I'm told there's some improvement. He's apparently accepted Princess Amelia is dead instead of insisting she's away."

Martin and Blair turned to Roger, who shrugged. "He's out of the straitjacket, at least."

"How do you know this?" asked Martin

"Friends among the Tories."

"Don't let Mother hear you. She'll forbid you the house, then write a mournful letter to your mother sharing her grief."

Roger rolled his eyes, acknowledging he knew Martin's words were a joke. At least partially. "But if the King is improving, the Prime Minister will get leverage for another two weeks."

"If both houses take him at his word," Blair said. "Some members won't." He turned his head toward Martin. "You know what His Highness wants."

"I do, but I doubt he's going to get it. He's still at Windsor?"

Blair nodded. "Mourning his sister, but setting himself up as the exemplary son. Whether he wishes to or no, Perceval must move soon. If Napoleon senses weakness, he may grow even more ambitious, especially if the child his wife carries is a boy."

"So, we need to ensure if he obtains an adjournment for another two weeks, it is the last." Martin sighed. "I'll to talk to our friends. If Everly was here, we could count on his voice, but given the fool stunt his son pulled in Horse Guards …"

Roger nodded. "Small wonder he decided to take the boy home. There are a few folks I can speak with. Not all the Tories agree we should wait."

"I'm willing to wager the vote will give the Prime Minister his adjournment," Blair said, "but we can try to make sure this is the last one."

The orchestra struck a chord, couples began to make their way onto the floor. The crowd was still respectable despite official mourning for Princess Amelia being in effect. "Then we should do it," Martin said. "Be prepared for a long evening on Wednesday."

They separated, each heading their own way. Roger speaking with his Tory friends would be useful, but Lady Abernathy wouldn't take kindly to learn he was consorting with "the enemy."

No, the Tories were simply annoying. Lady Wilmont was the enemy, a threat on par with Bonaparte as far as his mother was concerned.

CHAPTER 2

Purposefully moving about the edge of the room, Martin fixed his first target in his sight, only for Lady Knowle to bear down on him like a French frigate. "My dear Lord Abernathy," she gushed. "How is your poor sister? Hopefully, she didn't find this incident too upsetting."

The old cat was hoping for some fury she could report on. She and Manville worked in concert, trafficking in scandal. If Lady Knowle was a man, someone would have called her out some time ago. But, Martin reflected, no one had called out Manville to his knowledge, so perhaps not.

He quelled the urge to tell her to go to hell, struggling to keep a smile on his face. "My sister is well, my lady, but thank you for your concern."

The polite bow and mild words were clearly not what Lady Knowle wished. She leaned in, lowering her voice. "Are you certain? She is not on the floor while the Duke of Stockwood seeks partners."

Across the ballroom, Martin spied Stockwood surrounded by ladies, a grin plastered on his pleasant, if silly, face. Aware he was being watched for his reaction, Martin casually flicked an imaginary piece of lint from his sleeve. "He told me he intends to escort Cecilia into supper this evening," he said in a bored tone. "He finds her company most enjoyable. Now, if you'll excuse me, there is a lady I must speak to before all her dances are taken."

He bowed then made his escape. Lady Knowle's eyes were still on him; he could feel them boring into the back of his head. To allay her suspicions, he stopped before a young lady who stood on the edge of the floor to beg a dance for later. Miss Hickinbotham seemed a bit surprised as Martin had never spoken to her before, but, with a beam of approval from her mama, she accepted.

Looking back, he found Lady Knowle had disappeared into the crowd, likely in search of new prey or to spread the story further. Taking a deep breath, he made his way to Stockwood, currently surrounded by a muslin army.

The duke appeared almost grateful for the sudden arrival of a male presence. "What ho, Abernathy? Doing some shopping on the mart?"

The young ladies giggled. Martin wished them all to perdition. "A word, Your Grace, if you can spare one."

"Plenty of words to spare. The ladies here have been listening to them for the last ten minutes."

"I'm afraid these are not words for ladies. I would not bother you, but—"

He trailed off solemnly, hoping his tone would impress Stockwood. The man just stared at him. Martin lifted his eyebrows, jerking his head to one side in hopes the duke would take the hint about private conversation.

Understanding dawned visibly across Stockwood's face. "My apologies, ladies. I'm afraid Lord Abernathy has some business we must discuss." He gave a broad conspiratorial wink. "Affairs of state and all that."

"So why all the secrecy?" the duke asked once they were away from the ladies. "Bonaparte descending on London as we speak?"

"Not yet. I need a favor. Have you asked anyone for the supper dance yet?"

"Haven't had a chance. Didn't think it'd be polite with all the ladies about to ask one without asking the others."

Thank heaven for simple politeness. "Would you consider asking my sister?"

Stockwood's face lit up. "Miss Cecilia? Delighted. She's always good for some conversation." He leaned in conspiratorially. "Your sister is about the only girl in London who isn't trying to hook me into matrimony. Puts one off one's feed for some girl to make moon eyes at you while you're trying to eat. I take Miss Cecilia into supper, we can enjoy a jolly time without all the matchmaking folderol."

So much for his mother's grand plans. "Thank you, Your Grace."

"Not at all, not all. Here is the fair Cecilia now."

Cecilia had indeed returned, Lady Abernathy immediately behind her. She didn't appear thrilled when Stockwood made a beeline for her, but whatever nonsense he uttered coaxed a slight smile. A nod of acceptance and Lady Abernathy sighed in relief just behind her. If Martin was lucky, his mother would realize allowing this old feud to flare again wouldn't help her plans, even if she thought she was in the right. It certainly didn't help him.

With his sister settled, Martin turned his attention once more to his task, only to find his way blocked by Lord Manville. "Stockwood found your sister. I was under the impression he'd already asked her for the supper dance."

"Where did you get such an impression, sir?" Martin did not bother to keep the frost from his tone,

Manville smiled, a hint of malice hovering about his lips. "A little bird, perhaps, who received the information from an excellent source. Given all this attention, has the Duke of Stockwood come up to scratch yet? If he hasn't, many women won't stand idly by. It'd be distressing if Miss Drayton ends yet another season with no offer in sight."

Meaning Lady Wilmont and her daughter. The words were less subtle than Manville's usual work, which meant he was enjoying himself immensely. "I'm an old-fashioned man, Lord Manville. I prefer my sister's suitors come to me regarding an offer of marriage before they speak to her. You have no idea what gentlemen might have been turned away. London abounds in rogues, after all. Now, if you'll excuse me."

He didn't wait for a response but bowed curtly before walking away. There had to be better ways to spend an evening than being polite to a herd of jackals intent on tearing the flesh of helpless victims.

Only one way to deal with this situation, so he set his feet on a course toward Lady Wilmont.

Easy enough for Martin to find Lady Wilmont's party, as they'd taken up position in a prominent, almost showy spot. The Wilmont daughter was on the floor with a partner, leaving Lady Wilmont to converse with the other young lady in the party. She diligently made notes in the book she carried, occasionally offering her own comments.

Martin paused for a moment. It would be better if Lord Wilmont were present to exert some influence over his wife. But, as much as he might wish otherwise, he needed to deal with Lady Wilmont, for better or worse. A deep breath, then he made his approach.

"Dorothea, I fear I must retire for a moment. Stay here in case Alyssa returns."

Moving quicker than expected, Lady Wilmont departed. Martin stopped, uncertain whether it was a cut. She'd seen his approach—he wagered those eyes missed little—but moved before he drew near enough she must acknowledge his presence. To her credit, Lady Wilmont executed the maneuver far more skillfully than his mother's attempt.

"You appear puzzled, sir."

Dorothea watched him with an amused expression. Here was an opportunity to speak to at least one of the Wilmont clan. "Have I been insulted or no?"

She chuckled. "If you must ask, there is your answer."

Her expression was sympathetic, as if she understood his quandary. That sympathy caused him to push on to his purpose. "I wish to offer apologies for my sister's behavior."

"Which you are not responsible for."

"Also to ask if there is anything I might do to ease this feud," he finished, attempting to ignore her interruption.

"Is Lady Abernathy willing to let the feud drop?"

"No," he admitted with some reluctance.

A regretful smile crossed full lips. "Then I see little hope my aunt will be willing to make any effort. You do realize this began before either of us were born."

Her words did not sound encouraging, but he had to acknowledge the truth of them. "Something to do with their season. Ridiculous some triviality should provoke such acid response years later."

A frown crossed her face, her eyes dropping as she plucked at the cover of her notebook. "This may seem ridiculous to you, but a season is one of the few times a woman has the chance at some control over her destiny. She can encourage or discourage gentlemen, try to exert influence over who will be her husband. If either Lady Wilmont or Lady Abernathy felt those chances interfered with by the other, they might well nurture such a grudge across the years."

A perspective he'd not considered. Still, given his parents had enjoyed a happy marriage, might his mother be the one to sin against her rival?

"Ballrooms are battlefields, my lord."

The humor was back in her voice, her gaze meeting his without the missish demureness most unmarried ladies affected. Her attention, though, wavered every so often, watching something else in the room. Most likely keeping an eye out for Lady Wilmont. Given her plainer dress, Martin wagered she was a poor relation who earned her keep by doing small tasks and being useful. Which meant she lived on the Wilmonts' charity, needing their continued good will if she wished to retain her situation.

"My lord, I hope your sister does not feel too badly about her outburst. I fear Lady Wilmont did her best to provoke it."

Sometimes poor relations proved surprising. "I did not suggest Lady Wilmont did anything wrong."

"Because you are too much of a gentleman to do so. I was present, remember? I'm afraid both parties were at fault." Dorothea leaned forward. "I briefly considered fainting to end the scene."

Martin stifled a laugh. "Why did you not try this heroic measure?"

"Your sister spoke before I had fully steeled my resolve. I wish I had, though. My actions would be of less interest to certain parties than hers."

She wrinkled her nose and Martin found himself again intrigued. This was no pale-faced companion content for what crumbs might fall. Dorothea had both wit and intelligence. It was surprising no gentlemen sought her company, even if only for the amusement of her conversation.

The music ended, sparking a general exodus from the dance floor. Which meant Miss Wilmont would be returning. Which meant Lady Wilmont would be forced to rejoin Dorothea to supervise her daughter's next choice of partner.

Dorothea took a half-step toward him, closer than truly proper. "I urge you not to try my aunt tonight, sir," she said, her voice quiet enough the words would not carry beyond them two. "She is vexed from the encounter with Lady Abernathy, among other things. An attempt to force conversation would not go well."

A meaningful glance was cast to one side. Turning his head slightly, Martin found Lady Wilmont hovering. She looked away before he could meet her eyes, but not before he caught the unhappy expression on her face. "She's not pleased we're speaking."

"Why I ask you to go. Please. There is much she will allow me, but I fear we are stretching her patience. We are not chaperoned, and this conversation has gone on longer than is proper."

He accepted she spoke the truth. Any attempt to speak with Lady Wilmont would only fan the flames higher, as well as potentially offer consequences for Dorothea. "I will take my leave. I hope we meet again under better terms.

The moment he was safely out of range, Lady Wilmont returned to Dorothea as Miss Wilmont arrived with her partner. A quick glance, and Dorothea stepped back, making room for Miss Wilmont's suitors.

He sought out more gentlemen whose vote might make a difference in Wednesday's session. But he also found himself glancing back to where Dorothea stood. She continued to make notes, always on the fringe of conversation. Lady Wilmont did not appear angry, but one never knew what happened behind closed doors, nor was he likely to learn.

Across the room, Stockwood hung about Cecilia, perhaps seeking a shield from other ladies. Roger was beside her as well, leaning in to say something. Cecilia laughed in response, her face much more relaxed now. Despite the incident earlier, all seemed right with the world.

He couldn't shake the nagging feeling it was going to be a long season indeed.

It's going to be a long season. The thought floated through Dorothea's brain as the writing in her notebook blurred before her eyes while she struggled to remember which gentleman Lady Wilmont was asking about.

The lamps in the study had been burning since their return from Lady Dilmore's but there'd be no need for them soon. The gray light of dawn peeked through the slight gap in the curtains, signaling the servants would soon be up to start their day.

With effort, she forced herself to focus on the various sheets of paper spread across the desk, each bearing the date of a planned dinner. "William Hartsfield is considered something of a leader among the Tories with reformist leanings. He wields more than a little influence. While he does not oppose the idea of a regency, he wants considerable restrictions placed on the Prince of Wales if a bill is presented."

A stifled yawn before she continued. "Mrs. Hartsfield is pleasant, not inclined to gossip. She seems to want to think kind things about everyone."

"She'll be an excellent partner for the Duke of Stockwood." Lady Wilmont made a note on one of the sheets. "We can make certain they sit at the opposite end of the table from Mr. Hartsfield."

Dorothea frowned -- then yawned again. "That will put the duke some distance from Alyssa. She won't be happy."

"I told you I've no intention of encouraging her. She's dazzled by the idea of a duchess' coronet, but would quickly grow bored. You know how dangerous things can be when Alyssa is bored." Lady Wilmont shook her head. "No. Alyssa needs a gentleman who will handle her with a firm hand. Firmer than her father or I managed."

A shadow passed over Lady Wilmont's face for a moment, then her jaw tightened. "As long as we invite no one who will openly offend His Grace, we'll make him a guest at the table." She made another note. "It will bother Lady Abernathy. Also, continued exposure to His Grace might do more to direct Alyssa's attentions elsewhere better than any objections I might manage."

Dorothea chuckled, which turned into another yawn.

"Enough for now," Lady Wilmont said. "We can finish tomorrow." She glanced at the window then yawned herself. "Or at least after we've had some sleep. Oh, these hours were easier when I was younger."

"We're used to country hours," Dorothea said, gathering the sheets together to one side before she rose, notebook in hand. "I still find myself waking early, no matter what time we go to bed."

"And have sense enough to go back to sleep, I hope." Lady Wilmont began to rise as well, only to sit again. "One more thing. Lord Abernathy."

With a sigh, Dorothea returned to her chair. "As I told you, he wanted to apologize for his sister's behavior. I said I would convey the sentiments."

"You spoke much longer than such a conversation required."

Of course she noticed. "Lord Abernathy is … unhappy with the situation. He asked if you might be willing to end the feud with Lady Abernathy."

"He sought to gain information to himself by exposing you to gossip by conversing without a chaperone present." A censorious sniff. "Why should I expect better from him or his family?"

Dorothea blinked in surprise. "He did not behave in an untoward manner."

"Given how many were about, not surprising. The dance floor might prove a different matter. A gentleman and a young lady are away from her protectors. All manner of suggestions might be made.

But he took advantage of the situation without a thought to how his actions might reflect on you."

As Dorothea began to stutter a response, Lady Wilmont held up her hand. "The fault is partially mine, as I left you standing alone longer than proper. The wiser move would have been to take you with me. I am used to you being able to navigate the waters of our village. London is a different place. I've been so focused on ensuring Alyssa is launched properly, I fear I let my duties to you slip."

The insinuation Dorothea didn't realize when she was being propositioned pricked at her pride, perhaps more than it should. "I have no illusions about any social niceties Lord Abernathy offered. His station is so far removed from mine as to make the merest thought otherwise foolish."

Lady Wilmont leaned forward, reaching out her hand to squeeze Dorothea's. "I am only attempting to do my best for you. I wouldn't want malicious gossip making its way back to Mr. Shipley, giving him pause. Or, worse, make him think you need to be redeemed."

Dorothea could easily picture the Reverend Mr. Shipley, vicar of St. Michael's, Buxdale, thinking exactly that. Hardly her idea of a grand future, but she was a realist. Her choices were limited. She was lucky to have a choice at all, given her circumstances.

Lady Wilmont squeezed her hand again. "I also don't want you caught in a position where you might be forced to seek shelter in the future with Alyssa and whomever she marries."

The words sent a child down Dorothea's spine. Mr. Shipley was definitely preferable to being "poor Cousin Dorothea," little better than an unpaid servant subject to Alyssa's whims to earn her keep. "I will keep your words in mind."

Alone in her room, Dorothea swiftly crawled under the covers. The evening's flirtation with Lord Abernathy had been a pleasant diversion, nothing more. Best not to repeat, either, so she would keep her distance as best she could.

That her mind lingered on piercing blue eyes and a diverting smile as she drifted off did not help.

CHAPTER 3

"And so, with the division showing three hundred-forty-three in favor of the motion and fifty-eight opposed, this Honorable House is adjourned until the Twenty-Ninth of November," the Speaker intoned. "God save the King."

"God save the King," the Commons chamber echoed back before they began to move from their places. In the visitor gallery, Martin sighed before moving himself. Things had played out exactly as they'd expected, even if some members were beginning to question the wisdom of continued adjournments. The Prince of Wales might want a Regency Bill presented but more members needed to question the wisdom of continued adjournments before such a prospect could be raised.

The crowd was thick in the Commons lobby, but Blair's height made him easy to spot. "So, Perceval got his way," Blair said as Martin approached.

"Did we doubt it?" Roger asked, standing next to Blair. "The news of some semblance of recovery gave credence to the government's assertion His Majesty would soon be recovered."

"But even the most optimistic can hardly argue he'll be well enough to return to his duties in the space of two weeks."

"He doesn't have to be," Blair countered. "He only needs be recovered enough to give his consent to prorogue Parliament. He signs, the Chancellor attaches the seal, we all go home until February as originally planned." He glanced at Martin. "I thought you'd be happy. Would certainly put a temporary truce to the fight Lady Abernathy's having."

Martin resisted the urge to grind his teeth. "I've had enough jokes already, thank you. Too many in Lords remember the feud in painful detail."

"You learned what started this all?"

"Let me clarify. They remember what each did to the other, but no one remembers—or is willing to tell—what set things off." Martin turned to Blair. "Newlyn wants us to meet at the Cheshire Cheese tomorrow, determine next steps. Depending on whether or not the news from Windsor stays the same, we may be able to use those questions to convince others we can't keep adjourning."

Blair nodded. "I'll speak with some folks tonight, test the waters, then report tomorrow."

When Blair was gone, Roger asked, "Are you away home?"

"Not quite. If I delay at least an hour, Mother and Cecilia will leave for a musical evening at Lady Thirsk's. If I'm not there, I can avoid going with them."

Roger fell in step beside Martin. "I can think of quite a few things I'd rather sit through than a musical evening with Lady Thirsk. Is it me, or are the entertainments more wearisome this season?"

"We're not in the season, remember? Everyone assumed the King would prorogue Parliament until February, plus we're supposed to be in some kind of mourning for Princess Amelia, poor girl. So entertainments are more intimate or thrown together, no proper balls."

"But if more people show up than were officially invited to, say, Lady Dilmore's, it simply happened." Roger chuckled. "Despite sufficient food and the floor prepped for a decent-size crowd. God, I love society."

Martin's response was rude enough to set Roger laughing again as they headed for where the carriages would be waiting. "Speaking of

Lady Dilmore," Roger said, "how is Cecilia doing? Recovered from the incident?"

"Cecilia wants to forget the whole thing. Unfortunately, Mother wants to remember until she wrings a victory from the situation. Said victory being Stockwood asking for Cecilia's hand. Spot of supper? Or do you have somewhere to be."

Roger thought for a moment. "Supper sounds like an excellent idea. If your mother hears you dined instead of coming home, you can say we were discussing the King's illness."

Once they were in Martin's carriage, heading towards Brook's, Martin said, "I'm surprised you didn't come around to check on Cecilia yourself."

"Lady Abernathy would rather your sister's time not be taken up with old friends who might distract her from new suitors."

Martin sighed. "I swear, Mother's completely lost her reason. She's become fixated on this idea of Cecilia marrying the Duke of Stockwood, which is not going to happen. Not unless she's lost her mind and fallen for the git."

"I wouldn't worry too much," Roger replied in an offhanded way.

"Then there's the ridiculousness of this feud from over a quarter of a century ago flaring to life with all the fury of a military campaign. She and Lady Wilmont act like children squabbling over a toy. Why am I not surprised Lady Knowle couldn't wait to tell her Lady Wilmont had arrived in town?"

"Because you know she's a meddlesome busybody who lives to make other folk miserable?"

"Yet she is allowed to be a constant visitor in our home." Martin shook his head. "I don't understand."

He fell into silence for the rest of the short journey. As he'd told Dorothea, there must to be a way to stop this feud. All he needed was to find the key.

"I want to ask you something," Roger said as they alighted at Brook's. "But let's find a table first."

Roger's tone hinted at a secret he needed to impart. Curious, Martin began to ask what weighed on his mind, but as they crossed the dining room, a voice hailed them. "Abernathy! Phipps! Come have a drink with us!"

Martin turned to Roger. "We need Moulton on our side," Roger said reluctantly.

Which meant conversation must wait. "You seem in a jolly mood, Moulton," Martin said as they approached.

"Had a bit of luck." Moulton's words were slurred. "Thought I'd share."

He indicated those with him with a sloppy wave of his hand. "Looks as if you've been enjoying it," Roger commented.

"So I have. But I'm glad you're here, Abernathy, because only right I share with you."

"Moulton," another, more sober voice said warningly.

"See, I won twenty pounds on a bet from White's." Moulton continued on, oblivious.

Martin went still, certain what the bet concerned. "We should leave you to your enjoyment." Best to extract himself before anything was said.

"But I won because of you. Rather, if Lady Abernathy hadn't been the first to insult --"

Another gentleman reached out to pull Moulton back, handing him off to their fellows. "Get him away," he hissed. "Else he'll be called out for being a drunken fool."

The man turned to Martin. "I hope you can forgive what was spoken when deep in his cups. I don't think any insult was intended."

Intended or no, by the rules of honor, Martin was within his rights to demand satisfaction. Not that any was to be gained from beating a fool like Moulton. "As long as I don't hear more of him bragging about how he won the bet. Better he not cross my path again when he's in this state."

The gentleman bowed and hurried away. "You could ask him to face you in a friendly bout of foils," Roger pointed out. "He's a rotten swordsman, so it'd be humiliating at however many points you set."

"So stir more gossip, and annoy him when we need him in the debate? No, his friends will be happy enough they escaped, he'll make certain the matter's not discussed. The story will die. Much preferable."

"You knew there was a bet on the books at White's?"

"As to who would insult whom first?" Martin nodded. "I imagine more are being entered. I can't do anything about fools wanting to waste their money -- but I can try to do something about stopping this damn thing before it gets any worse. The only question is how."

We're going to be on the tongue of every gossip in London. The words seemed to burn into Dorothea's brain as she sat on one of the chairs in Lady Burkle's reception room, her eyes firmly fixed on Alyssa. Somehow, her cousin had managed to arrange things so Dorothea served as an unwilling buffer between her and Lady Wilmont. Which meant the last ten minutes had been spent listening for anything Lady Wilmont might want noted on one side, while watching Alyssa flirt with Viscount Tilney on the other.

Flirting was what Alyssa was supposed to do. But not with gentlemen who had little money and a reputation many deemed less than savory.

"But why would you want to find other entertainments at a ball?" Alyssa asked Tilney, sounding sweetly innocent. Too sweet, too innocent.

"There is always … promenading," Tilney gave the word weight. "Not after a dance, but during. Conversing while dancing, a couple can exchange only brief snatches before the figure demands they part."

He leaned in, a bit closer than proper. "If one promenades during a dance, one has a chance for more … private … conversation."

Alyssa giggled in response, inviting him to lean in closer.

Turning to her other side, Dorothea cleared her throat to attract Lady Wilmont's attention. She didn't need to converse, only for Lady Wilmont to glance in her direction.

Lady Wilmont didn't turn from her conversation, nor showed any sign she heard Dorothea when she cleared her throat a second time. "My lady."

A slight movement of her head. "In a moment, Dorothea. I'm speaking with Lady Dorrit."

Frustrated, Dorothea sat back. Lady Dorrit was busy discussing her charitable efforts back home. Laudable, yes, but not anything Lady Wilmont would find enthralling. Sitting back in her chair, she pondered her next step, keenly aware Tilney was inducing Alyssa to "promenade" with him at the next gathering. Worse, he hinted they might find other delights in their time together.

Why wouldn't Lady Wilmont turn around? Lady Dorrit was not on their lists as necessary for invitations or other connections. What was so fascinating?

With a sigh, she let her gaze travel over the other guests assembled for Lady Burkle's salon. The guests were an eclectic mix of society and intellectuals. Dorothea would have enjoyed speaking with some of the others, or, at least, listening to their conversations. Snatches floated across the room, discussion of the king's illness dominating, along with what the government should be doing to deal with this potential crisis. Some complained the crisis was a personal inconvenience, with so many in London three months earlier than they'd planned.

Then she caught sight of Martin, leaning against the wall almost directly opposite, in conversation with another gentleman. Upon arrival, he had acknowledged the company generally, but not approached Lady Wilmont in an attempt to force conversation, for which Dorothea was glad.

Now, though, where he stood would put him in Lady Wilmont's direct line of sight if she turned, which accounted for her ignoring Dorothea's requests for attention. When Dorothea's gaze settled on him, he bowed his head politely, a slight curve to his lips showing the acknowledgement was not unwelcome. She bowed her own head in reply, though her response was not a smile when his eyes slid over to the conversation between Alyssa and Tilney. If he had noticed, others in the room had as well.

Again, she tried clearing her throat at Lady Wilmont, hoping her insistence would signal something required attention. No such luck.

Out of the corner of her eye, Dorothea saw two other ladies watching Alyssa as well, exchanging quiet comments with one another, accompanied by malicious smiles.

The small sideways kick to Lady Wilmont's shin caused her to start, turning automatically. "What do you—"

The complaint stopped the moment she caught sight of Tilney. "Alyssa, my dear, come join Lady Dorrit and myself. She's arranging for some ladies to sew garments for unfortunate children. I think your nimble fingers would be most welcome." When Alyssa did not move immediately, she added. "*Now.* Dorothea, please change places with Alyssa."

Alyssa reluctantly rose as Dorothea did the same, giving in to the inevitable with a somewhat sullen expression on her face. Tilney, on the other hand, didn't seem particularly bereft of Alyssa's presence. "We have so seldom had a chance to exchange words, Miss Hindley. I find that regrettable."

"But not surprising," she countered. "I am not in London to catch a husband."

"You're not? I thought it the dream of every young girl who enters into the season."

"This is not my season, but my cousin's. Besides, an understanding is in place between me and the Reverend Mr. Shipley, vicar of our parish. So you see, when the season is over, my future is settled."

He shifted, somehow moving himself closer to her. "Betrothed to a vicar. Forgive me for saying so, Miss Hindley, but I'm afraid that sounds like a very dull future, full of psalms and sermons. Don't you ever long for some excitement?

Dorothea shifted away from him, the new distance ensuring any attempt by his fingers to caress her hand would not be subtle. "Being even on the fringes of society during the season is quite enough excitement."

Tilney's reaction was to lift his eyebrow and smile as if she'd offered him a challenge. Lovely. Just what she needed.

"Tilney! Come speak with us. You've been with the Prince lately."

Martin's voice was loud enough Tilney had no choice but respond. "Of course, sir," he said, rising smoothly. Turning to Dorothea, he bowed over her hand. "I look forward to our future conversations, Miss Hindley."

Dorothea barely resisted the urge to jerk back when his finger caressed her palm through her glove. Instead, she presented a blank expression, offering no encouragement. He merely chuckled before strolling across the room to join the other gentlemen. No sooner was he gone than Alyssa hissed in her ear, "Don't think of trying to steal one of my suitors."

Tempting as it was to say Alyssa was welcome to him, she knew any response would only provoke the scene she hoped to avoid. Instead, she ignored the words, opening her notebook to read her notations for the day. They had several other calls to make and Lady Wilmont would undoubtedly be calling for their departure soon.

Sure enough, within a few minutes, Lady Wilmont thanked Lady Burkle for her hospitality. Still managing to cast her gaze everywhere but in Martin's direction, she swept the three of them out of the room. Dorothea couldn't help throwing one last glance over her shoulder in his direction. *Thank you*, she mouthed, and was rewarded with a gentle nod of his head.

Once in their carriage, Lady Wilmont let her annoyance show. "I told you to stay away from Viscount Tilney," she scolded Alyssa as the driver moved the vehicle into traffic. "His reputation hardly lifts your own, even if he is friends with the Prince of Wales."

"He's not seriously courting me, Mama," Alyssa replied, shrugging her shoulders. "But he is highly entertaining."

"Not in a way proper for an unmarried woman. You'll stay away from him in the future. I don't want you thinking about going through with whatever assignation you and he planned."

Alyssa glared at Dorothea. "Snitch."

"Did you hear me say a word to Aunt Honoria? Because that would expose you were speaking to Lord Tilney quite intimately."

"But you were quick to speak with him when I was forced to move."

"No, he spoke to me," Dorothea corrected. "I did not invite the conversation. I certainly didn't encourage him." At Lady Wilmont's raised eyebrow, she added, "When I said I had an understanding with Mr. Shipley, he asked if I ever longed for excitement."

Lady Wilmont did not ask further, but her lips grew thin, tightly pressed together. "I think," she said at last, "the driver will drop us at Lady Shaeffer's then take you on to Hookham's. You have the list of books? Of course you do. He'll return for Alyssa and me, then take us on to Lady Baker's. Then, he can fetch you. By the time he returns, it should be time for us to leave."

She turned toward at Alyssa, next to her. "While we drive, Alyssa and I can discuss her behavior."

Dorothea had some sympathy for the carriage driver who would be making these various trips, but knew better than to argue. Lady Wilmont seldom got that expression in her eye, and she did not envy Alyssa the discussion to follow.

CHAPTER 4

"The folly of all this is she doesn't have the slightest understanding of the issues surrounding the issues. She's decided to be 'fashionable' by aligning herself with the Prime Minister's faction rather than those who support the Prince."

Cecilia shook her head, wondering why her mother had insisted on visiting the galleries of the British Museum. All she and Lady Agatha had done since their arrival was discuss the same topics they would discuss in any drawing room.

Lady Abernathy's expression bore a certain smugness as she said, "That Woman won't find favor with His Highness if she continues on such a course."

"That is the most delicious part." Leaning in conspiratorially, Lady Agatha lowered her voice to a dramatic whisper which carried across the room. "She would dearly love to receive the Royal nod and find herself invited into the exalted circle."

The response was a noise just this side of an impolite snort. "How droll. But not surprising. Back when we were in our Season, she frequently tried to catch the prince's eye, along with any other man she could find."

Lady Agatha' face grew sharp with anticipation. "Do tell."

Lady Abernathy shook her head. "It is old gossip, long past, with no bearing now save for showing a lack of constancy or understanding in her character. It is Lord Wilmont I feel sorry for. He deserved better, but he made his choice."

"One wonders why he made such a choice." Lady Agatha slipped her arm through Lady Abernathy's as they made their way down the display cases.

How long would she be forced to listen to this incredibly boring conversation? At least her mother decided against bringing one of her suitors along, so no gentlemen walked beside Cecilia, making meaningless small talk.

She slowed before a case of Egyptian jewelry. Had the woman who wore these pieces found herself in such a situation?

"They've moved into the next gallery and haven't realized you're not with them."

Cecilia started a little as the words interrupted her thoughts, but relaxed when she saw Roger, watching her with an amused smile. "You came," she breathed with relief.

"I take it things are been going swimmingly?"

She rolled her eyes. "Mother is driving everyone insane with this silly feud."

Roger frowned. "Given gentlemen are willing to put down sums of money as to which one will be triumphant, I wouldn't term the feud silly. Ridiculous, yes, but we've moved beyond silly. Martin's right to be worried this will reflect badly on the family."

The words weren't comforting, but little was these days. A glance over her shoulder to ensure her mother hadn't returned, she stepped closer. "I hate this," she said, her voice hushed. "I hate we must be so formal when we see one another, then steal moments to talk."

"I know," Roger said. "I've tried twice already to speak with Martin. I have every confidence he'll agree to our marriage, but he's distracted by the situation in Parliament. Plus, the way your mother is behaving has him tied in knots."

Cecilia sighed. "She'll object. If Martin says yes, she'll throw a fit because her sights are set on the Duke of Stockwood. It was bad enough before, but with Alyssa Wilmont throwing herself at the poor man …"

She started to turn away, unable to put her frustrations into words, but stopped when Roger caught her arm. "Don't lose hope. Sooner or later she's going to have to admit Stockwood isn't going to ask. Perhaps when she realizes he's unlikely to ask Miss Wilmont, she'll relax."

His lips quirked slightly in amusement. "My bet's he'll fall out of infatuation before the end of the month."

He stopped, looking over Cecilia's shoulder. "I think they're coming. Be strong, my love."

Roger hurried away as Cecilia settled her gaze on the case, smoothing her skirts. Mere moments later, Lady Abernathy appeared. "There you are. I turned around to find you gone."

Cecilia turned away from the case. "I'm sorry. I'm afraid I was thinking which of these pieces I preferred."

Was the lie obvious on her face? Cecilia had never been expert at deception, and she swore her mother seemed suspicious.

After a moment, Lady Abernathy turned to Lady Agatha, who had joined them. "Perhaps there is hope for the young after all. I can understand why you enjoy the jewelry, Cecilia, but please try to keep up. It's not proper to linger here alone. You might be accosted by anyone."

"Yes, Mother." Cecilia uttered the words meekly, falling in step behind the two other ladies as they proceeded. Within, she had a small glow of hope. If her mother didn't suspect what she and Roger felt for one another, they might be able to secure Martin's approval before she could interfere.

❧

"You're late," Martin said, slipping his watch back into his waistcoat pocket. "I thought you wanted to pick up something here before we went on to the tailor."

Roger's chuckle did nothing to make Martin feel better. "You sound as if you've had a fine afternoon."

"Just lovely. One conversation after another trying to convince the flower of England to stop waiting for Divine Providence to deliver His Majesty from his current trials. 'We waited in 1788.'" Martin rolled his eyes. "No Bonaparte trying to gobble Europe twenty years ago. But, no, these men see no reason for concern as long as Perceval says the king is improving."

He broke off to glance up at the sign over the door to Pastor's Chocolate Shop on Bond Street where they'd agreed to meet. "What did you need to buy?"

"A box of Cecilia's favorites." Roger said. "She's been having a hard time lately."

Martin snorted. "That's for certain. With Mother having lost her reason over not just Stockwood, but this damn feud, I'm sure she'd rather be back in the country. Come on."

They stepped inside, past the customers at the scattered tables in the front sipping at warm chocolate drinks while sharing gossip. "Do you realize Mother started ranting about Lady Wilmont when she learned the woman had accompanied Lord Wilmont to town?" Martin asked. "Kept saying she wouldn't let it happen again. Naturally, Lady Knowle couldn't resist reporting every movement."

Two ladies were at the counter before them, so Martin and Roger took up a position to one side. The clerk acknowledged their presence with a nod before returning to his customers. "Why am I not surprised she's in the mix?"

"Because Lady Knowle's a meddlesome busybody who lives to make other folk miserable. If every member of the aristocracy was a model of moral rectitude, the woman would invent some trifling sin to feed her need for gossip. If Mother had only done what I'd asked, simply given Lady Wilmont a nod of acknowledgement before moving on, none of this would have happened."

"To be honest," Roger offered, "Even if Lady Abernathy had moved on, this would flare up at some point. Lady Wilmont's more than eager to score points."

"So even if I managed to speak with her, you don't think it would help."

When the ladies finished, the clerk gestured for Martin and Roger to step forward. They placed their order, then Roger said, "If you spoke to Lady Wilmont, she would be forced to either cut you directly, or play nice and try to make up with Lady Abernathy. I think she would rather eat broken glass. Miss Hindley did allude to your attempts to make remonstrances when I dined with them. Lady Wilmont wanted none of it."

Which meant the girl had been as true as her word, though Martin wasn't surprised at the lack of success. Given her actions earlier, she was as invested as him in preventing her family from looking foolish. "The bets haven't slowed down," he said, almost to himself.

"Afraid not."

"Viscount Tilney took some glee in telling me His Highness is highly amused by the news of the feud, following the game with much interest."

"Tilney's an ass. Why, in the name of heaven, did you waste time speaking with him?"

The clerk returned with the order, indicating he'd be more than happy to deliver the package as the gentlemen required. Address provided, they stepped out of the shop, moving down Bond Street toward Martin's tailor. "I did a favor for a lady in need of rescuing."

Roger nodded knowingly. "So, if you can't reach Lady Wilmont, any ideas on convincing your mother to let things lie fallow? What if your sister was betrothed? Wouldn't she focus more on the wedding than fighting with her rival?"

"She would, but Cecilia's not showing a particular inclination toward any of her suitors and Mother is fixated on Stockwood. She might—*might*—settle for a marquis, but nothing else."

"But you're the one who has to approve the match. You're Cecilia's guardian."

"You know my mother. I agree to a match she doesn't approve of, she would make life a living hell for both Cecilia and I. Things get bad enough, Cecilia might decide to take matters into her own hands." He shook his head. "No. I'll have a difficult enough time standing my ground if Stockwood does come up to snuff.

Roger made a bit of a noise, but didn't continue. They walked on in silence for a few moments, then Roger said, "Miss Hindley! This is a pleasant surprise seeing you here?"

Pulling himself from his thoughts, Martin realized Dorothea had alighted from a carriage outside Hookham's Library. The smile she offered Roger as he stepped forward to bow over her hand was less fixed than at Lady Burkle's, but he saw still a hint of stress. "You as well, Sir Roger."

Reclaiming her hand well within the proper time, she turned to make a curtsey to Martin. "Lord Abernathy. I did not expect to see you again so soon."

"Nor I you. You're not accompanying your aunt and cousin on their other calls?"

"Aunt Honoria remembered some books she wished from Hookham's.

"Lady Wilmont does not strike me as a reader."

The words were said without thought, surprise at the idea the loud, overblown woman would take the time to turn the pages on anything except the latest trash from Mrs. Radcliffe or Mrs. Parker.

Dorothea, frowned, drawing herself up slightly. "There are a number of things about Lady Wilmont you do not know. I am sorry she has not shown herself to her best advantage with you, my lord. Now, if you'll excuse me, I'll be seeing to my task."

Another slight curtsey, and she disappeared inside the library before further words could be exchanged. "Well," Roger said with a chuckle. "She told you."

He hadn't meant to offend, but somehow he had. Perhaps, like him, she found herself overly sensitive to anything from the other camp which might be construed as such. A reminder he was not the only one impacted by this feud. Lady Wilmont had ambitions for this season. If those ambitions were not achieved, Dorothea would likely pay some price.

Someone who had as much to lose in her sphere as Martin had to lose in his.

"Why don't you go on to Old Hart's," Martin suggested to Roger. "I'll meet you there."

Roger looked suspicious. "What about your appointment? You know how he gets when someone's late."

"Keep him busy. You said you wanted a new suit; this might be the time to browse the fabrics. I won't be long. I just remembered a book Mother wanted."

He headed for the door, ignoring Roger's call of "I thought Lady Abernathy patronized Dutton's." Speed was of the essence. If she was merely picking up new books, she would be in the open areas. He'd have no chance to speak to her with others around.

Luck was with him. No sign of her near the central desk, so more than a simple exchange. Now he needed to find her within the shelves. A few fruitless moments of searching, he spotted the simple bonnet with a jaunty feather he recognized from earlier.

Inspiration burning in Martin's head, he followed, only to slow his steps once he turned into the row. He had gotten her back up once, so this needed a delicate approach. Being evicted for making improper advances to a lady within the shelves would do nothing to help his cause.

He was delaying, doubts creeping in. She had no real reason to help him and hell to pay if caught doing so. "Miss Hindley?" he asked, doing his best to keep his voice unthreatening.

She started at the sound, the volume plucked from the shelf fumbling in her hands. Recovering herself, she turned, her face a mixture of surprise and annoyance. "I'm sorry, my lord. I didn't realize you were there."

She replaced the book on the shelf, dropped a curtsey then began to move past him. Quickly he said, "I did not mean to catch you unawares, but I wished to speak with you."

Her face immediately grew guarded, but she did not move. "Really?"

The words that had sounded so perfect in his head, he now found difficult to say. He knew the idea was insane, but he could think of no other solution. But she might not agree. If she didn't and decided to tell Lady Wilmont, things would only be worse.

He had to risk this. He needed this damn feud to end. Dorothea Hindley was the only one who understood the stakes.

Taking a deep breath, Martin plunged ahead. "Miss Hindley, I have a proposition for you."

CHAPTER 5

No. Lady Wilmont couldn't have been so correct in her insinuations about Martin. But what could Dorothea think, given what he'd said?

Conscious of staring, she stammered out, "I—I beg your pardon?"

Annoyance flashed across his face. Did he hope she would fall into his arms? It didn't fit with what she knew of him, yet …

"I phrased that badly," he said. "What I mean to say is I have an idea which might be mutually beneficial to us both."

Dorothea found herself unwilling to drop her guard quite yet. "And what would that be, my lord?"

Offering a conspiratorial smile, he stepped closer. Dorothea stepped back. He stopped, took a deep breath, and did not move again. "Lady Wilmont is attempting to marry off her daughter while achieving social success and, I'll wager, using your talents to facilitate her goal."

His words were the truth and nothing Lady Wilmont tried to hide, but Dorothea didn't care to admit this to the son of Lady Wilmont's greatest rival. "You give me too much credit, sir. The gentlemen of London have recognized my cousin's beauty and charm."

"Launching a beauty in society takes more than mere outward affect. But I will not quibble. Suffice to say you are interested in seeing Miss Wilmont ends the season betrothed to a gentleman of sufficient station and wealth who will make her mother happy."

This she would admit to, though still unsure as to his purpose. "My mother," Abernathy continued, "wishes to see my sister betrothed. These goals should not conflict."

None of this required him to speak with her in a clandestine manner. "What is your idea, my lord?"

He checked to make certain they were not observed, then leaned in quite close. This time, she did not move away. "We need to make this easier," he said.

"How?" she whispered in return. This close, she detected the faint smell of soap, clean, fresh. Her heart fluttered slightly. She told herself to stop being ridiculous.

"We get them to stop feuding."

He was so earnest in importing this piece of heretofore unknown piece of wisdom, Dorothea couldn't help laughing. He pulled back abruptly, puzzlement turning to hurt. "It is not my intent to entertain you, Miss Hindley."

She did her best to stifle her laughter behind a gloved hand, not wanting to draw attention their little tête-à-tête in the bookshelves, but unable to stop. When she took her hand away from her mouth, she found herself stuttering and giggling again.

"May I ask what is so amusing?" Martin asked dryly as he favored her with a disapproving gaze.

"I'm sorry," she managed at last. "It's quite clear you don't know Lady Wilmont very well."

"Enlighten me."

His voice bore a tight edge, indicating patience wore thin. Dorothea made an effort, taking several deep breaths to help her reach a point where she might speak with something resembling coherency. "Lady Wilmont does not take kindly to those who cross her, and at some point in the past, Lady Abernathy crossed her."

"So she tries to steal my sister's suitor."

Dorothea decided not to admit Alyssa's determination to do just that. "If you're referring to the Duke of Stockwood, I will give you this. Lady Wilmont is not in favor of a match between her daughter and His Grace, but she's determined not to make the road easy for your sister out of sheer spite."

"And you intend to help her?"

She didn't like the turn the conversation had taken. "Are you seriously suggesting I undermine my aunt's efforts because you are discomfited? I don't like this feud any better than you, and I do not bear Miss Drayton any malice. But I also understand where my loyalties lie: with the woman who took me into her home and treated me well these last six years. I will not repay her by undermining her plans."

"And you don't care how ridiculous these plans make her family appear?"

"On the contrary. I urge against this feud when I can."

This time she stepped closer, head tilted back to meet Martin's gaze. "And what are you doing, sir, to actively end this feud? Are you attempting to reason with your mother, try to get her to stop glaring daggers from across the room each time she sees my aunt? Or are you expecting the work to all be done on one side, not caring how others might be impacted? Or what consequences I might suffer if I agree to this nebulous plan of yours?"

Silence fell between them. Dorothea sighed. "I understand. Good day, my lord."

She scriggled past, one sleeve brushing across his coat. Headed for the central counter, Dorothea cast a glance about and found, to her relief, no one watching her. She might escape with her reputation intact.

Lady Wilmont's order waited at the counter. As the clerk finished with paperwork, she saw Martin emerge from the bookshelves, his eyes fixed on her.

She tried to push him from her mind as the clerk secured the small stack of volumes with a string. Dorothea thanked him and took the books, not looking back as she headed for the door.

Given how long all this took, the Wilmont coach would be

arriving soon, but she still had to pause on the sidewalk, waiting. Which meant she had nowhere to go when she heard Abernathy's voice behind her. "Miss Hindley. A moment."

She shouldn't speak to him on the street. A greeting was one thing, but a prolonged conversation without a chaperone another. This left her with two options: ignore him or walk away. Neither would solve the issue, especially when he said, "I want to apologize for my behavior inside."

"You seem to apologize quite frequently, Lord Abernathy."

The words evoked a chuckle. "I don't. But every time we speak, I'm attempting to. This time, the fault is most definitely mine."

Turning to face him, she found one side of his mouth quirked upwards, as it had the night they'd met. There was humor in that smile, a bit self-mocking. "Will you accept, or must I make continued applications?"

Dorothea laughed. "I will accept. I'm afraid my behavior was not what it should have been either."

"You're being kind, Miss Hindley. You were right; if Lady Wilmont thought for a moment you were trying to do something which undermined her efforts on behalf of Miss Wilmont, things would not go well for you."

He sounded genuinely concerned, though she didn't necessarily believe him. "But you were also right. This feud serves no one."

"Except Lord Manville and Lady Knowle, and I doubt either of us truly wish to help them."

"A lady's not supposed to say what I'd like to do with those two."

His smile grew broader. "A woman after my own heart. We must be able to find some way we can achieve our mutual goals and effect a reduction in hostilities."

The Wilmont carriage appeared, much to her relief. "If there is such a way, I cannot see one," she offered. "Neither can you, I imagine. Else you would not have come to me."

"Too true."

The doorman stepped forward to open the carriage door, and Martin offered her his hand to help her enter. "Do you think my idea has any merit?" he asked.

She leaned forward, resting her hand on the edge of the window. "I think we would all be well-served with this feud ending. I doubt there is any easy solution. But," she added, "I will think on this."

"I can ask no more." He reached out to lay his hand over hers, and gave a quick squeeze. The touch was a conspirator's, but before she could react, he stepped back and signaled the driver. As the carriage pulled away, Dorothea found herself more confused than before.

Try as she might, Dorothea could not shake the conversation with Martin from her mind. It niggled into her brain, awakening doubts and concerns which had long lain dormant.

She found herself watching Lady Wilmont with a careful eye, noting every "point" scored greeted with a certain malicious glee. Such behavior had always been present, but Lady Wilmont exerted enough social dominance in Buxdale, there'd been few to challenge her.

That wasn't quite true. She had been challenged from time to time, but crushed her rivals with deadly force. Here in London, her arsenal was not the largest or most effective. Around them, Dorothea noted the smiles behind hands, the way some chose not to come near, or did so only to add fuel to the fire.

Such as Lord Manville. At yet another glittering gathering, he appeared at her side once Lord Wilmont hid in the card room, encouraging Lady Wilmont as she watched Alyssa on the dance floor. "Notice how His Grace is more interested in her than the Abernathy chit he's partnering," she told him smugly.

A lively country dance was in progress, and the movement brought Alyssa and her partner into contact with Stockwood and Cecilia. The quartet joined hands and circled halfway around, then dropped hands so Alyssa and her partner could move about the other two before moving up the set.

The steps took the dancers close to one another, but Alyssa circled Stockwood closer than proper. The difference in their heights meant Stockwood founded himself forced to gaze almost directly down at her—and straight into her bosom. Not surprisingly, this earned a rather broad smile from the duke, as it likely would from any gentleman. She followed this up with a haughty, dismissive glance at Cecilia, as if daring the girl to respond, then continued up the set.

"You can see the sour expression on Lady Abernathy's face," Lady Wilmont chortled. "She should take a care; frowns only accentuate the lines."

Across the way, Lady Abernathy indeed wore a sour expression, no doubt assisted by Lady Knowle whispering in her ear. If she hadn't seen the exchange between Alyssa and Cecilia, a blow-by-blow replay was being provided. For a brief moment, Lady Abernathy happened to glance in their direction. A smug expression on her face, Lady Wilmont offered her the mockery of a bow. Quickly, Lady Abernathy turned away, much to Lady Wilmont's glee.

Not that Dorothea expected Lady Wilmont to address Alyssa's behavior in front of Lord Manville, but her aunt showed no sign she found anything wrong.

The dance moved on, and shortly Alyssa and her partner found themselves with Viscount Tilney and the lady he escorted. The steps repeated, and as she had with Stockwood, Alyssa moved closer than proper around the man. Much closer. Tilney, on his part, enjoyed the view and made no effort to hide the fact.

Casting a glance over her shoulder, Dorothea discovered Lady Wilmont deep in conversation, eyes not following the action on the floor. Manville had, given how his eyes glittered.

Lady Wilmont was usually careful about keeping watch on Alyssa's behavior. But the feud caused her attention to slip away in an ever more consuming drive to score points. If Alyssa realized her mother's attention was not quite so focused, there would be more than simple embarrassment.

Deciding best to take advantage of the distraction herself, Dorothea asked, "May I be excused to the retiring room for a moment, Aunt?"

Lady Wilmont, looking somewhat irritated at being interrupted, nodded her assent. "Don't take too long, but if you can, ask if Lady

Foster is available next Wednesday before you return. She'd fit in with the group quite nicely."

No, she wouldn't, but Lady Foster had no love for Lady Abernathy, which was undoubtedly the reason behind the invitation. Dorothea also knew better than to argue in public. She just hoped Lady Foster would be otherwise engaged.

Lady Foster nor the retiring room was her true target, though. She spotted Martin on other side of the room and hoped he would still be there by the time she reached him. Making her way through the crowd without attracting attention was not easy, nor would speaking to him without Lady Wilmont noticing. She had to try, though.

Keeping her eye on him, and shifting course as he moved, Dorothea at last came into his orbit. Of course he was engaged speaking with a gentleman. All she could do was put herself in his eyeline and hope he would guess she needed to converse.

The moments dragged on, and Dorothea would have to make her way back to Lady Wilmont after stopping to speak with Lady Foster, of course, or questions would be asked. Questions she didn't want to answer.

He saw her, giving the smallest nod. A few moments later, he ended the conversation, and stepped toward the wall, moving close to a potted fern.

Dorothea slipped behind the fern, grateful for the cover. "You don't want to be seen," he said, his eyes focused toward the floor, not on her.

"Lady Wilmont would not be pleased. But I've given your idea some thought."

He started to turn toward her but stopped. "And?"

"I think you're right. I don't know how, but we need to stop this feud, or at least bring the temperature down. It's … allowing things to flourish which should not."

This time he did turn. "You're serious."

"Very much so. Yes, Lady Wilmont will be furious if she learns of this, but I see no other way. Her attention has become too focused on scoring points against your mother and she is not seeing things she should."

He nodded solemnly. "This will not be easy, Miss Hindley. We may not succeed."

"We may not, but I think we can agree it is best if we try."

He offered her that wicked conspiratorial smile. "Partners, Miss Hindley?"

"Partners, Lord Abernathy."

CHAPTER 6

It was one thing to agree with Martin something needed to be done to cool the feud. Another altogether to accomplish that objective.

Another evening, another event. Once more, the Wilmont and Abernathy camps stood on opposite sides of the room, ignoring one another except when points were to be scored. If they continued to ignore one another, things would be much easier. Unfortunately, too many people wanted to stoke the fire for idle amusement.

Martin had removed one irritant by ceasing his efforts to offer an apology. Trouble was, Dorothea found she missed the conversations she enjoyed with him.

A shift in the pattern caused Dorothea to glance towards her cousin, only to see Viscount Tilney with his hand toward her. Worse, Alyssa looked as if she intended to accept his invitation. This time, thankfully, Lady Wilmont was watching. "I do believe Mr. Knighton asked you previously for this dance, Alyssa. Did you not, sir?"

Knighton offered Alyssa his hand. Viscount Tilney did not remove his. Alyssa paused, caught between obeying her mother or taking the more interesting choice.

Lady Wilmont cleared her throat. With visible reluctance, Alyssa placed her in Knighton's. "I'm afraid I did promise."

"Perhaps later."

As Alyssa was led away, Lady Wilmont turned to him. "A word, if I may, Viscount?"

A bemused expression on his face, he joined her. The other suitors quickly dispersed, removing themselves from any potential line of fire. Dorothea distanced herself as well. She had no wish to be privy to what she assumed would be an unpleasant conversation.

"You're looking rather pensive, Miss Hindley. What has happened to wipe away your lovely smile?"

The Duke of Stockwood's voice lightened her mood. "Reviewing some arrangements, Your Grace. They are of no importance."

"You're being polite. I'll wager you were contemplating how Lady W's next supper should be arranged, a matter of the utmost importance. Fine meals they are, too, very convivial. Haven't had a chance to compliment you on the work you've been doing. Yes, you'll lay everything at Lady W's door." He leaned in and lowered his voice. "But we both know, don't we?"

Dorothea laughed as she slipped her notebook into her petticoat pocket. "Thank you for the compliment, Duke."

"I was going to ask your cousin to dance, but I couldn't catch her attention."

"The press of the crowd must have been too thick," Dorothea assured him. "Otherwise, Alyssa would have been certain to accept your invitation."

"There's the thing, Miss Hindley. She did see me. I think she took me for granted."

A trick Alyssa often pulled in the country when too sure of a suitor, certain they would be available when she deigned to notice them again. "You may wait with me. I'm certain she'll be happy to dance with you once this set is done."

Stockwood pondered this for a moment. "I've got a better idea. Instead of the two of us standing here with nothing to do, looking like a right pair of ninnies who can't catch partners, why don't we dance?

All other thoughts vanished. "Pardon?"

"I want to be here first for Miss Wilmont, but I don't want to just stand about. I ask another girl to dance, she might be miffed the set's already started. Dance done, I take her back to her mama then make small talk before I could depart. This way, I'll be here because I'll return you to the tender mercies of Lady Wilmont. You wouldn't be offended if I tried to claim Miss Wilmont's hand directly?"

"Well—"

"Please say yes, Miss Hindley. You never seem to enjoy yourself, which I find a shame."

Stockwood meant nothing but a pleasant time for both of them. Alyssa would throw a fit, but Alyssa had thrown many fits of late. What was one more? "Thank you, Your Grace, but I should—" she began.

"Right. Here we go."

He didn't let her finish, but took her by the hand and nearly dragged her on to the floor. Behind them, she heard the shocked cry of "Dorothea!" from Lady Wilmont and knew they'd been spotted. Nothing to do now but dance. A retreat would cause a larger scene than a nobody dancing with the man half the mamas in London society were chasing for their daughters.

They took up position at the bottom of the set, and as the current measure finished, Stockwood swept her a broad bow. Dorothea responded with a curtsey and laid her hand in his as they faced the couple who'd been moving down the set. The next measure started and they were away. Lady Wilmont did not forbid her to dance, but Dorothea frequently found herself too busy. Now she found herself grateful Stockwood had insisted.

The duke was not a bad dancer. Not marvelous, but he launched himself into the country measure with infectious enthusiasm. Two and a half figures in, she wondered why she had hesitated.

Halfway up the line, she found herself face to face with Martin. "I thought you didn't dance, Miss Hindley."

She allowed herself to gaze upward flirtatiously. "There are a number of things you don't know about me, Lord Abernathy. "

"I'm beginning to realize that."

A laugh as she moved back into place, enjoying Martin's eyes lingering on her. She'd dreamt of just such a moment when Lady

Wilmont told her about the London season. If she did not dance a step again before they returned to Buxdale, there would be tonight.

He deserves better than Alyssa, she couldn't help thinking. Alyssa would be thrilled by the title, despise her husband, and the duke would be miserable. Hopefully Stockwood would fall out of infatuation with Alyssa soon, even if it'd be easier on her if he waited until after Lady Wilmont's entertainment in two weeks.

That hope only firmed when they moved into the same figure as Alyssa. Dorothea enjoyed a certain smug pleasure seeing the shock on Alyssa's face at her poor cousin on the floor with one of London's most sought after bachelors. The shock was followed by a flash of pure, naked fury, quickly covered with a smile meant to dazzle Stockwood. Then, as the figure caused Alyssa to pass close, a vicious pinch to Dorothea's arm.

Dorothea winced, but she wouldn't let Alyssa spoil the fun. Even so, when the movements spun her and Stockwood away, she was relieved. They started the next figure, bowing to a new couple, and Stockwood said, "Did that hurt?"

"I'm not quite sure what you're referring to, Your Grace." Dorothea replied, covering automatically.

The figure took them apart, circling with their opposite number. When they came back together, Stockwood said, "I had a nurse when I was small. Nasty woman. Just before delivering me to my parents, always gave me a right old pinch so I arrived blubbering into their presence. Not surprisingly, Papa promptly sent me back to the nursery. Never a happier day than when she left."

The dance called for them to take one another's hands, and she squeezed his. Perhaps he wasn't such a fool as everyone assumed. "I am not hurt, Your Grace. Do not worry yourself."

"That's the problem. I do. Don't care for such behavior."

"I would not want you to think the Wilmonts cruel. They have been kind to me."

He nodded. "I'll not say a word if it will cause you trouble. However, the scales have fallen from my eyes."

Oh, dear. So much for hoping for a delay.

Those thoughts put a bit a damper on the rest of the set, but she pushed them aside until the music ended. "That was capital, Miss Hindley. We should do it again."

"I fear a number of ladies will hate me if I take your attention away from them," Dorothea said as she rose from her final curtsey.

He waved the objection away. "Can't dance more than twice with any of them, and don't want to dance more than once with most. Take Miss Hickinbotham, for example. Charming girl and her mother desperately wants to snare me, but I fear she doesn't care a fig and is only flirting because she's told to. Rather dance with someone like you or Miss Drayton."

Stockwood offered his arm and they proceeded. She hadn't counted on Alyssa intersecting with them halfway back, Knighton firmly in tow. Fury still glowed in Alyssa's eyes, but now her face wore a mask of false concern. "I thought you weren't going to dance tonight, cousin. Remember what the doctor said about overexerting yourself."

Dorothea bristled at the lie. Alyssa had steered her partner to meet her and Stockwood safely away from Lady Wilmont's eye. "I am quite well, and since His Grace asked me to keep him company on the floor, how could I refuse?"

Her voice dripped with sweetness, hoping Alyssa would understand she would not back meekly down as she often did to keep the peace. She didn't dare a direct challenge, but she didn't have to quietly consent.

"Miss Hindley honored me," Stockwood said. "She should dance more."

A muscle in Alyssa's cheek twitched, as if she physically restraining herself. "Dorothea loves to dance," she said before Dorothea could respond and reached out to lay a hand on Dorothea's arm. "But you do tire so easily."

The touch was tight, not quite squeezing, but enough to convey Alyssa's message she brooked no opposition. She turned her head toward Stockwood, pulling the trick of looking up through her lashes. "You said something about a dance earlier this evening, Your Grace?"

Stockwood did not eagerly accept Alyssa's offer to pay attention to him. "I should escort Miss Hindley back to Lady Wilmont, especially if she is tired. By the time I'm done, no doubt some other gentleman will have claimed your fancy."

"I'm certain Mr. Knighton would be happy to escort Dorothea back to Mama." She locked eyes with Dorothea. "You are ready to sit, aren't you?"

More than a hint of Lady Wilmont was present in Alyssa's voice and manner at this moment. The longer Dorothea stayed on the floor, the more likely her cousin would throw a tantrum. "I'm ready," she said, reluctance coloring her words. "If His Grace is willing to release me."

"You said there was no reason for you to hurry back and we might promenade," Knighton said.

Alyssa turned all her charms on him. "How I wish I'd remembered before I accepted His Grace's invitation." Again, she reached out a hand, but this time the touch was coy, resting lightly on his arm. "Later?" she pleaded. "After supper? A promenade will be most pleasant."

Knighton wavered, softening as many men before him. Why did Lady Wilmont make an effort? Alyssa was in her element here, bending suitors to her will with ease. Oh, right. Because Lady Wilmont worried a scandal might break out if left to her own devices.

Knighton might be softening, but Stockwood still seemed torn. "What would you think best, Miss Hindley?"

Dorothea took a deep breath. "You wanted to ask Alyssa to dance. I believe she would be most pleased if you did so now." *Things would go easier for me if you did.*

He caught her meaning, though showed no joy. "Well, then, Knighton, would you—"

"I would be happy to escort Miss Hindley back to your mother," Martin said, drawing nearer.

Alyssa stiffened visibly as Martin bowed pleasantly to her, showing no indication he noticed her discomfort. "Of course, I would like to claim a dance as my price. Later in the evening when you are free."

The feud belonged to Lady Wilmont, not Alyssa, and no more than a second passed before she smiled consent at her new conquest. Dorothea wondered where her cousin had picked up the trick of looking coyly up at a man from under her lashes. With Alyssa, the gesture appeared just short of provocative. "I would be happy to pay your price, Viscount Abernathy."

Knighton still seemed irked. "And a promenade with me after supper," he insisted.

Alyssa spared him a smile. "Of course. Until then."

Knighton bowed and moved away, not as happy as a man promised a promenade should be. "You are so kind to be of assistance," Alyssa told Martin as she slipped her arm through Stockwood's.

A curtsey and Alyssa led the duke away, chattering cheerfully about Lady Wilmont's upcoming dance. "He doesn't appear particularly happy," Martin noted.

"He caught a glimpse of Alyssa's true nature."

Martin did not press but offered her his arm. Slowly, they turned in the direction of Lady Wilmont. "Stockwood is right," he said after a moment. "You should dance more often."

She couldn't help a short, sarcastic laugh. "I tire myself too easily, remember?"

"Your cousin aside, I saw a young woman who displayed grace enough on the dance floor to please many a gentleman here."

Once more, something flashed in his eyes, a look to cause small shivers to run beneath her skin. This time, no easy figure pulled her away, able to revel in the triumph but not deal with the consequences. Letting her eyes drop to the floor, she focused on the pattern passing under her feet as they moved

"There are some who might be willing to try to win you away from the good reverend," he said.

The words were enough to make Dorothea stop, still some distance from their destination. "My cousin would then consider me competition, same as any lady who causes a gentleman's attention to focus anywhere except on her. I have no desire to find myself cast as her enemy." She shook her head. "No, Lord Abernathy, I know what I am. A poor cousin who is lucky to spend time in this glittering gathering. Memories to treasure when I return home to a quieter life."

She tried to smile. "When I am older, I can tell my granddaughters one night I danced with a duke."

At that moment, the plans offering security and a home of her own, something seemingly impossible six years ago, sounded unappealing. "I think we best continue," she said at last, her voice quiet. "Lady Wilmont is watching and I wouldn't want to her to think you're making an untoward suggestion."

Martin lifted an eyebrow. "Would she really think so?" he asked, "With the two of us in public in the middle of a crowd?"

Dorothea fixed him with a steady stare. He considered for a long moment, something different in his gaze. "I believe she would," he said with a heavy voice.

As they approached, Lady Wilmont's expression was a mixture of annoyance and horror, with no polite escape possible. Martin bowed. "Miss Wilmont asked I return Miss Hindley to you."

Lady Wilmont's smile froze upon her face. "Did she? How kind."

He inclined his head in response. "I am grateful for the opportunity to rectify a situation which distresses me greatly. Since the night we met you and your charming daughter, I wished to make apologies for my sister's behavior. She did not intend to offer offense and regrets her words. She would like to offer you these sentiments herself, but worries you might not wish to receive her."

He hit all the right notes, especially with the reference to Alyssa as "charming." Perhaps Lady Wilmont wouldn't want him numbered among her daughter's suitors, but she wasn't going to object to the compliment. "Well," she said, softening a touch.

"Please, Lady Wilmont. I escorted Miss Hindley with the express hope of speaking with you. I only thought it proper since I requested a dance from Miss Wilmont, I attempt to make peace between us."

Suspicion in Lady Wilmont's eye, but she also realized if she sent him away now, the social approbation would be more on her head than his. Taking a deep breath, she said, "You are correct, Lord Abernathy. Let us put this misunderstanding behind us. Poor girl; she found herself overwrought with the excitement of the occasion. I remember how overwhelmed I felt my first season under the glow of the candles and with the pride of the Ton spread before me."

Not a complete acceptance of his story as Cecilia Drayton was in her second season. But an acceptance nonetheless, and the condescending generosity with which Lady Wilmont spoke made Dorothea turn away momentarily. Surveying the dance floor, she spotted Alyssa with Stockwood. Her cousin worked hard to exercise her charms, but he didn't appear as … enthusiastic as on prior occasions. Perhaps that would help salve any annoyance in Lady Wilmont.

"Dorothea, will you please stop woolgathering!"

Or perhaps not. Turning back, she focused all her attention on her aunt, offering up an expression of being eager to be of assistance. "Lord Abernathy graciously consented to join us for our assembly. His invitation went astray somehow."

Another social lie. The three of them understood damn well no invitation existed. Still, Dorothea offered a curtsey. "My apologies, my lord. I will ensure the oversight is rectified."

Abernathy waved his hand. "No harm done. We've spoken and all is well. Now, if you will excuse me, ladies."

He bowed to Lady Wilmont, then to Dorothea. He wore an air of triumph about him, as if he'd accomplished some Herculean task. She wondered how long that would last once he got back to Lady Abernathy and gave her the news.

"Such lovely manners," Lady Wilmont said once he was gone. "He certainly didn't learn them from his mother."

She turned back to Dorothea. "Now, I would like to know exactly how this happened."

CHAPTER 7

Dorothea hesitated before speaking. There'd be trouble from Alyssa over Stockwood, and now she might face consequences from her aunt as well. "The Duke of Stockwood missed asking Alyssa for a dance, and decided he would ask me. He hoped when he returned me, he would be first in line to claim her. I didn't have a chance to refuse before he whisked me on the floor."

Lady Wilmont waved a hand. "I don't think he meant anything other than to pass the time." She gave Dorothea a sharp glance. "I'm more concerned about Lord Abernathy and why you returned with him.

"Once the dance finished, the duke and I started back, but Alyssa and Mr. Knighton met us on the way. Alyssa spun some yarn about my needing to sit down because the doctor worried about my health." Lady Wilmont's eyes narrowed further and Dorothea hurried on. "She asked him to return me to you while she danced the next set with His Grace. Mr. Knighton objected, but she promised to promenade with him after supper. That's when Lord Abernathy appeared. He said he would bring me back, if Alyssa would give him a dance later this evening, which she said she would."

"Without speaking to me, naturally. What am I going to do with that girl?"

Exert more discipline? popped into Dorothea's head, but she knew better than to speak the words. "Lord Abernathy brought me back and spoke with you," she concluded, knowing she hadn't covered everything, but hopefully enough to make her aunt happy.

"You did not come directly back."

Trickier ground here. "He asked me if you would receive him," she lied. "He … also asked why he had not seen me dancing before and thought I should do more. A pleasant compliment, nothing more."

Lady Wilmont nodded, her face thoughtful. "I suppose it couldn't be avoided," she said at last. "Shrewd man, pushing me into this, and ill of him to use you in such a fashion. At least you recognized the compliments for what they are; the means to an end. I'll speak with Alyssa before she dances with him, though. I don't want her thinking this is another conquest, because no daughter of mine will be caught aligned with that family."

No immediate explosion, no insistence on dragging Dorothea to a more private place so she could administer a proper tongue-lashing. One might be coming later, but Dorothea had likely escaped the worst.

Looking back at the dance floor, a curl of irritation and jealousy grew inside her, wishing she could enjoy this as much as Alyssa, and resenting she would forever be on the fringes. These scenes would be vanished all too soon, existing only as memories she might dwell on from time to time once she was a vicar's wife. Something to remind her that, once, she had been young, and enjoyed the attention of wealthy and aristocratic gentleman.

"What were you doing speaking with That Woman's daughter?"

Lady Abernathy's words came tight and angry before Martin could open his mouth. His first reaction was she hadn't objected to him speaking with Dorothea, which pleased him more than he imagined. "Trying to calm down this damn feud of yours," he said, determined to remain calm. "Since you refuse to do anything, I decided it best to take matters into my own hand."

Lady Abernathy sniffed. "I thought you realized some time ago she didn't have the simple courtesy to speak with you."

"I'll admit pinning her down proved difficult, but I finally achieved success. She is willing to admit perhaps Cecilia did not mean any insult, but merely overcome by the excitement of the evening." Martin didn't hide the edge in his voice. "And, when we attend the dance the Wilmonts are hosting, I expect you to behave with all the social niceties as well."

He had the entire party's full attention now. Cecilia looked surprised, but Lady Abernathy appeared frozen. "I will not."

"You will. Lady Wilmont extended the invitation, which I am certain gave her no joy, and I told her we will be happy to accept. All of us. So no discovering an ague or a conflicting engagement. We. Are. Going. You and she will give one another the kiss of peace and everyone can stop placing bets on who's going to come out on top with this damn feud."

"Oh, well done," Roger, standing next to Cecilia, said, which earned a glare from Lady Abernathy. Cecilia appeared somewhat relieved. If he couldn't dissuade his mother from the idea his sister would snare the Duke of Stockwood, at least he could take this stress from her plate.

Lady Abernathy began to protest, but quickly closed her mouth as Lady Knowle descended. "Is it true? You tendered your apologies to Lady Wilmont and accepted an invitation to her assembly?"

The woman wore an openly predatory air tonight, as if she sensed blood in the water. Martin guessed what answer she hoped for: Lady Abernathy had no intention of attending Lady Wilmont's assembly, had not apologized, would not apologize, and Lady Wilmont could go to hell.

Lady Abernathy sat a little straighter. "Martin spoke with Lady Wilmont, yes. They agreed the incident nothing but a misunderstanding and Lady Wilmont graciously allowed herself to be lenient over a bit of overexcitement. Such things happen to young ladies. I'm sure you remember."

Here was the political hostess, the woman with no intention of ceding any ground she considered hers. Perhaps she realized no matter what her personal feelings, the image must be maintained.

The look of disappointment on Lady Knowle's face made Martin more than a little happy. "But you are attending? I thought you and she——"

A slight flutter of Lady Abernathy's fan. "She is willing to offer the olive branch, so politeness requires we accept. I don't hold out hopes for an exciting or spectacular evening, but I think she shows a certain maturity to make the offer."

Lady Knowle's disappointed expression deepened. "Most mature of her. And of you to be willing to accept. Ah, there is Lord Blair. I must ask him how Lord Chalton is doing. Pray excuse me."

"Well done, Mother," Martin said when the woman departed. "What she wanted was you to stamp your feet and throw a temper fit."

"As if. I learned one thing early on. Show no weakness. Once you do, your enemies and others will use that as a weapon against you."

"Why do you put up with her, Mama?" Cecilia asked.

"Better to know what's she saying about others. Might tell you what she's saying behind your back." Lady Abernathy glared at Martin. "I am still vexed with you for putting me in this position."

"You may be vexed as much as you wish, as long as you appear at the Wilmont's ball and do so with a pleasant expression."

There would be more discussion. Not now and not here, though, since the Duke of Stockwood, released from his duty with Alyssa Wilmont, appeared. "Any chance of a dance, Miss Cecilia? Or, if not a dance, a promenade? I find the need for some pleasant company."

Protection more likely. "A promenade and then a dance?" Cecilia put her hand in Wodehouse's. "Taking a turn might be pleasant."

"Capital. Want to come along, Phipps?"

No, not the romantic expression Lady Abernathy undoubtedly hoped for. "Cheer up," Martin said once the three departed. "He opted to come to her directly after dancing with Miss Wilmont. Must count for something."

"You're being flippant. I just wish he would propose. I'd like to see Cecilia settled. Properly."

Something about the way she said the last word, looking after Cecilia walking between Stockwood and Roger made him think she'd seen something he did not. He didn't care to argue. "I'm going to go rescue Blair MacDonald from Lady Knowle."

Before she objected, he moved away. There'd be hell to pay at home, but the invitation was worth the pain. For the moment, word would spread Lady Wilmont and Lady Abernathy had ceased hostilities far more peaceably than the Plantagenets and Lancasters.

Lord Blair had escaped Lady Knowle's clutches by retiring to the card room, where Martin finally found him. "Blair, you're looking for a wife, aren't you?"

Blair paused in the act of lifting a glass. "Odd question to ask a man."

Damn, he must not be thinking clearly and too focused to ask in such a way. "I thought you evidenced interest in Miss Dorothea Hindley at some point."

"Ah. Lady Wilmont's ward." Blair took a drink. "A slight interest, but some understanding exists back home, according to Lady Wilmont. Pity. Girl would make some ambitious MP a fine wife."

"So Lady Wilmont told you." Martin remembered what Dorothea said earlier about her future being settled. "Not Miss Hindley."

"Miss Hindley seemed not averse to my attentions when I visited the Wilmonts. Not that she acted forward, mind you. Annoyed the Wilmont chit, but the girl thinks the sun should rise and set with her."

More pieces of the puzzle, but the picture wasn't becoming any clearer. It didn't help when Blair leaned in to ask, "What's the interest? I thought the Abernathys and Wilmonts were at drawn swords."

So Lady Knowle had not bothered to impart news of the truce. Interesting. "I think we're managing to at least lower the temperature. Miss Hindley has been something of a help. I can't picture her as the wife of a country parson. Can you?"

"Horrifying thought." Blair reached for the decanter and poured himself another drink. "One of those prim, pale creatures who sits in the front pew every Sunday gazing at the pulpit with adoration as her husband reads out some appalling sermon? The one who supposedly runs the altar guild, but is cowed by the wife of the gentleman with the living in their gift? No, I cannot see Miss Hindley enjoying such a life. Is that the understanding waiting for her?"

Martin nodded. "With the reverend in question being local so Lady Wilmont keeps Miss Hindley at her beck and call. Probably why she doesn't want her ward courted by respectable gentlemen."

His words earned him a lifted eyebrow. "Thinking of courting her yourself, Abernathy?"

"What? No!" came the immediate response. "Can you imagine what my mother would say at the mere thought?"

The problem, Martin admitted to himself, was he became involved with Dorothea the moment he asked for her assistance. Now, with their objective obtained far more easily than anticipated, he couldn't cut her loose to a life which would ultimately crush her spirit. "No." A little slower, a little more firmly. "I am not courting Miss Hindley myself."

Blair shrugged, finished his drink, and put his glass down. "I have something I need to discuss. When Parliament reconvenes, Lord Grey will request Lords appoint a panel of physicians to examine His Majesty. The prince would like you to immediately rise in support of the motion."

"I thought Glossop had been tasked with that," Martin said.

Blair grimaced. "Glossop made a joke about cuckolded husbands in His Highness' presence. When His Highness wasn't in a humorous mood."

"Never said Glossop was the cleverest man in the world. Why me?"

"You have tact, discretion, not a breath of scandal attached to your name, and you're respected on both sides of the house." Blair examined his fingernails. "He also thinks highly of your mother."

Martin didn't want to dwell too long on the images those words conjured up. "I'm flattered His Highness holds me in such esteem, but I can't guarantee results. The government is going to delay as long as possible. They'll try to convince everyone of no need for a regency as long as the king continues to improve."

"The news the Prince is getting is not necessarily what is being told to Parliament." Blair glanced around, then leaned in and lowered his voice. "They put the king in a straitjacket again. What happens when spring comes and Bonaparte takes to the field?"

Blair's words summoned up an unpleasant image. "Tell him I'll do what I can."

"The effort's the important thing. You carry weight within Lords." Blair gave him a cheeky grin. "Even with this feud your mother's involved in."

Of course that had to be mentioned. Blair added, "His Highness also asked to be remembered to your mother. He's apparently looking forward to her ball in February."

Conversation done, Martin returned to the salon in fine spirits. Greetings from the Prince of Wales would make the idea of being polite to Lady Wilmont a bit easier. Hopefully.

The trust of princes and a truce in the feud. The evening was going well. As he pondered whether to seek more discussion or another partner for a dance, he couldn't help glancing toward the Wilmont party. Neither Lady Wilmont nor her daughter appeared happy, which he hardly found surprising. Dorothea stood well behind the pair, her ever-present notebook hugged against her chest as if a shield.

Miss Wilmont, momentarily bereft of suitors, turned and said something to her. What Martin saw of Miss Wilmont's expression suggested the words were far from pleasant. Dorothea's hands grasped her notebook tighter and lifted her chin, but did not reply. Trouble he'd had a hand in creating, he suspected. Little he could do, certainly where Miss Wilmont was concerned, no matter how unfair that might seem.

"The Duke of Stockwood is not dining with us Thursday. This is all your fault!"

The last words were practically shrieked, causing both Dorothea and Lady Wilmont to look up from their lists for the dance. "I can't believe you would do this to me. He was so attentive until you danced with him and now he's turned down our dinner invitation."

"Alyssa, be silent," Lady Wilmont's tone was sharp. "I don't want the servants listening to you complain because a gentleman decided against being in your company for an evening." Her eyes narrowed. "And how did you learn this information?"

"This note arrived from him." She thrust the paper in her mother's direction. "How am I going to be a duchess if he won't dine with us? He's paid more attention to Cecilia Drayton than me at the last two events, along with that nobody Miss Hickinbotham. Who does she think she is, making eyes at my duke?"

She glared down at the table, scattered with notes, menus, and seating plans for the small private supper being hosted before the event. "You are putting him next to me at supper, aren't you? I need him next to me so I can win him back."

"No, you will not be seated next to His Grace at supper," Lady Wilmont said. "He tendered his regrets earlier, citing a prior engagement. I wouldn't have seated you next to him anywise as a punishment for reading things not addressed to you."

She laid the note down on the table. "Time you accept he is not 'your' duke. Perhaps His Grace realizes this as well. Shrieking at Dorothea will change nothing."

"Everything was fine until she danced with him." Alyssa moved closer to the table. "What did you do? What did you say to him?"

"I didn't say anything," Dorothea did her best to keep her voice calm. "His Grace asked me to dance so he might have a better chance of securing a dance with you."

"Is that the lie you're telling now? Because I can't imagine why he would want to dance with someone like you. More like you twisted things so he had no option but to ask."

A raised hand and Dorothea scrambled from her chair before the slap could be completed, but Alyssa pursued.

"Stop it!" Lady Wilmont stood abruptly, followed by a crash as the table overturned. "What do you think you're doing?"

"Giving Dorothea what she deserves. What she's deserved ever since we arrived in London! I should have slapped her so hard she cried instead of pinching her."

Lady Wilmont grabbed Alyssa's upraised arm as Dorothea moved backward, wanting to put as much distance between herself and her cousin as possible. "Will you calm down? Dorothea has made every effort to ensure this trip is a success. How dare you treat her like this."

Alyssa tried to twist away, but Lady Wilmont's grip prevented her. "Why are you taking her side? She's little more than a servant, someone we're saddled with."

"Doesn't give you leave to pinch her."

Alyssa's eyes widened, narrowing as she tried to free herself. "You went running to her, didn't you?"

"Dorothea didn't say a thing," Lady Wilmont said. "You told me." She glanced at Dorothea. "Did His Grace witness this?

"Yes," Nothing would be gained by avoiding the truth with the subject raised.

"Liar!" Alyssa hissed.

"As we moved up the set, he said he doesn't care for such behavior."

"Why didn't you tell me?" Lady Wilmont asked. "I should have dealt with her."

She released Alyssa and moved between her and Dorothea. "Go to your room. You and I will talk more on this later, and be grateful I don't cancel everything and send you home." She raised a finger as Alyssa opened her mouth. "Say one word and that is exactly what I'll do."

Alyssa closed her mouth, glared at Dorothea, and stomped her foot before flouncing from the room. Lady Wilmont turned her attention to the debris from the table, frowning at the upset ink bottle. "Damn. Ring for the footman. They'll need to clean this up. Let us see what can be rescued."

The next several minutes were spent cleaning, rescuing some pages and discarding others. Dorothea's notebook was among the casualties, ink disfiguring a fair amount of information. When the servants left Lady Wilmont said, "Now what are we going to do with you?"

Gingerly laying her book down on the now-righted table, Dorothea stood with her hands clasped before her. "I am entirely at your command, my lady."

"Don't sound so meek. It doesn't suit you. Do we have more of these cards? No, leave them. I imagine you ensured there are extras. I can always count on you to think ahead." Lady Wilmont reclaimed her chair. "But we have a problem. Seems Alyssa's decided your presence is unacceptable."

"You may not appreciate hearing me say so, my lady, but the problem is not new." Her words were careful, formal.

"I'm painfully aware of that. But we must survive this season and get her settled with a husband. I doubt she'll wear well on the shelf for a second year." Lady Wilmont thought for a moment. "Perhaps you not coming with us again until after the assembly is over would be the wisest choice. That might convince her to behave better."

"And if it doesn't?" Undoubtedly, Alyssa would turn her ire and blame somewhere else if Dorothea were absent.

Lady Wilmont sighed. "I fear we must send you home. Please understand. Your future is settled. As much as I value you, if your presence interferes with Alyssa behaving, I'll be forced to forgo the help."

"So you're suggesting I stay out of sight as much as possible? Confine myself to the house?" Dorothea struggled to keep the bitterness from her voice.

"Until the ball is over at least. Let Alyssa enjoy her triumph and perhaps a favorite will emerge from the pack, aside from the Duke of Stockwood. She's become too fixed on the idea of marrying him."

Dorothea bit back the temptation to say there was no surprise. Alyssa wanted to be the center of all things, and bitterly resented anyone who had the tiniest light shined on them. There seemed no check from her acting out at the slightest opposition.

Not her problem at the moment though, as she and Lady Wilmont sat down to begin recreating the cards ruined with the ink spill. For now, Dorothea had her marching orders: stay out of sight and still be helpful.

She couldn't help the growing bitterness inside, that she was not allowed to enjoy even a small part of the season because Alyssa threw a temper fit.

This meant she would disappear from Martin's view without explanation. For all the strangeness of their situation, he was the bright spot she would miss. In her wildest dreams, things would calm down enough after next week and she might be able to partner him for a dance if he asked.

Better not to hold her breath.

CHAPTER 8

"I don't understand what Martin was thinking when he accepted That Woman's invitation." Lady Abernathy complained to Lady Agatha.

Standing on the dressmaker's platform, trying to hold still as the modiste pinned the hem of her new gown, Cecilia sighed. While Lady Abernathy presented a pleasant face to most folk about the ordeal, behind closed doors and with intimate friends, nothing had changed. If anything, her disdain increased.

"He put you in a position where you had no choice but to accept." Lady Agatha sighed. "She hasn't changed since our days on the marriage mart."

"Not a whit. But he insists if we don't accept the olive branch she's chosen to extend for whatever reason, we will be the ones seen as ungracious."

The mirror showed her mother looking more than a little smug. "Given he wants us to put on a proper show, why shouldn't Cecilia and I order new gowns? I'll remind him he insisted we attend when he gets the bill."

How long must she continue to listen to this incredibly boring conversation, and would it be too much a breach of manners to scream in frustration? Of course, folk in the outer area of the shop would likely hear and earn Cecilia a scolding.

The modiste asked her to turn, then declared herself satisfied with the hem and other alterations. She clapped her hands and an assistant stepped forward to help Cecilia from the dress, making certain no pins dislodged. Once done, another assisted Cecilia back into her day dress. "And now you, *Madam Le Viscomtesse* Abernathy." The modiste laid on the faux French accent. "If you will step on the platform, we will ensure all is well with your gown."

"It best be," Lady Abernathy warned as she rose. "I don't want a panic at the last minute."

"Even with something from the back of your closet, you'd still be better turned out than Honoria Wilmont," Lady Agatha said.

Settling her hat, Cecilia said, "Mother, I'm going to browse the ribbons."

"Just don't leave the shop, dear."

She had no intention of leaving the shop. She wanted five minutes without hearing her mother complain.

One of the assistants was happy to show Cecilia the ribbons, and more than happy to hover nearby in case she needed assistance. Fortunately, to her relief, the shop door soon opened, admitting a woman with two daughters in tow. "We are here for our fitting," she announced grandly.

Cecilia didn't recognize the party as part of her social circle, which eliminated the need for greetings and conversations. The hovering assistant moved to help the new customers, leaving her with peace, glorious peace.

Then she spotted Roger outside the shop, watching her through the window.

A quick glance over her shoulder to ensure the assistant was still occupied and Cecilia was out the door. "What are you doing here?" she asked in a surprised whisper.

"Martin complained your mother insisted on new dresses for the Wilmont affair. Easy enough to get word from him you had a fitting this afternoon. I hoped we might steal a moment. You don't need to whisper. We're standing on the street." He paused. "Why are you holding a roll of ribbon?"

Glancing down, Cecilia realized she'd walked out with a roll in hand. "Pretending to look at the color in sunlight, make certain I have the right shade. I suppose must buy a length now. If Mother finds me—"

"So I will be quick. I almost spoke to Martin, but we were interrupted by a drunken idiot who insulted him. I'll wager, though, if Martin gives his consent, your mother will try to stand in the way."

"You could be an earl," Cecilia said, "and I don't think Mother would approve if there was the smallest chance the Duke of Stockwood would offer for me."

"Which means, once we gain Martin's consent, we need to move quickly." Roger took a deep breath. "I'm going to talk to Thomas about getting a Special License."

"Those are expensive and hard to come by."

"Which is why I'm going to my dear brother. Remember Mother bursting with pride at him being given a place with the Archbishop of Canterbury? If anyone can procure us one, he can. He'll understand the problem. And you are worth every penny."

She wanted to kiss him, but knew she couldn't. Not here in public, where anyone passing might see. All she could do was reach out to squeeze his hand. "I'd best go back in," she said, unable to say more for fear of her emotions betraying her.

Roger nodded. "Once I have the license in hand, I'll force the issue if I haven't had a chance to speak with him before then. Just don't agree to marry any dukes in the meanwhile."

His words made her laugh, and with one last glance, she hurried back inside. "I will need a length of this," she said to the assistant who regarded her suspiciously. "I stepped outside to check the color in the sunlight. I'm sure you don't mind."

"Of course not, miss. I had no worries as you were in my sight." A pause. "Two lengths, you said?"

"I think three," Cecilia said. "And one for yourself of any color for being so helpful."

The assistant smiled. "You're very kind, miss."

As the assistant measured out the ribbon, her mother and Lady Agatha emerged. "I like that color," Lady Abernathy said. " A bit dark for you, though."

Cecilia shrugged. "It may serve for smartening one of my bonnets. And Martin is paying for this."

Lady Abernathy smiled. "So he is. They swear the dresses will be done in time. I have every confidence you will outshine Miss Wilmont considerably. Don't you agree, Lady Agatha?"

"I do." The older women waited while Cecilia's order was wrapped. "Shall we stop at the delightful little sweet shop down the street. I find myself in need of something restorative."

"An excellent idea. Come along, Cecilia."

Dutifully, Cecilia joined her mother as instructed, in a much better mood than when she arrived.

◈

For the amusement of the gossips, Lady Wilmont formally welcomed Lady Abernathy and her family. Kisses to the air beside one another's cheeks were exchanged, sealing the deal. A truce was now in place. For the duration of the evening, at least.

His mother stepped away with a touch more speed than necessary. He turned his attention to Miss Wilmont, all smiles, shimmering in her white gown shot through with strands of silver. This was her moment and she knew it, and so should everyone else. "May I claim a dance later>" he asked. "Although undoubtedly you are besieged with requests."

"I am." She batted her lashes as she gazed up at him. "But I would be more than happy to save one for you, Lord Abernathy."

Dear lord, an actual simper. Did she think he would fall under her spell with that trick? He did not trust himself to respond, but bowed and proceeded on, taking his mother's arm as they made their way into the ballroom proper, Cecilia trailing behind. "I suppose you had to ask the girl." Lady Abernathy sighed. "Be careful. She seems the type who'd deliberately put a man in a compromising position."

67

"I'll stay well away from any dark corners. Besides, I think Stockwood has more to worry about than me."

"Rumor is His Grace 'developed' a cold and sent his regrets he wouldn't be here this evening. So much for Lady Wilmont's vaunted campaign."

The acid in her voice didn't surprise Martin. Lady Wilmont likely expressed similar thoughts to Lord Wilmont. What did surprise him was Dorothea's absence. He'd not expected her in the receiving line, but he thought she would be nearby, within call if Lady Wilmont required anything. Nor had she been at her aunt's side the last week or so.

"I want to depart as early as we can," Lady Abernathy said as they claimed a spot along the wall. "Best arrange your set with Miss Wilmont earlier rather than later. Then, we can leave after whatever they're going to pass off as supper."

Martin made a bit of a face at the idea, only for Lady Abernathy to rap him sharply on the arm with her fan. "You're the one who wanted us here, and you're the one who asked her not five minutes ago. Time for you to reap what you sowed."

Martin took the dismissal and moved away. At least now he could hunt for Dorothea without risk of his mother's questions.

After a few minutes searching, he spotted her in conversation with a somewhat harried-looking upper servant, almost hidden in the shadows at the edge of the room. As he approached, Dorothea was saying, "We're going to need more chairs for the chaperones. They're nearly full and the dancing hasn't begun."

The man's face twisted unhappily. "I'll do my best, Miss Hindley, but I don't think her ladyship will appreciate if we start pulling chairs which don't match."

"I'll tell her we have a crush and she is a success. Fetch all you think will serve, and you should open the small library for those who want a brief respite. Dispatch two footmen to stand duty, which will eliminate the chance of impropriety, and make certain there are enough candles." A notation in her ever-present notebook. "Thank goodness I ordered flowers."

"Always busy," Martin teased as the man departed to do her bidding.

Dorothea turned with a bit of a start, but relaxed at the sight of him. "Ensuring everything runs smoothly while Lady Wilmont greets her guests." A pause. "Did everything go well?"

No need to ask what she meant. "They behaved themselves, though things were said as we walked away."

A slight laugh. "So long as they didn't break into hostilities. Lord Manville's been dripping poison about the fact Aunt Honoria felt compelled to invite your family."

Martin snorted, "Manville would shrivel up and die if he didn't drip poison about something. Hopefully, no new fuel will be added tonight."

She laughed again, which pleased him. She seemed to light up when she laughed, which made her shine despite with the simplicity of the dress she wore. One far too simple for a dance in her own home. "Lady Wilmont lacked her right hand at events of late. You are well?

The laughter stopped and Dorothea's smile faded. "With so much to do, I begged leave to stay home and complete some tasks in relative peace."

There was more to the story; something about her manner hinted much more than she let on. But he couldn't press, not here, not now. "Are you allowed to enjoy yourself tonight? Or will your duties prevent you?"

Surprise lit up her eyes. "I am allowed, but later. After supper, when there is less to worry about."

Which meant his mother would be forced to linger longer than she wished. Too bad. "Might I beg a dance then?"

Her smile returned, warm and genuine. "I would be honored."

He bowed over her hand, and squeezed gently. "For luck," he said before moving away to do his social duty.

Dorothea understood she risked potential wrath by accepting Martin's invitation to dance, but with luck, Alyssa would be too busy with other triumphs late in the evening. It wasn't that she wanted to dance; she wanted to dance with *him*.

"You think you're so smart, don't you?"

Her shoulders tensed at the sound of Alyssa's voice behind her. Calm, she told herself. Stay calm.

Taking a deep breath, she turned to face her cousin. "Is the receiving line done?" she asked with deliberate casualness. "Should I send word to the musicians dancing will begin momentarily?"

Alyssa's eyes narrowed, giving her a hard, unyielding appearance. "Mama says I should be grateful, but I don't know why. All you've done is prevent me from having fun and make people pay attention to you instead of me."

The words were on the tip of Dorothea's tongue to say fetching Alyssa away from potentially embarrassing circumstances at her mother's insistence did not count as "preventing her from having fun." She restrained herself, knowing a fight or tantrum would not be viewed kindly.

"I'm glad Mama hasn't allowed you to attend events," Alyssa continued, "but I think it'd be better you went home, and I will tell her so. Given you fancy a man who couldn't possibly be interested in paying any honest addresses, I think she'll agree. Wouldn't want a scandal, would we?"

"I have no idea what you're talking about." Dorothea's hands tightened around her notebook.

"Don't you? I watched you and Viscount Abernathy just now, listened to him ask you to dance, and you accepted." Alyssa leaned in, her voice lowered to a hiss. "This is my ball. You're a poor relation. What makes you think you have the right to do anything but the tasks my mother sets you to?"

"I didn't realize you despised me so much."

The words slipped out and Dorothea regretted them instantly, more so with the gleam in Alyssa's eyes. "Mama thinks so highly of you and she doesn't understand you're kissing up to her, making your-self useful so she won't send you away. I won't have it. Not during my season. You'll go home and if you're lucky, perhaps I won't ensure Mr. Shipley learns you've been throwing yourself at a man ridiculously far above you. He desperately wants Mama's favor, but even he must have his limits."

Despised her enough to destroy her future. "I'll not dance with Lord Abernathy if that's what you want," she said, hating every word. She needed to defuse the situation somehow, salvage something. Martin was a dream, one she needed to let go to survive, no matter how much the idea hurt.

"Of course you won't." Alyssa's expression was smug. "Because I'll have him eating out my hand before the evening's done, and you'll get to watch. When I'm through, he won't remember who you are."

She turned away, but turned back. "And you're still going home. You came to us with nothing and you'll leave with the same."

Alyssa glided away without another glance. A gentleman bowed to her and she gave him the sweetest smile in response, as if her tongue had never uttered a cruel word. Dorothea pitied the man who married her smile, only to uncover her true nature later.

And that nature might bring Dorothea's world crashing down about her ears. Perhaps returning to Buxdale would be for the best. Getting word to Mr. Stickley would require effort and Alyssa had never been the most enthusiastic correspondent. If Dorothea was not in London, perhaps something else would take Alyssa's attention and her threats no longer of such interest to her.

So return to Buxdale she must, to wait in fear a silly, nasty girl would try to blacken her reputation because she could. Unless Lady Wilmont chose to take a stand, there'd be regret, but agreement as well. Within a few days, Dorothea would likely be on the road.

And the thing she would regret most was missing the chance to dance one dance with Martin.

CHAPTER 9

Claiming Alyssa for a dance proved more difficult than Martin antici-pated. A crowd of gentlemen clamoring for her hand this evening was no surprise. But each time he tried to ask, she turned to someone else, almost as if intent on keeping him dangling as long as she could.

He filled some of the time by dancing with several of the young ladies his mother favored. He also spoke with gentlemen regarding the upcoming report from His Majesty's physicians. Already, sentiment ran hot at the possibility the Prime Minister and Chancellor had not been as forthcoming as hoped.

More than once during these conversations, he found himself watching the edges of the room to see what task Dorothea engaged in. She wore a tension about her he had not seen earlier. As much as he wanted to dance with her, perhaps he would ask if they could prome-nade instead. Conversation would be easier if they walked. More folks promenaded after supper as well, which meant they would draw less attention.

The thought made him realize how close they were to the supper dance. If he weren't careful, he might find himself squiring Alyssa for the meal. Turning his steps deliberately toward her, he found her once again in the center of a gaggle. Maneuvering his way to the front of the group, he held out his hand. "I believe this is our dance, Miss Wilmont."

Alyssa appeared a bit surprised at his tone, and he thought she might demur, putting him off once more. She tilted her head at a practiced, fetching angle, and gazed up at him through thick lashes. After a considered hesitation, she laid her hand in his with a feigned meekness.

Fortunately for Martin, the dance was lively rather than stately, which made conversation limited as the figures frequently pulled them apart. Not that he needed exert much effort; Alyssa happily bore most of the burden, all her words aimed at showing him how fascinating she found herself to be. He understood for the first time why his mother had such a distaste for Lady Wilmont if her daughter was a reflection of her younger self.

Near the end of the set, Martin caught sight of Dorothea on the edge of the dance floor. He didn't know what to make of the jealousy on her face, but when their eyes met, he found anger. Anger at who or what though?

She broke the connection first, turning away to exit through a door designed to blend with the wall. Martin shifted his steps to follow, only to find himself faltering in the dance. Cursing under his breath, he recovered his place, and saw the annoyance in Alyssa's eyes. His misstep had not gone unnoticed.

The music mercifully ended with the next figure, and as Martin began to escort Alyssa back to Lady Wilmont, she said, "Would you care to promenade? Such an excellent way to cool down after such vigorous exercise."

Given how many guests crowded into the ballroom, Martin doubted a stroll would provide much relief. Also, how Alyssa laid her hand on his arm brought to mind his mother's warnings about dark corners. "The idea is lovely, but I'm certain other gentleman are eager to claim you for the next dance."

She pouted, but did not object too strenuously as he steered them directly to where Lady Wilmont sat. Martin didn't care if she found him a disappointing suitor. After tonight, he would avoid partnering her on the dance floor. She was exactly what he wanted to avoid in a marriage, because he couldn't face the idea of twenty years of a woman like her at breakfast. Her focus would be purely social, and he doubted she had the interest in political maneuvering he needed in his wife.

He offered up all the appropriate compliments in returning her to Lady Wilmont, earning a not completely stiff smile. Miss Wilmont appeared somewhat vexed he hadn't proved more pliable. Free to escape, he made his way through the crowd toward the door Dorothea disappeared through. It opened into a servant's corridor, plain walls with plain doors which ran to the far edge of the house, ending in a staircase. If she didn't want to be followed, Dorothea had certainly chosen the right path.

After opening doors a crack for fear of disturbing a private scene, Martin found what appeared to be Lord Wilmont's private study, a room paneled in dark wood and lined with bookcases. Only a few candles in glass chimneys burned, giving the room a dim, private air.

Dorothea was on the far side of the room, her head tipped back, shoulders hunched, and arms hugged tightly about her. The sight made him ache in sympathy and he wanted nothing more than to heal her pain.

Quietly, he closed the door behind him and took a few steps further into the room. "Are you well, Miss Hindley?"

She started, turning in surprise, traces of moisture at the corners of her eyes. "You shouldn't be here," she stammered out, the words nervous and awkward. Was there panic as well?

"I was concerned," he said. "You appeared angry watching the dancing, as if someone had done you an injury."

"Why should I be angry?" She tried to smile. "Everything is going beautifully. Alyssa is much admired and Lady Wilmont will enjoy a social triumph."

"For which you labored, but will receive no credit."

"And what else should a gentlewoman of twenty-two who is dependent on the charity of others do? I am here for the express purpose of assisting in the launch of my cousin upon society. I should not be attempting to catch the eye of eligible gentlemen above my station. Else I might jeopardize the match with a respectable cler-gyman my aunt graciously arranged."

The mask began to fall away, hurt and anger coming to the fore. Dorothea turned back to the window, scrubbing her hands over her face as if to erase any traces. "In the country," she said, her voice tight, "I may dance with the younger sons of the local gentry or some honest clerks. Here, best I keep to the shadows, and see to the arrangements. Most importantly, I must not do anything to upset Alyssa or make her think I am trying to take attention away from her."

He found nothing he could say, certain anything he might offer would sound like hollow platitudes. "I shouldn't be complaining. The Wilmonts take care of me, and often treat me as if I were another daughter. I am clothed somewhat fashionably, fed, and have a roof over my head. I am an orphan with no fortune and must count myself lucky they brought me to London and arranged for a marriage when I return home."

Turning back, she said, "Am I wrong that just once, I find it unfair Alyssa does not care who she hurts, and faces no consequences? She dances with men she does not give a fig about save they are many and suitable enough in title to elevate her? She blames me for the Duke of Stockwood losing interest, though her own actions are the cause. Even Lady Wilmont realizes this, but she also knows Alyssa to be a spoiled, willful child. The only way to get her to behave in a civilized manner is to let her have her way, so I must be sacrificed. Being dressed like this," she swept a hand down her all-too-simple gown, "and staying to the shadows does not appease her. I am to be sent back to Buxdale in disgrace. Worse, if she has her way, a disgrace with no reputation, no matter what lies she must tell."

Her voice broke on the last words, the tears that had been threat-ening now flowing hot and fast. Without thinking, Martin stepped close and reached out to hold her as she gave way to the storm inside.

They stood thus for some time, her face buried against his chest, sobs coming in ugly gulps. She needed this, but she also felt right within his arms. *As you knew she would*, a voice inside his mind whispered. Several times she tried to speak, but he shushed her, telling her to cry herself out. Only when she thoroughly dampened the front of his jacket and her breath came more calmly as she regained control of herself did he loosen his grip.

She shifted back, far enough to glance up at him. "You're too kind," she said, still snuffling somewhat. "I can't continue to take advantage of you."

"You're not taking advantage," he told her, fishing a handkerchief from his pocket. "You needed someone to comfort you. I would do the same for my sister."

She took the linen square, dabbing at her eyes. "But I'm not your sister and do not have a claim on your affections.'

Dorothea gazed up at him, longing and sadness behind the tears. What she longed for, he was not certain, but he understood what he longed for. "No, you're definitely not my sister," he said, his voice rough with emotion.

His arms tightened about her again and Dorothea did not object when he pulled her closer and lowered his head to hers. Their kiss was sweeter than he'd imagined, though he was only now fully aware of the desire which had haunted him these past weeks. Dorothea returned the kiss with at much eagerness as he gave, pressing close, her arms sliding about him.

They paused to catch a breath of air, then kissed again. This time, her lips parted beneath his, giving him silent leave to explore. He took permission without hesitation, stretching out the tip of his tongue to gently circle the edge of her mouth. In response, her grip grew tighter, providing encouragement as the entirety of the universe shrank to only they two.

"Oh, I beg your pardon. I didn't realize anyone was in here."

Martin reacted on instinct, releasing Dorothea and thrusting her behind him. With luck, neither Manville nor Lady Knowle had recognized her. "Do you require something?"

The pair didn't bother pretending to show regret at disturbing the room's occupants. "Me? Nothing." Lady Knowle fluttered her fan. "You, on the other hand, Lord Abernathy, appear to have everything you require."

Martin's face grew warm, part from embarrassment, part from anger. "Is there a reason to disturb a private moment."

"Very private," Manville's expression barely concealed a leer. "I understand. I was young once."

He and Lady Knowle laughed, closing the door to the study as they left.

"I'm sorry," Dorothea said from behind him. "This shouldn't have happened."

He turned back to her. "Don't blame yourself." He reached out to gently caress her cheek. "It's long been rumored that pair spend their time at gatherings opening doors to catch someone in a compromising position."

His words only agitated her more and he reached out to run his hands up and down her arms. "If anyone's to blame, I am. After all, I followed you without an invitation."

They both knew who followed whom would matter little to the gossips with a juicy piece of scandal to sink their teeth into.

Martin pushed the thought aside in favor of dealing with the difficulty at hand. "What we need to do now is get you back to the floor before anyone realizes your absence." He took a deep breath. "Best we aren't seen together."

The words felt cold and callous, but Dorothea nodded, her face grim. She had told him malicious gossip could ruin her life. He didn't like his hand in creating some. "I can return via the servant's corridor. You, though …"

She took a deep breath. "Go out through the card room. We may cast some confusion on the story if you are seen. That's the best we can hope for. I'll show you the way."

Dorothea grabbed his hand and pulled him into the servant's corridor, stopping before a door quite close to the one which led to the ballroom. "The door opens behind the screen in front of the chamber pot so the servants can empty it discreetly," she told him in a soft voice. "Pass through, then back to the ballroom. Poke enough holes in the story and many will doubt the truth of Lord Manville and Lady Knowle's words. Likely won't stop the gossip, but we can perhaps mitigate the damage somewhat."

"You have experience with this."

She met his gaze, straight and steady. "Think about my cousin. Yes, I've had experience."

A chilling tale in those words, and a secret entrusted. He wanted to kiss her for luck, but didn't dare. All he did was squeeze her hand.

She squeezed back, then carefully opened the door a sliver. "Go," she whispered, stepping back to so he might move.

Move Martin did, slipping through the door, which closed behind him. He paused for a moment, took a deep breath, and stepped out from behind the screen, his movements deliberately calm. Nodding to various gentlemen, he made his way back to the ballroom. Once inside, he found Manville and Lady Knowle busy oiling the gossip machine. Lady Knowle stood in the middle of a circle of ladies, who hung on every word. Manville had headed straight for Lady Wilmont. Whatever his words, they didn't meet with her approval. Her eyes blazed as she spotted Dorothea, and summoned her with an imperious gesture. Dorothea didn't hesitate, but as she began to make her way toward her aunt, Martin moved as well. He would not let her face this wrath alone.

He arrived as Lady Wilmont told Manville, "I thank you for your concern, sir. I will deal with this personally. Pray, continue to enjoy your evening."

Manville took the dismissal, but moved only a short distance away, still close enough to catch what transpired above a whisper, with a clear view of how they reacted.

Lady Abernathy did not acknowledge Martin's presence, but turned to Dorothea. "Well? Were you caught kissing Lord Abernathy?"

"I was checking on the supper," Dorothea began, but stopped at Lady Wilmont's glare.

"I do not doubt that, but do me the courtesy of an honest reply. Were. You. Seen. Kissing. Him?"

Dorothea began to reply, but then only nodded. Lady Wilmont's face turned a particularly unattractive shade of dark red, as if she might suffer an attack of apoplexy. "Go to your room," she said, her voice deadly still. "I do not want you to set one toe outside until I send for you. Do I make myself clear?"

Much brewed on Dorothea's face, as if she wanted to argue or offer explanation, but she curtseyed and hurried away. She cast one last glance over her shoulder toward Martin, but Lady Wilmont filled his frame of vision. "I do not take kindly to having my hospitality abused, Lord Abernathy," she said in sharp, clipped tones. "I ask you take your family and leave my house. If you possess any decency, you'll do so with as little fuss as possible."

"If I can explain --"

"Yes, your actions do demand an explanation, but this is hardly the time or the place. Please try to show a modicum of discretion; you've caused enough trouble."

Sense told him he should leave, tail between his legs, but he couldn't, not now. "The problem, Lady Wilmont, is the tale Lord Manville is spinning is wrong."

Out of the corner of his eye, Martin spied Manville inch closer. Of course. "How was he mistaken in seeing you kiss my niece, sir," Lady Wilmont asked, "when she herself admitted it was so, or are you saying they are both lying?"

Damn. "No, he did see that,"

"Did you arrive with the intention to take advantage of a member of my family? Or did the idea come while you danced with my daughter."

Everything was spiraling out of control and he found himself groping for a possible solution. The only words which came were, "I kissed Dorothea—Miss Hindley—because she agreed to become my wife."

He did not quite understand where the statement came from, but it was the only thing with any hope of salvaging the situation. Lady Wilmont's face grew redder, her knuckles white around the fan she carried. "You what?" she managed.

Manville had to be loving this, but Martin plowed on. "I understand this is somewhat irregular, but I wanted to ascertain if Miss Hindley would accept my suit. It was my desire to speak to her before the ball, but as she found herself busy with preparations—"

Lady Wilmont lifted her hand stop him before he dug himself any deeper. "Call upon us at one tomorrow and we can discuss what agreements are to be made. I still ask you and your family depart as this ball is in honor of my daughter and she should not be forced to share with your happy news."

She glanced sideways at Manville. "Though I am certain the news will spread, no matter what I wish."

Leaning in, she said in a voice meant for only they two, "Be on time, Lord Abernathy. Be ready to make this right or I will destroy you. Do not think you can toy lightly with someone in my care."

Having no doubt Lady Wilmont would do as she promised, Martin bowed stiffly and moved away to fetch his mother. By some miracle, the gossips had not yet reached her, and she chatted politely with Lady Devon. Giving the other woman a nod and slight bow, he leaned down and whispered in Lady Abernathy's ear, "Time to go."

"Go?" Lady Abernathy regarded him with surprise. "Supper has not been called. We will appear rude."

"I'm afraid you don't have a choice in the matter. Where's Cecilia?"

"Dancing. Martin, what is this all about?"

"I'll tell you later. Ah, the dance just ended."

He did his best to stand still as Cecilia's partner escorted her back to her mother, hands clasped behind his back, one curled in a fist. As she arrived, several young men appeared, eager to claim the next set. Before she spoke, Martin smiled and declined on her behalf. "I'm afraid we must be going," he told them. "Do come to call."

Even as the gentlemen gaped, he hustled his mother and sister from the ballroom, aware of Lady Wilmont's gaze on them like daggers.

CHAPTER 10

"What happened?" Lady Abernathy asked the moment they were in the carriage. "Did Miss Wilmont attempt to back you into a dark corner?"

Martin winced at how close to the mark the jibe had come. "Lord Manville and Lady Knowle," he said, each syllable dragged from him, "found me alone in Lord Wilmont's study with Miss Hindley.

He swallowed. "They found me kissing her."

A moment of deadly, dreadful silence as his mother and his sister stared at him in shock. Then Lady Abernathy exploded.

"That hideous, evil woman! She did this. She sent the girl to lure you away from the ball so you would be found in a compromising position. She's trying to bring ruin and scandal to this family."

"Miss Hindley did not 'entice' me into the study."

"You just happened to casually wander into the room where the girl was conveniently waiting?"

Martin realized nothing he said would be to his credit. "No, I followed her."

"I didn't think I raised a fool for a son. They set the trap and you walked into it."

She fixed him with an all-too-familiar expression, the one which said he'd disappointed her. "Please tell me you did not compound one stupidity with another and decide you were obliged to be honorable."

Martin tensed at this casual dismissal of consequences. "I meet with the Wilmonts tomorrow to discuss the marriage settlement."

The words came more easily than expected. "Perhaps a proposal was not my original intent, but having said so in the presence of others, I have no intention of going back on my word."

"You. Will. Not."

The words were a command. But Martin was no longer a boy. "I will. It may not be the most auspicious beginning, but Miss Hindley is a capable, intelligent woman who will make a fine wife."

"I'm certain Miss Hindley possesses all the virtues." Lady Abernathy's words dripped with sarcasm. "Which is why she let a man to whom she is not engaged make free with her. I suppose I shouldn't be surprised. Look at the Wilmont girl. She'll be a scandal before the season's done, mark my word. And if you marry this Miss Hindley, we'll be tied by association. Did you stop and consider what this will mean to your sister? What man is going to want to associate himself with a family tainted with scandal? She could end up on the shelf, or find her only choice is someone of much lesser rank and fortune. Is that what you want for her?"

"Martin's landed himself in a terrible position," Cecilia said, "and you're worrying about whether or not a man I won't accept will offer for me?"

A crack of thunder rent the air outside, followed by the sound of rain falling, the storm which had threatened all day bursting forth. "Cecilia, you're overwrought." Lady Abernathy's voice took on a soothing tone, one hand reaching out to pat her daughter's, but Cecilia jerked her hand away.

"I'm not. I think Martin has more pressing matters." She glanced across to him. "You're really going to marry her?"

Martin nodded. "If she'll have me."

"Of course, she'll have you," Lady Abernathy said. "You're titled and rich and she possesses nothing."

Lady Abernathy turned her head away. "Of course, if she or the Wilmonts break things off for one reason or another, you would be free, honor intact and the Ton would understand the family for what they are."

"Don't even think it."

"I'm just saying --"

"You'll not try to get the Wilmonts or Miss Hindley to break the engagement. Do you understand me?"

This time, she bowed to his role as head of the family, though he knew her silence would not last. Nothing to be done now, though, and he turned his head away, trying to make some sense of the chaos in his thoughts.

He did not accept the idea Dorothea had been anything but open and honest with him. The pain in her eyes had not been feigned, of that he was certain.

Closing his eyes, he could once more see her looking up at him, the need to be comforted, pleading not to let her be lonely, if only for a moment. Kissing her had been such a simple matter.

Martin stared at the rain for the rest of the short journey home, hoping he might find some answer to his troubles in the tumbling waters. He found none.

◈

"I hope you're satisfied." Alyssa stood on the threshold to Dorothea's room. "You planned to ruin things, didn't you?"

Dorothea turned from the window, but didn't bother to respond. What did it matter? Alyssa wouldn't even need to invent gossip for Mr. Shipley now.

Her silence only served to annoy Alyssa further. "I should have guessed," she continued, stepping across the threshold. "All the times you've spent talking to him at events, seeking him out. I bet the two of you planned this the evening he escorted you back to Mama."

"I planned nothing of the sort," There'd be no escaping the coming inquisition from Lady Wilmont. Why should she endure one from Alyssa as well?

"Of course you claim that now, having been caught. To think I once considered asking you to come with me once I marry the Duke of Stockwood. I wanted you to help me set up house and manage things. Out of the question now. I won't allow a person with such loose morals around me."

Alyssa wanted her to plead with her to change her mind. Any such efforts would only serve Alyssa's vanity and her desire to rule over those she considered her inferiors. Dorothea found no use in doing so. Not anymore.

The lack of response turned Alyssa's expression more petulant. "They're waiting for you downstairs. Mama and Papa. They sent me up to fetch you before I retired."

Dorothea rose, steeling herself for judgment. "Good night, Alyssa,"

Alyssa didn't respond, throwing a nasty stare before she flounced out of the room. Dorothea followed at a more sedate pace, not hurrying her steps as she made her way downstairs to meet her fate.

She barely stepped through the door of Lord Wilmont's study when Lady Wilmont started. "How could you? I thought you had more sense than to be seduced—and to be seduced by Lady Abernathy's cad of a son." She turned back to Lord Wilmont. "This is why he wanted an invitation, I'll wager. He planned to embarrass us in the most public manner possible."

"And cast aspersions on himself in the process. Think for a moment, Honoria. Do you think Lady Abernathy would agree to such a plan?"

"It'd be just like a man to come up with such a plan," Lady Wilmont countered. "He has a title and a fortune. Yes, his reputation will suffer, but many young ladies will still be eager to line up for the chance to be the next Viscountess Abernathy."

Lady Wilmont spun back to Dorothea. "If you must be so foolish as to be seduced, why tonight? You not only ruined yourself, but everything we've worked for. The only thing anyone will speak of is you caught practically stretched out on the desk. Who you were caught with gives this added fuel."

"We were just kissing," Dorothea said, stirred to speak by this description.

"The two of you could have been saying prayers," Lady Wilmont shot back. "What you were actually doing won't matter once the gossips are done."

"Honoria, enough," Lord Wilmont held out his hand to his wife. "I want to know Dorothea's side of the story."

Lady Wilmont hesitated for a moment, then took one of the two chairs before the desk. Dorothea noted she was not invited to take the other. "Some grave charges have been made against you, young lady. You were observed in improper behavior with Lord Abernathy, and the actions grow worse with each retelling. What happened?"

Dorothea did not doubt most of the Ton would be more willing to believe the juicy story rather than the distraction she'd tried to arrange. "They found Lord Abernathy kissing me. Nothing more."

"Did Lord Abernathy lure you in here?"

"No," Dorothea's voice was a whisper.

"Did you lure him?"

She shook her head, her face growing warm at the suggestion.

"Why were you in the library?"

No getting around this. "I … was unhappy. I didn't want to be in the ballroom. Everything was going well, so I thought no one would miss me if I slipped away for a few minutes. Certainly, Alyssa wouldn't be grieved if I absented myself," she couldn't help adding.

Lord and Lady Wilmont exchanged a glance between them. Alyssa's behavior being a topic of conversation offered small comfort now. Dorothea took a deep breath. "I don't know why Lord Abernathy followed me. He said he worried about me. We talked. I cried. I didn't plan on kissing him and I don't think he planned to either. Everything … happened. Lord Manville and Lady Knowle interrupted us, and—"

Lord Wilmont raised a hand. "We can guess the rest. You should have left the room when he came in, not allowed yourself to be alone with a man who is not family. Why didn't you?"

Dorothea could only offer a shrug. "I was upset and not thinking. We began to talk, and things happened swiftly."

He didn't ask another question, but pondered what she had said for a minute or so. "You are not going to like this, my dear, but I don't think there were ill intentions."

"Then why did Viscount Abernathy insist he proposed to Dorothea?" You did not see his face, husband. He found himself caught and willing to say what he must to lessen the shame to himself."

Dorothea's head jerked sharply toward Lady Wilmont. "He … said he proposed?"

Lady Wilmont frowned. "You had no idea, did you? I sent you to your room before he offered up that particular nugget. He said Lord Manville misinterpreted what he'd seen, and you and he kissed because he offered you marriage and you accepted."

"I take it there was no offer," Lord Wilmont said.

Dorothea shook her head. Why would he say such a thing, unless he was so concerned about his honor, he saw no other way.

"Better hope he will hold to his word," Lady Wilmont said. "I told him to call upon us this afternoon to settle details. If he doesn't show, you are well and truly ruined."

Lord Wilmont leaned forward. "If Abernathy doesn't come up to scratch, you won't be able to stay. Your presence will reflect badly on Alyssa. I don't know what we're going to do with you, but best you stay in your room as much as possible. Your meals will be sent up to you. I think we can all agree any guests who pay calls today should not see you."

Dorothea took the words as a dismissal and made her curtsey. Things could have been worse, she reflected as she climbed the stairs to her room. She still had a roof over her head.

She was painfully aware all that might change in an instant.

❧

Martin presented himself at the Wilmont townhouse at the appointed hour. "You are expected, my lord," the butler said once he proffered his card. "Lord and Lady Wilmont will be with you shortly."

He didn't miss the overt hint of disapproval in the butler's tone as he was shown into Lord Wilmont's study. The room seemed different now, the soft sunlight, tinged with winter gray, coming through the window rendering the setting less intimate than mere hours before.

He did not wait long. "I'm pleased you were prompt," Wilmont said as Martin made his bow to the baron and his wife.

"There is business to discuss and futures to decide. I think you'll agree this is something to be dealt with promptly."

Wilmont nodded, even as Lady Wilmont glared, and he gestured for Martin to take one of the two chairs before the desk. Lady Wilmont took the other as her husband claimed the chair behind the desk. The arrangement did not make him comfortable. Too easy for Lady Wilmont to lunge at him if she so desired. He did not doubt she was perfectly capable of doing so if she thought the occasion warranted.

"Before we start anything," Lord Wilmont said, "I want your version of last night. Not what you tried to peddle to Lady Wilmont, but what happened."

Clearly, they weren't going to allow him to make his offer without considerable effort. He edited the tale somewhat, speaking of the concern which prompted him to follow Dorothea, but not offering exact details of what she said. Saving that, he offered as clear and honest accounting of the events as he could, including Dorothea's attempt to muddy the waters. "My worry for Miss Hindley's reputation caused me to say I had proposed," he concluded. "While I did so to help her, let me be clear I do not count it a hardship to offer her marriage."

Something unspoken passed between husband and wife and Martin wondered if his tale tallied with what Dorothea told them. He hoped so, and she had not altered the truth in a misguided attempt to protect him.

"I'm pleased you're willing to do the right thing by Dorothea," Lord Wilmont said at last.

"If he was interested in doing the right thing," Lady Wilmont snapped, "he wouldn't have followed her out of the room to where being caught would mean she's compromised."

"I erred in doing so," Martin let his own tone be tart. "But what is done is done and I am more than ready to deal with the conse-quences. Naturally, my solicitor will speak with yours, Lord Wilmont, to hammer out the details of the marriage settlement. I understand there isn't money on Dorothea's side."

Wilmont held up his hand. "Dorothea will not be coming to you in her shift. We have put aside a dowry for her. Perhaps not a grand dowry, but I'll not have her completely beholden to her husband. Every woman should possess some competence which is her own. My solicitor will ensure it."

"Dorothea comes from solid gentry stock and traces her ancestry back to a knight who fought with King Henry at Agincourt," Lady Wilmont said. "She is fine enough to stand beside any peer of the realm."

Many might say otherwise, but Martin couldn't help counting the fact Lady Wilmont stood by her ward as something in the woman's favor. Perhaps the first thing. "And I will be proud for her to stand beside me."

"Honoria, why don't you go fetch Dorothea?" Lord Wilmont said. "Only right we get her formal agreement."

Lady Wilmont rose and departed, though not without giving Martin one final glare. Once she departed, Wilmont leaned forward. "Let us speak frankly, sir. I don't like this at all. You put Dorothea in a difficult spot and only out of concern for her are we agreeing to the match. I don't need to tell you what a scandal can do to a young woman of little fortune, no matter how proud her lineage might be."

Martin nodded, but said nothing, sensing Wilmont had not finished. "I understand the control the law gives a husband over a wife. I will tell you, though, if I learn she has been mistreated under your roof, it will not go well for you. You have my word."

If anything is left once your wife's done with me. "It is not my intent to mistreat her." Martin met Wilmont's eye with a steady gaze. "As I said, I do not count it a hardship to marry Miss Hindley."

CHAPTER 11

Dorothea put aside her book at the tap on the door, rising to her feet as Lady Wilmont entered. "Lord Abernathy's proved true to his word, much to my surprise. You're going to be a viscountess instead of ruined."

He wants to marry me. The thought flitted through Dorothea's mind, only to be revised to *His honor obliges him to marry me.* "Better than having Mr. Shipley hold rescuing me over my head for the rest of my life," she muttered, trying to wrap her head about the idea.

To her surprise, Lady Wilmont laughed, the annoyance on her face dissipating. "There is that." Her frown returned. "His sermons and platitudes might be preferable to dealing with That Woman on a daily basis. At least you're dressed and not wallowing about in a dressing gown."

She started for the door. "You need to formally give him your consent. Then we can start planning the wedding and the solicitors can hammer out the details. Don't worry. You're not going to him in your shift. May cost us a bit more than planned, but you'll be able to hold your head up. Plus, I think Abernathy's in a mood to be generous on settlement, and don't scorn the idea. You need to make certain you're not dependent on them."

Her words sounded rather mercenary, but Dorothea knew only a fool would refuse, no matter what Lady Wilmont might think about her future mother-in-law.

Both Wilmont and Martin stood when she and Lady Wilmont entered the study. "I think we should leave them alone to talk," Lord Wilmont said, as he emerged from behind the desk and ushered his wife toward the door.

Lady Wilmont began to protest, but Wilmont didn't stop moving, closing the door firmly behind them.

"They sound certain this is settled," Dorothea said.

Martin blinked. "Are you saying you don't want to marry me?"

She shook her head. "I've been the subject of so much charity in my life and I couldn't bear to face the same in my marriage." The words were awkward on her tongue. "Am I making sense?"

"Some." He gestured to the chaise against one wall. "Would you rather marry your vicar?"

Dorothea couldn't help making a face. "That's charity, too. Reverend Shipley wants the link to our family, so he might still take me even with this scandal, but …"

She sighed and settled on the chaise. "No, I don't want to marry him."

A hint of a smile on Martin's face and a bit of relief as well. "This isn't charity, Dorothea. Yes, I'm doing what is considered the right thing because society perceives I'm responsible for the ruination of your reputation."

"Or I lured you into a compromising situation where you find yourself forced to marry me because you're a man of honor," she countered.

"We know the truth. What happened in the library when we kissed … I do not think this would be a bad marriage between us. And I expect this to be a full marriage. You'll take your place as the Viscountess Abernathy and act as my hostess, which I know you can do."

He took a seat on the chaise as well, so close their knees almost touched, his face serious as he reached out to take her hand. "But I also mean the marriage bed. I expect children, an heir for the next generation. And everyone will be counting on their fingers the moment they suspect you're with child."

"A relation once told me a babe could be born a year or more after a hasty marriage and the gossips would still count on their fingers."

Martin snorted. "Certain truth in those words. But you understand." He rubbed his thumb slowly along her forefinger. "I think the two of us can face the Ton together. Are you willing to try with me?"

For a moment, Dorothea hesitated. This was not what she pictured her life would be like, a man such as this offering marriage, even if not under the best of circumstances. She had no desire to trap him into something he didn't want and a little seed of doubt nagged at her.

But she could also picture what her life might be like if she didn't marry Martin. Seeing him waiting, she thought, *At least we're being more honest with one another than most couples are at this point.* "Yes."

The smile on his face as he pulled her to her feet and into his arms told her he was glad she'd agreed. His kiss hinted desire might well play a part in things as well, the passion of last night coming through as she wrapped her arms tightly around him.

This time she had no thought anything was wrong with what they were doing, no worries they might be discovered. At this moment, there was just the two of them and the world ahead. Eventually, though, breathing became an issue and they reluctantly parted. "We'd best call your aunt and uncle back in," Martin's words sounded a bit ragged. "They're probably listening at the door."

Dorothea giggled, and couldn't help continuing when Martin opened the door to find Lord and Lady Wilmont standing quite close. If they weren't listening now, they might well have been earlier. "Miss Hindley has agreed," Martin said.

Lady Wilmont embraced Dorothea and kissed her on the cheek. "I hope you are happy." Turning to Martin, she added, "And if she is not, you will hear from me, sir."

"You should be grateful ladies can't fight duels," Wilmont commented dryly. "I believe, besides the settlement, there is the date to be determined. Which is the purview of the ladies, though they might allow you some input."

"I suppose you'll want a special license," Lady Wilmont sniffed. "Done quickly to damp down talk."

"I think such a move would increase talk. But a Common License to avoid waiting on the banns. The day after Christmas, perhaps?" Martin smiled at Dorothea. "Would that please you, my dear?"

Out of habit, Dorothea mentally reviewed the calendar in her mind. "You'd planned an open house, Aunt Honoria."

"We can host a wedding breakfast instead," Lady Wilmont said. "Three weeks should give us enough time. We'll start spreading the news to our acquaintances and whoever calls this afternoon." She considered for a moment. "You should come later yourself, sir, so you are seen. I would ask you to bring your mother, but …"

Martin bristled, which was hardly surprising. "I believe Mother planned on paying her duty call today. So she will be accompanying me. And, of course, you should pay us a call as well. Next week. For maximum effect."

There was another detail or two discussed which Dorothea did not find herself able to pay close attention to, focused more on Martin, studying him closely. Then he bid farewell to Lord and Lady Wilmont and turned to her. "I will return in a few hours."

She smiled. "We'll be able to speak. And dance together."

A broad grin split his face. "I'll hold you to that, Miss Hindley."

He bent down to kiss her, a lighter touch than when they'd seal their pact, but the touch still filled her with warmth after he disappeared through the door. "I'll give him this," Lady Wilmont said. "Even if he's only doing this out of a sense of duty and honor, he's determined to put on a good face."

She turned to Lord Wilmont. "Don't embarrass us with the settlement. Abernathy isn't expecting Dorothea to come with much and she needs to be able to hold her head up before That Woman."

"You might want to stop referring to her as such since she's going to be Dorothea's mother-in-law," Wilmont said.

"And I don't envy her. Lady Abernathy will find fault with everything she can. She'll criticize Dorothea's conversation, suggestions, her dress—"

Lady Wilmont stopped to run a critical eye over the simple gown Dorothea wore. "Come with me."

Knowing any protest would be useless, Dorothea allowed herself to be pulled out of the study and up the stairs. "Mary, put down your mending," Lady Wilmont called to her maid as they entered her chambers. "Go to Miss Alyssa's room and fetch me the pink gown with flowers, the light gold, the blue with the ruching about the bottom." She stopped and waved her hand. "Whatever else you think might be suitable for Dorothea and be quickly altered. Also, a green embroidered shawl Miss Alyssa never wears. Kate will know the one. Be quick about it."

With Mary out the door, Lady Wilmont turned her full attention to Dorothea. "You'll need new gowns for evening, but your day dresses will serve. We'll need to brighten them with ribbons and shawls." With a sigh, she indicated Dorothea should make a turn. "You'll need at least one or two new of those as well, and something for the wedding. Today, we need to make certain Lady Abernathy can find nothing to pick at."

She frowned. "Mary should re-do your hair. The style's too simple."

Self-consciously, Dorothea patted at the knot she wore most days as Alyssa stormed in. "What's this about Mary needing some of my dresses for Dorothea? I thought you were sending her away."

"Circumstances have changed," Lady Wilmont said, not bothering to turn her attention from Dorothea. "If only you had a bit more height."

"One thing I cannot alter, no matter how much I might wish."

Lady Wilmont chuckled. "Mama!" Alyssa stamped her foot. "Last night, you agreed Dorothea's behavior was horrible. She ruined my ball!"

"Which was unfortunate. But many eligible gentlemen still sought your attention." Lady Wilmont turned toward her daughter. "Fortunately, Lord Abernathy offered Dorothea marriage, which will help put the scandal to rest. We need to put our best face on this betrothal."

"What does that have to do with my dresses?" Mary arrived, arms laden with gowns, a green silk shawl on top of the pile. Alyssa snatched it as the maid passed. "And why does Dorothea get to be a viscountess? She's supposed to marry Reverend Shipley, which is better than someone like her could expect."

No surprise Alyssa would not easily accept the idea of Dorothea standing higher in rank well. "Things have changed," Lady Wilmont repeated, her voice even, but firm. "Perhaps they are not as we planned, but we move forward and adjust. "

She reached out to take the shawl, but Alyssa drew back, pouting. Throwing up her hands, Lady Wilmont said, "I'll lend Dorothea one of mine. But we need some of your outfits altered until we can acquire some from the modiste."

Lady Wilmont turned to her maid. "I need you to send to Mlle. Lisle and ask her if she can call on me at six. Tell her to bring any gowns she has available suitable for a young lady. I'll make it worth her while."

She considered for a moment, then said, "Best convey the message yourself, after we finish. We need to see if you can alter any of these for Miss Hindley by tomorrow and she'll need her hair redone before callers arrive."

Mary laid the dresses across the room's chaise and held up one in a pale gold. "Kate said this is a bit loose across the bosom on Miss Alyssa, so it might suit Miss Hindley."

As Lady Wilmont held the dress up against Dorothea, Alyssa said, "Not that one, Mama. I want to wear it to the Rothman's assembly later this week."

"You own plenty of others to choose from. Take off your dress, Dorothea, and see if this fits."

"Mama!" The word was accompanied by another stamp of a foot.

"Don't sulk," Lady Wilmont said. "It's unbecoming."

The advice had no effect, Alyssa's pout becoming a scowl. "Don't you have anything to say, Dorothea? Don't you think the dress is wrong for you?"

Dorothea didn't respond as she was helped into the gown. A bit tight in the bosom, but one glance in the mirror told her she appeared far grander than she could ever remember. *I wonder if Martin will like it.*

The thought reminded her she would soon be his wife, with things she never dreamed of within her grasp.

"Well?" Alyssa demanded. "Say something."

Taking a deep breath, Dorothea turned back her aunt. "I think you're right, Aunt Honoria. I think this will do quite well."

"Mama, do something!"

"Be quiet or go to your room! I will not tolerate these tantrums while I'm trying to work."

Alyssa hovered, shocked for a moment, then turned and fled, weeping noisily. Dorothea tensed, wondering if Lady Wilmont would break off to appease her daughter.

Lady Wilmont shrugged. "She'll recover. You're not to let yourself be vexed. Worrying about Alyssa is not your problem. You have other things to think about."

She stepped back, considering Dorothea critically. "Yes, this will do. Mary, can you move the hooks slightly in the back? Come up with a trim or drape to cover things if necessary. The hem will need to come up a touch as well; that should give you extra fabric if necessary. Pin it this evening after the modiste leaves. Now, we need to get ready for calls."

As Mary helped Dorothea out of the dress, Lady Wilmont began to tick items off on her fingers. "We'll need to make a list of all the other things you'll need for your trousseau. Hats, spencers, nightgowns …"

Dorothea reached automatically for her notebook, only to realize it was still in her room. Soon, there'd be no more late-night sessions going over notes as they plotted the next step in Lady Wilmont's social campaign. the idea of the loss as she stepped into the unknown bothered Dorothea more than she would have thought.

Martin had no sooner handed his hat to Farthing than Cecilia appeared. "Are you really going to marry the Hindley girl?"

"I said so last night." Martin ushered her toward the morning room so they could speak privately. He stopped when he realized his mother would likely be waiting, ready for calls. Instead, he pulled her into the alcove created by the curve of the staircase. "I just came from the Wilmonts' and the date's set for the day after Christmas." He smiled down at his sister. "I think you'll like her."

"That's not what's worrying me," Cecilia said, her face solemn. "I don't want you unhappy, trapped in a marriage because you feel honor-bound. I don't want that for either of us."

"I respect Miss Hindley. She has wit and intelligence and I like her." He couldn't help offering a lopsided grin. "I must marry at some point. Think of some of the women Mother wants me to court. They'd all make a fine viscountess, but do you think they would make me happy?" He shook his head. "This is different, and I want to think it's the right thing for me."

Cecilia smiled, though her eyes still showed concern. "Then I will do my best to welcome her. And once you're wed and can think about other things, I'm hoping—"

"You're back."

Martin and Cecilia turned at the sound of Lady Abernathy's voice. On her face was no sign of last night's potential scandal, her demeanor as cool and collected as always. "Cecilia, will you please go to the morning room in case any guests arrive?"

Brother and sister cast a wary eye at one another. Without bothering to argue, Cecilia did as bid, leaving Martin to face his mother alone.

"I suppose you've done it," Lady Abernathy said once Cecilia was out of earshot. "So? A hasty wedding and send her to the country so she's not an embarrassment to the family?"

Her tone betrayed no more emotion than if a servant had broken a piece of porcelain or somehow torn some fabric. Perhaps less. "Private license," he replied, doing his best to keep his voice calm despite his annoyance. "The ceremony will be December 26, with the wedding breakfast at the Wilmonts'. We can't take a proper wedding trip, I'm afraid, but I thought perhaps four days away at the lodge in Hertfordshire."

He flicked a speck of lint from his sleeve. "Miss Hindley and I will have a chance to become acquainted as a husband and wife should."

"You cannot seriously be considering treating this—this abomination of a marriage as something normal."

No, an emotion lurked under her words: pure anger. It wouldn't be the last time, Martin was certain. "Don't you realize if we're going to weather this scandal, the best way is to act is as if there isn't a scandal. Yes, the gossips will have a field day I found myself enamored of a poor relation with little fortune who is linked to a woman you despise." Martin leaned forward. "But we will have a bigger one if I don't carry through on what I said last night. Not only would I be a cad who tried to seduce your enemy's ward under your enemy's roof, but I reneged on a promise I publicly made. Is that what you want?"

As she chewed on his words, he pressed his point. "Are you going to let everyone see you're furious and don't care for the idea of this marriage? Or are you going to show no weakness where the gossips are concerned?"

Lady Abernathy glared over his shoulder and Martin became aware of the hall boy retreating. Of course the servants hung on every word. His marriage would mean changes. "I suppose I have no real choice," she said. "For Cecilia's sake, I will do as you ask. But if you think I'm going to be happy, you're sadly mistaken."

None of what she said surprised him. "I trust you won't let your unhappiness show when we call on Lady Wilmont this afternoon."

The cool facade now showed cracks. "Why on earth would I deign to pay a call on that ..."

She stopped speaking as the door knocker sounded. As the servant moved to answer, Lady Abernathy pulled Martin in the direction of the morning room, out of view of the front door. "I will not," she hissed.

"You will too. I've already told Lady Wilmont we'll attend when thank you calls for the ball are being made. She's agreed to present a united front, which I think you'd want to do. For Cecilia's sake."

A furious glare, but she did not reply as Farthing approached with the card tray. Lady Abernathy plucked the card from the surface, then nodded after a momentary perusal. "We'll need the carriage at four. Please do not admit visitors after half-three."

Farthing bowed and departed. Lady Abernathy opened the morning room door and led the way in. "For Cecilia's sake, and nothing else."

Cecilia glanced up from her embroidery, her expression curious. "We're paying a call on Lord and Lady Wilmont this afternoon," Lady Abernathy said. "It is only polite after they invited us."

Cecilia didn't appear to believe this excuse, but Lady Hennings appeared in the doorway, ending the discussion. "Is it true?" the woman asked after exchanging pleasantries. "Is Lord Abernathy betrothed?"

Lady Abernathy gestured graciously toward the chairs set out for visitors. "A surprise but he is determined. Not that I know Miss Hindley beyond the briefest acquaintance, but I suppose I will have many opportunities to rectify the lack in the future."

Martin tried not to grit his teeth too hard. The next three weeks would be long ones. He had saved both Dorothea's reputation and his family's with his proposal. But what type of life would he bring her to?

CHAPTER 12

"Proposed to at a ball—how romantic!"

Lady Rossiter leaned in confidentially, placing her hand on Dorothea's. "I want all the details."

Of course she did. Everyone Dorothea had spoken to wanted all the details. Each word, inflection, gesture and expression would be weighed and dissected at other calls. Dorothea had observed this game from the fringes often enough she'd been expecting it. Didn't mean she had to like it.

Like it or not, though, this was the game she had to play.

Conscious of Lady Rossiter watching, she let a smile cross her face. "I'm afraid I don't remember most of the details," she said, letting a hint of embarrassment color her voice. "It happened so fast. I remember Lord Abernathy's face when he asked, I said yes, and he kissed me." She paused for a moment. "Then I remember us being interrupted by Lord Manville and Lady Knowle."

She fiddled with the ends of the shawl Lady Wilmont had loaned her. "I'm afraid it was not how either of us wished for our families to learn of our news. We did not intend to distract attention from Cousin Alyssa."

"Of course you didn't, my dear." Another pat of her hand and the smug expression on Lady Rossiter's face hinted the woman found Dorothea's story satisfactory. "So naughty of them to interrupt you at such a private moment and make the worst possible assumption without bothering to wait for explanation." A pause. "Will Lord Abernathy will be joining us today?"

That question had been asked as well, more than once. "He will." Dorothea tried to sound certain. "That was his plan when he spoke with Lord Wilmont."

Another nugget to make Lady Rossiter's eyes light up, another piece of the story being built. Now, if only Martin would arrive, with or without his family. At least Alyssa wasn't visibly sulking, a small consolation. Surrounded by young men, she was all smiles. The few times she glanced in Dorothea's direction, though, the expression in her eyes warned Dorothea she was not forgiven, nor likely to be in the near future.

"Is the date set?" Lady Rossiter's question Dorothea's attention back to the conversation. "Has there been any discussion of the wedding trip? I understand he only proposed last night, but—"

She broke off as the butler entered the room and announced, "Viscount Abernathy, the Viscountess Abernathy, and Miss Cecilia Drayton."

Every head swiveled toward the door as Dorothea tensed. Martin was a welcome sight, but she found herself uncertain how to respond to Lady Abernathy. The woman gave no sign whether she considered this marriage good, bad, or was indifferent to the entire prospect. Behind them, Martin's sister gave the impression her most recent meal might be vexing her.

Lady Wilmont rose from her chair and stepped forward with her arms outstretched. "My dear Lord Abernathy. So glad you could join us this afternoon. Dorothea, come and greet Lord Abernathy."

Dorothea did as bid, not objecting as Martin took her hands and planted a chaste kiss on her cheek. Lady Abernathy's face remained impassive as Lady Wilmont turned to her. "And it is lovely to see you as well on such a happy occasion. There is much to discuss and I'm certain the children would like to chat."

Doubtful Lady Abernathy wanted to discuss anything with her

archrival, but she played the game, allowing herself to be led to a seat next to Lady Wilmont, Cecilia following. Martin drew Dorothea toward the windows, away from the crowd. "She's not happy to be here," Martin said. "But she'll play her part."

"As will Aunt Honoria. I think both of them hold their desire to minimize the scandal higher than their distaste for one another. We'll probably enjoy a truce until after the wedding."

She stopped, the word strange in her mouth. Martin slipped his hand under her chin and tipped it upward. "Then we begin a new story."

The words were said with a certainty Dorothea wished she felt. A certainty reflected in his eyes as he gazed down at her. "They're all watching us," she said, not knowing how else to reply.

"Of course they are. We had a steady stream before we left, all asking if the betrothal rumors were true."

A sideways glance to where most of the guests sat and he dropped his hand, offering her a lopsided smile. "The story I proposed seems to have travelled much quicker than the idea I attempted to debauch you."

Dorothea wanted to suggest she wouldn't have minded being debauched, but remembered they were not alone.

"You're thinking," Martin said. "If I know one thing about you, it is that expression."

His words coaxed a smile from her. "Am I so obvious?"

"Only to someone who's paying attention."

Which meant he'd been paying her closer attention than she thought during the past weeks. She liked that. "It feels strange, being able to talk to you openly."

"And about something other than how we're going defuse this damn feud." Martin nodded. "I understand." Another glance over towards the others. "Though, I must wonder if this truce will survive until the wedding."

She followed his gaze and saw Lady Abernathy appeared even frostier than when she arrived. Lady Wilmont did her best, but signs of strain were visible, as if she bit her tongue on every other word.

With barely a thought, Dorothea reached for his hand, taking comfort in the warmth of his fingers around hers. "Here's hoping."

In the nearly two weeks since the ball, there'd been the appropriate calls back and forth between the families, as well as other encounters. At events where the Wilmonts weren't present, Lady Abernathy still let her dislike of the woman be known, though she assured listeners she found Dorothea "charming."

Martin did his best to ignore the insinuation Dorothea would be much more charming once removed from Lady Wilmont's influences.

The Wilmonts now sat in the Abernathy Drawing Room, Lady Wilmont and Lady Abernathy tossing oh-so-polite barbs at one another, much to the amusement of the other guests. To one side, Dorothea's smile appeared fixed as she suffered through an interrogation from Lady Knowle, who'd somehow managed to return to his mother's good graces. Making matters worse, Alyssa Wilmont appeared determined to catch the attention of every man who came calling on Cecilia.

And no chance to speak with Dorothea this visit beyond the barest of words. Martin was not a happy man.

Farthing entered with a card from another visitor. With only the briefest of glances, Lady Abernathy gave her nod of approval. Moments later Lord Blair MacDonald entered, making his way first to Lady Abernathy, who happily disrupted her conversation with Lady Wilmont to greet him. Her relief was short-lived, for once the social pleasantries were done, he turned to Martin. "Abernathy, a word if I may?"

They withdrew to the far end of the room. "Perceval approached His Highness with a proposal for a Regency Bill," Lord Blair said.

"Not surprising. After the physicians' report, he wants to protect his position because he knows a Regency is inevitable this time."

Blair nodded. "I know you've been busy," he glanced back toward Lady Abernathy, "but will you be at Lords this evening?

"As soon as I can escape this." Looking toward the other end of the room, he saw Dorothea had escaped her conversation with Lady Knowle. She now sat on the fringes of whatever disagreement Lady Abernathy and Lady Wilmont where having. And it was a disagreement. Poor girl. "You can assure His Highness I'm doing what I can."

"His Highness understands you're otherwise occupied at the moment. But he wondered if you'd heard about the reaction of Commons to the report of the King's Physicians."

"That members are annoyed the Prime Minister and the Chancellor lied to them about the seriousness of His Majesty's condition?" Martin sighed. "I'll be here for as much debate as I can be until Christmas, and back again on the Thirtieth. If I'm needed --"

"Don't joke," Blair said. "Someone may be here when you arrive to convey you to Parliament. I doubt we'll give your bride any joy."

Martin doubted that as well. Dorothea was speaking now, her posture respectful. Lady Wilmont seemed pleased with her, even proud. Lady Abernathy did not.

Blair leaned in. "Given his own unhappy state, His Highness is suspicious of sudden, unexpected betrothals. He hinted he might say a word if you feel trapped."

Which would thrill his mother beyond telling. Another reason for the wedding to happen soon. "Tell him the wedding's my wish. You can tell him my mother is not happy, but mostly because of the Wilmont connection and I didn't pick one of her choices."

The words earned a chuckle. "I suspected so and told him someone was likely trying to make trouble. But he also said he looked forward to seeing you panting at the altar for a blushing young maiden."

"He's not angling for an invitation, is he?" Martin asked.

"He's bored to tears at Windsor, but he can't come to town merely for his own pleasure. It wouldn't give the right appearance. Your wedding would be an excuse."

The royal presence would make both ceremony and breakfast much larger than Martin intended or Lady Wilmont planned for. But it would also mean the match would be accepted at the highest level of society, putting paid the gossip this was something shameful which needed to be hidden away. He suspected such news would also cause his mother and Lady Wilmont to put aside their feud for a while longer. "You may tell His Highness Miss Hindley and I would be honored."

He turned to face the assembled company. "Wonderful news. Lord Blair tells me the Prince of Wales would be pleased to grace us with his presence at the ceremony and wedding breakfast."

Everyone's attention focused on him, small gasps and murmurs running about the room. On Dorothea's face was a thoughtful expression, as if trying to puzzle out why they would be so honored. "He wishes to be invited?" Lady Wilmont asked, her voice sounding both panicked and hopeful.

"We shall be glad to send him one." Lady Abernathy spoke as if such a request were the most natural thing in the world, but Martin saw the satisfaction in her eyes. She turned to Lady Wilmont. "I possess some familiarity with the kinds of delicacies His Highness prefers. Perhaps we should consult on the menu."

A clear power move, inserting herself into the arrangements normally the prerogative of the bride's family, but, for once, Lady Wilmont didn't appear to mind. "As I'm sure we both want the Prince to enjoy himself since he chooses to honor our families, I agree consultation is an excellent idea. Dorothea, did you bring your notebook?"

The question earned a lifted eyebrow from Lady Abernathy, but Dorothea reached through a slit in her gown and extracted the small volume. Looking toward to Martin, she gave him the smile belonging to a partner in a shared conspiracy. He liked her smile. No matter his mother's rantings, their partnership gave him hope they could make this work, no matter the storms gathered against them.

And his mother might be pleased at the idea of the Prince's attendance, but it didn't mean she held Dorothea in any less contempt. Another thing to deal with once they were through the wedding.

For Dorothea, the last week flew by. Before, her life had been focused on making Lady Wilmont's dinners a success and planning for any other events went smoothly.

Christmas passed and she found herself before the altar, a ring slipped on her finger. Martin smiled down at her as the minister pronounced them husband and wife. A curtsey to the Prince of Wales, then out of the church and into the carriage. For the first time since she accepted his proposal, they found themselves alone.

"You seem a bit dazed," Martin said, his tone teasing as the carriage with the Abernathy crest on the door began the short journey to the Wilmont townhouse.

"It's—" Dorothea took a deep breath. "Everything has been a blur the last few days. I found myself caught by surprise."

He squeezed her hand and lifted it to his mouth to plant a gentle kiss there. Turning it over, he kissed her palm, before drawing her to him. "I think I might like catching you by surprise."

He kissed her, gently at first, but slowly growing more demanding. Dorothea dropped the flowers she carried on the carriage seat to wrap her arms around him. A vague thought not to muss his neckcloth passed through her mind, but the press of his lips against hers drowned it out.

Her body wanted to do something as he drew his hand down her body and a settled in the place between her legs. When Martin pulled his lips away from hers, she began to protest, only for the words to turn into a gasp as he kissed her throat. Lady Wilmont had been thorough last night in explaining the mechanics of what passed between a man and a woman, but hadn't mentioned this stirring.

The carriage slowed and Martin pulled away. "I believe we're here," he said, his voice a bit rough.

Heat rising self-consciously in her cheeks, Dorothea reached for her bouquet. At this moment, she wished the breakfast was done. Also, why did Martin appear much calmer than she felt as he handed her out of the carriage?

Wilson opened the door, bowing with a smile as they passed into the entrance hall to be met by applause from the waiting staff. The smiling faces made Dorothea realize how many of these people she would miss.

"Enough," Wilson informed the staff. "His Lord and Ladyship will be here shortly, with the guests, and the Prince of Wales, directly behind."

The staff scattered as Wilson led Dorothea and Martin to the morning room, to receive their guests before they sat down to the wedding breakfast. "Would her ladyship care for a sherry after the rigors of the ceremony?" Wilson asked as a maid held out her hand for Dorothea's bonnet.

Automatically, Dorothea answered, "I imagine Lady Wilmont would appreciate a drink. Thank you, Wilson."

Martin laughed. "He means you, my dear. You're Lady Abernathy now, so you are a "ladyship.""

Dorothea's cheeks grew warm. "Yes, I think I would like a sherry."

Martin drew his arm through hers. "Don't be embarrassed. It took six months to get used to being called "Lord Abernathy" after my father's death. Sometimes when I hear it, I still expect him to be there."

This was why she hoped this marriage would work. Martin could be kind and deserved a wife he could be happy with. She hoped she could fill the role.

The Wilmonts appeared, Lady Wilmont still sniffing into her handkerchief. "It was a lovely ceremony. You are the very image of what a bride should be. How kind of you, Wilson."

As Wilson attempted to move past Lady Wilmont, she neatly snagged the glass of sherry from the tray. "Exactly what I need to restore myself."

Wilson rolled his eyes heavenward and retired, presumably to fetch another glass. "His Highness appeared pleased with the whole affair," Lady Wilmont continued. "And such a lovely gift. A silver punchbowl will make a fine addition to your parties, Dorothea."

"They're right behind us," Lady Abernathy announced as she entered the morning room. "We should probably form a receiving line for His Highness soon."

Lady Wilmont appeared a bit annoyed at the presumption of

Lady Abernathy, but agreed with a sigh. "Alyssa, you should freshen yourself before the guests arrive. I want you to be at your best."

"Dorothea's the one who should freshen herself," Lady Abernathy said tartly. "After all, it is her day. Why, thank you."

As Wilson paused at Lady Abernathy's side, unable to quite get to Dorothea, Lady Abernathy availed herself of the glass of sherry on the tray. "I must say, Lord Wilmont, your servants are excellent."

"Er, yes." Lord Wilmont grimaced at Wilson's rather annoyed expression as he retired to fetch a third glass. "Lady Abernathy is right, Dorothea. Need to, er, freshen up?"

When Dorothea shook her head, Martin said, "We'll use the Prince's punch bowl for the ball, of course."

"Since His Highness will be present," Lady Abernathy said, "it would be rude not to. I doubt he'll have forgotten it by February."

Martin must have noticed Lady Wilmont's expectant glance because he said, "I hope you will join us, madam."

Lady Wilmont preened, even as Lady Abernathy's lips thinned.

Wilson appeared, at her elbow. "Your sherry, my lady." He sounded as if this were a victory against the enemies of England. But no sooner did Dorothea raise the glass to her lips and take her first tiny sip, when they heard came noise in the hall. Lady Wilmont reached out to pluck the glass from her hand. "No time with the guests arriving. Take it away, Wilson."

Years of experience brought the tray upright in time to catch both Dorothea and Lady Wilmont's glasses. Experience couldn't keep the somewhat annoyed expression off Wilson's face as he retreated, pausing only to retrieve Lady Abernathy's glass as well.

For the next several minutes Dorothea and Martin greeted guests. If she had married the Reverend Shipley, it would have been a small wedding with a small party for breakfast. This was much grander, Martin's friends and those who might be advantageous to either side making up the bulk of the attendees.

Wilson appeared in the room's doorway to formally announce the next guest. "His Royal Highness, George, Prince of Wales."

Lady Wilmont's sigh of pleasure was audible as the prince swept into the room with his entourage. Dorothea sank into a deep curtsey while Martin made a formal bow. Wreathed in smiles, the prince raised her almost instantly. "Come, come, Lady Abernathy—for you are Lady Abernathy now—none of that. It is your wedding day, when every bride is a queen. In fact, it is I who should bow to you."

Still holding her hand, he gallantly bowed over it as deeply as his girth would allow. All eyes focused on this action, which was nothing more than a dramatic gesture meant to quell gossip. She knew better than to trust it too far. "Your Highness flatters me," she assured him. "I hope we will have the pleasure of welcoming you to our home as one of our first guests. We would consider it an honor."

The smile on his face when he straightened with a slight wheeze showed Dorothea had picked the right words. "I might take you up on the invitation, my lady, once you return from wherever Abernathy is whisking you off to. Just don't be gone too long, sir; I need you in Lords."

As the Prince moved away to greet others, Martin squeezed Dorothea's hand. "Well done, Lady Abernathy. Well done."

She squeezed back and decided to take this as a promising sign.

CHAPTER 13

Dorothea found herself unable to enjoy the breakfast. There'd been a week of hard work preparing for this event. Even now she found her mind ticking off every detail, a habit she imagined would not break any time soon. She was also keenly aware of every eye on her, watching her every move. Martin ate light as well, not partaking much of the wine. She opted to do the same through the toasts offered.

With the meal done, they mingled, but soon Lady Wilmont swooped down to insist she change into her traveling clothes. Halfway up the stairs, though, Lady Wilmont groaned. "Oh, she isn't."

Dorothea turned her head to find Alyssa below them, doing her best to back the Duke of Stockwood into a corner. "Someone needs to stop her," Lady Wilmont said.

Instinctively, Dorothea began to move. "Not you, silly goose," Lady Wilmont said. "You have other things to do. Wilson!"

The butler, ever attentive, appeared almost magically a step or two below them. "Wilson, tell Miss Alyssa she is required upstairs in my room to help Lady Abernathy change. Do not take no for answer."

"Understood, my lady."

Without waiting to see the results of her command, Lady Wilmont shooed Dorothea onward. Once they achieved Dorothea's room,

Lady Wilmont began to undo the spencer worn over the satin wedding dress, while Mercer, Dorothea's new maid, stood by to assist. "This gown will serve you well for evening if you take care of it, and you always take care."

Lady Wilmont pressed her hand to Dorothea's cheek, her eyes glistening. "I do want you to be happy, even if your path is different from my plans."

Finding herself unable to respond, Dorothea covered Lady Wilmont's hand with her own. She could feel tears threatening, but Lady Wilmont cleared her throat and returned attention to undoing the spencer.

Dorothea was nearly changed into her blue traveling gown when Alyssa appeared, her face arranged in a pout. "You told me to entertain our guests, Mama. You stressed we must make a good impression today."

"I did not mean causing a scandal with the Duke of Stockwood. A lady lets a gentleman pursue her, not the other way around."

"But he hasn't been pursuing," Alyssa pouted. "I can't let that ninny Cecilia Drayton catch him."

"You're speaking of Dorothea's sister-in-law, so take care. Besides, I already told you, your father will not give his consent to a marriage with His Grace."

Alyssa flopped into a chair, looking for all the world as if on the edge of a tantrum. "Did you notice how handsome Viscount Tilney is today?" she said as the maid did up the last of the hooks for Dorothea's dress. "Far more handsome than the Duke of Stockwood. His title's older than Lord Abernathy's, too, so I would stand higher than Dorothea. Perhaps he'll make an offer."

"The only offer you're likely to get from him is an indecent one," Lady Wilmont snapped. "He's in debt up to his eyeballs, only invited because His Highness wished to include him in his party."

"Well, Lord Tilney's asked me to dance with him at the Sidney's rout and I accepted," Alyssa said, her tone daring her mother to forbid it. "Why shouldn't I enjoy myself with a handsome gentleman? This supposed to be my season, even if Dorothea stole all the attention."

Pleasedon'tfightpleasedon'tfight. The words kept pounding through Dorothea's brain. The past weeks had been one long quarrel between Alyssa and everyone else. She found herself weary and ready to leave it behind.

The knock on the door came as welcome relief, and she turned eagerly, hoping to find Martin, only for Lady Abernathy entering. "Are you ready to leave?" she asked. "Martin has finally escaped from the Prince, who's agreed to formally take his leave so you can depart."

Dorothea reached for her bonnet, but Lady Wilmont said, "Almost. If I could beg a few minutes alone for some private words before Dorothea goes?"

Instead of objecting as expected, Lady Abernathy softened a little. "Of course. I'll send Martin up shortly."

As she left, Lady Wilmont dismissed the maid and told Alyssa, "Wait downstairs for me. Do not attempt to force yourself upon the Duke of Stockwood again. *Don't* go near Lord Tilney. I'll know if you do."

With a toss of her head to show how little she cared for the instructions, Alyssa left, offering not a word of well wishes.

Lady Wilmont settled on the bed, then patted the coverlet next to her. "Come sit by me, child."

When Dorothea sat, she said, "This is not how I pictured your wedding day. I wish it had happened in another way, not with this cloud."

She took a breath. "Begin well, and love and affection will hopefully grow, especially if you provide him with an heir. Also respect." Lady Wilmont smiled at her. "He does appear to hold some respect for you, or else I don't believe he would have gone to all this effort to smooth over this scandal. Hold that precious."

Dorothea nodded, unsure what else to say. Lady Wilmont frowned. "His respect is precious because you'll receive little from his mother. I'll wager she will try to thwart you at every turn. She'll cut you down to your husband without hesitation, so it is imperative you stay in his good graces. If you need advice, turn to me because I doubt you'll receive any from That Woman."

This sounded less comforting, though Lady Wilmont seemed to think it sound advice. It didn't paint a rosy picture of her new home.

A knock at the door and Martin stuck his head in. "Mother said you're ready."

"I am," Dorothea said, scrambling to her feet. "I just need my hat and cloak."

She was more than ready to leave, to stop this state of waiting. Lady Wilmont helped her on with a fur-lined cloak to keep her warm during the journey and tied the ribbons of her bonnet. With a smile and a kiss on the cheek, Dorothea found herself handed over to her husband.

"All is well?" he asked, and she knew some of her discomfort showed.

"Ready to be done with this," she whispered in return as Lady Wilmont proceeded them down the stairs.

Not an exciting thing to tell a new husband, but the time for explanations was later, if she shared it fully at all. Her instincts warned her Lady Wilmont's words against Lady Abernathy should keep close to her chest.

"They're coming!" she heard Lady Wilmont announce to the guests below. Martin stopped at the top of the stairs, holding Dorothea back before they came into the view of the gathered crowds. "This is the last gauntlet," he told her. "Ready?"

She nodded and he squeezed her hand encouragingly. They made their way down the stairs, a bow and curtsey before the Prince at the bottom. He beamed broadly as if he somehow had a hand in arranging the whole affair, then grandly led the way outside, technically departing before they did.

On the sidewalk final embraces from Lord Wilmont, who gave her a warm kiss on the cheek, before handing her over to Lady Wilmont. Alyssa had managed to somehow blend with the crowd, avoiding giving Dorothea any farewell at all.

This left her standing as Lady Abernathy embraced her son, eyes closed as if the emotion of seeing him off on his wedding trip too much to bear. At last she let go, fighting back tears as he offered some final words. Then, she turned toward Dorothea to offer a stiff embrace. "I expect you to be a proper wife to him," she murmured. It was a command, not a wish.

When Lady Abernathy released her, Cecilia gave her a quick embrace as well. Martin beamed as he took her by the elbow and helped her into the carriage. Then they were away, the wishes ringing in their ears as the coach drove through the streets of London.

❧

"The manor used to be a more strenuous journey, but as London grew, the roads were made better, Now it's a relatively easy jaunt."

Martin glanced toward Dorothea, who took in the scenery as they rolled into the drive leading to Drayton Lodge. The winter sun had begun to set, painting everything with a golden glow. "Sir Edward Drayton built it during the reign of Queen Elizabeth, hoping to entice her to visit him," he continued. "She did—three times, in fact—and it damn near bankrupted him."

As Dorothea laughed, he added, "What's worse, he didn't get the preferment he sought. His grandson became the first Viscount Abernathy under the Stuarts. Which, of course, was put in peril during the Civil War because he sided with King Charles."

She turned toward him, her face catching some of those golden rays. "Do you think Sir Edward would be pleased his descendant stands high enough in royal favor for the Prince of Wales to attend his wedding?

There was a certain teasing to the question, as if she hoped to lighten the mood. The journey had been easy, but the atmosphere within the carriage more awkward as they progressed. "I think he would warn me not to put too much trust in any prince for they are fickle creatures. Also, what was I doing to raise our family to an earldom."

Dorothea laughed, and this time Martin gave in to the urge to kiss her. He had restrained himself, aware what hours alone in a carriage with only brief breaks could lead to. The wedding night had to be on her mind; better to wait beyond the briefest of kissing until they found themselves somewhere with less jolting.

She melted into his arms without hesitation. It was she who pulled him closer, wrapping her arms around his neck and letting her lips part beneath his.

There was a sudden jolt, a small bump in the road, but enough to pull them apart. "Blast," Dorothea uttered, her tone one of frustration.

No sooner had the word left her lips than her eyes widened and she clapped her hand over her mouth. Martin couldn't help laughing at her reaction. "Blast, indeed."

Leaning forward, he gently pulled her hand away. "I'm flattered I provoked such a reaction."

This time, his kiss was gentle and much shorter, but he still sensed her willingness. Reluctantly pulling away, he told her, "We're almost there."

The carriage rounded a gentle curve and the house appeared in their view, gabled roofs and ornate carved chimneys silhouetted against the sky. "It's beautiful," Dorothea said.

"Not too old-fashioned for you?"

She shook her head, focused on the house. "Not at all. I wouldn't change a thing."

With a smile, Martin leaned back against the upholstered cushions. The old pile was safe for another generation from the new mistress wanting to remodel according to the latest fashion.

He pushed thoughts of his mother's reaction to "the new mistress" away as the carriage stopped before the front door, the graveled drive lined with torches to provide illumination. A footman stepped smartly forward to open the door and flip down the carriage's steps. Martin emerged first, then offered his hand to help Dorothea down.

The butler, standing on the stoop, made a deep bow. "Welcome home, my lord. I trust your journey was a pleasant one?"

"Pleasant enough, Rogers. The staff?"

"Assembled inside to welcome Lady Abernathy." The butler bowed to Dorothea. "I thought your ladyship would prefer not to linger outside."

"Very thoughtful of you, Rogers," Dorothea said. "I'm certain the staff doesn't object, either."

The words were spoken lightly, her tone approving. Rogers smiled, bowed again, and Martin knew she'd made a conquest in a way his mother never had.

Rogers indicated they should enter, falling into step with Martin as they did. "I dissuaded a delegation from the village appearing as I didn't think your lordship and Lady Abernathy would welcome the fuss after your journey. However, I have heard rumor there will be the traditional serenade tomorrow morning for the newly married couples. Shall I make certain ale is at the ready?"

"Probably best you do. If you would do the honors."

Martin had wondered how Dorothea would handle this, but she greeted the staff as if born to this. As she moved down the line, she offered a smile here, a word there, setting them at ease with this new and unexpected mistress.

Once through the introductions, Dorothea turned to take in the room's features, enthralled with the tapestries, carved staircase and painted beams of the vaulted roof. "It meets with your approval, I take it?"

"In my wildest dreams, I wanted to live in a house like this," she breathed, her gaze still fixed on the ceiling.

"I'll remind you of those words when we have trouble with the roof," he teased good-naturedly. "Mrs. Potter, would you kindly give Lady Abernathy a tour and show her to her room so she can freshen up before supper?"

He stepped forward and untied the ribbon which held her bonnet in place. "No need of this," he told her. After all, you're hardly a visitor."

Handing the hat off to whichever servant held out their hands to take it, he moved closer. "I'll give you some time before dinner."

Slipping two fingers under her chin, he tilted her chin up and back until their eyes met. Lowering his head, he placed a kiss on her lips. His intent had been simple, her response was more, lips parting, pressing against him as her arms slid around his waist. The sensations were heady, not unlike the rush of desire he had felt at the Wilmont ball.

For a moment, he found the urge to sweep Dorothea off her feet, march up the stairs and consummate their marriage now almost over-whelming.

But the pressure of desire brought another pressure as well, reminding him they'd spent hours in a carriage. Pulling back, he cleared his throat. "Why don't you go with Mrs. Potter now?"

His voice was lower and thicker than he intended, and he did not trust himself to say more. With a smile which promised all sorts of delight later, she slipped from his grasp and moved to follow the housekeeper. He watched her go, then shook his head in an effort to clear it. All the things he desired were coming to him, but not in the way he planned.

CHAPTER 14

Sometime after supper, Dorothea sat before the dressing table of her chamber, her maid brushing out her hair. Unused to having a maid, it was tempting to dismiss the girl so she could do the brushing herself. Lady Wilmont, though, stressed the need to begin as she meant to go on, which meant making use of her maid's services. Still, brushing her own hair would give Dorothea's hands something to do, a welcome distraction.

A tap at the door Mrs. Potter said connected her rooms to Martin's, followed by him entering. "Thank you … Mercer, isn't it? I'll finish Lady Abernathy's hair."

Mercer dropped a curtsey, giving Dorothea a knowing smile in the mirror as she left. Her image was quickly replaced by Martin moving to stand behind her, picking up the brush Mercer laid down. Slowly, he began to draw it through her hair, silent as he watched her in the mirror. He was wrapped in a dressing gown, with no shirt underneath. She tried to meet his gaze in the mirror, but her eyes kept dropping to the light brushing of curly hair visible just above where his robe met. Is he wearing anything underneath?

The thought flashed through her mind like lightning, illuminating the fact there was no turning back. They were married, bound for life.

Easy enough to agree theirs would be a full marriage sitting in the Wilmont drawing room, her choice wedding him or ruin. Even with the delicious kisses and touches in the carriage today, there'd always been a barrier of clothes and a certain amount of propriety between them.

Now, the last barrier was about to fall away, leaving her bare before a man she didn't really know.

"Mercer thinks," Dorothea began, but stopped. Taking a deep breath, she started again, this time trying to keep her voice lower, calmer. "Mercer thinks my hair is too thick. She believes I should cut it in the latest style when we return to Town."

"I'm surprised she didn't whisk you under the scissors of some hairdresser before the ceremony," Martin said, his words tinged with amusement. "Most ladies' maids I've known are fierce dragons when it comes to ensuring their ladies are shown to the best advantage."

She almost asked how many he knew, but stopped herself. "Mercer wanted to, but Aunt Honoria forbid it. She didn't think it was a good idea to make so drastic a change before the wedding."

"I never thought I'd say this, but hooray for Lady Wilmont." He considered her reflection. "A little trimming in the front, perhaps, but please leave the back as it is. I find it most attractive."

Setting the brush down, Martin ran both hands through her hair, letting them slide lower to caress her neck. Moving down to her shoulders, he pushed her dressing gown off her shoulders, playing with the neckline of her nightdress. Shivers ran in the wake of her touch, her nipples tightening beneath the silk.

Meeting his gaze in the mirror, she pulled her arms free from the robe, before undoing the ribbon which secured her neckline. The silk slid off her shoulders from the slight pressure of his hands, slithering down her arms to pool about her waist, leaving her exposed to him. *Don't be afraid to surprise him*, Lady Wilmont had said last night, as the hour grew late and her advice bawdier. *Never hurts to keep him off balance.*

His reflection's eyes grew wider, and hands moved from her shoulders to her breasts. Cupping them in his hands, he drew his thumbs across the nipples, smiling as she sucked in a sharp breath. "Stand up," he commanded.

She did as he bid, and the nightdress slithered down her legs to the floor. Turning to face him, she resisted the urge to cover her nakedness. They had dealt honestly with one another to this point; why should she hide now?

Was it the cold air which made her shiver, or how his gaze travelled down her body? "Beautiful," he said, his voice hoarse.

"I'm glad you approve," she said, doing her best to sound brazen. "I know the fashion is for taller ladies."

"If you were taller, your curves wouldn't be quite so … curvy."

As if to illustrate his point, he reached out to run a hand down her side before stepping closer to lower his head to hers. The kiss was thorough, her mouth opening to admit his tongue as he explored. All the while, his hands caressed her body, delicious tingles across her skin, a pleasure she didn't want to stop.

But he did stop, pulling back with a frown. "You're shivering. I shouldn't keep you standing here. Into the bed."

"Martin—"

"Bed."

Dorothea scrambled under the covers, glad for the lingering heat from the warming pan. Martin blew out the candles on her dressing table, leaving the banked fire and candles by the bed as the only illumination. He was a shadow as he approached, discarding his dressing gown before crawling under the covers. His face shifted into the light, his body close enough to warm her. "Better?"

"It will be if you kiss me again."

He laughed, leaning down for a long, lazy kiss as his hands stroked her side, just enough to make her squirm closer to him. "I don't know what to do," she said in frustration when he came up for air.

"Why don't you lie back and relax?" he suggested. "There's plenty of time to learn. Let me guide you."

Martin plucked at her nipple, causing Dorothea to gasp. "A little hard to relax when you're doing that."

"You're not nervous?" One hand cupped her breast as his thumb described lazy circles.

"Nervous, yes," she managed with some effort. "But not frightened. I agreed to this."

She hated how cold the word sounded as if this was some blood-less bargain. A slight frown on Martin's lips as well, which unsettled her. "So you agreed to this?" he asked before planting a series of small kisses along her jaw.

"And this?" He trailed his tongue down the length of her neck.

"And you agreed to this?" He lowered his head to suck her nipple into his mouth. Dorothea gasped again, shocked by the sensation.

"Was that a yes?"

"That was most definitely yes," Dorothea said, her voice breathy. "Is there more?"

Martin chuckled. "Much, more. But I want to make certain you're getting what you agreed to."

He shifted slightly, bringing up his other hand to capture her other breast. Lowering his head, he began to lavish attention on it as well, drawing more gasps from her lips. The sensations travelled through her body, down to settle between her legs. Squeezing her thighs together, she couldn't help wiggling, and the slight friction caused a little gasp as well.

The delicious touch of Martin's lips on her breasts stopped and Dorothea opened her eyes to find him watching her. She froze, wondering if she'd done something wrong. "Did you agree to this, Dorothea?"

One hand skimmed down her body, across her belly to coax her legs open. He began to stroke, delicately but determinedly, along her inner thighs. "Yes," she breathed, her eyes drifting close again to better lose herself in the sensations.

A gentle nip on her nipple and her eyes opened again to find Martin watching her, his eyes bright and hungry. "How about this?"

His hand shifted, sliding closer to her cleft. Carefully, his fingers began to explore, tracing the outer lips. "I think you're enjoying this, my lady. That's what your body is telling me."

"I—" A single finger slid between those lips, and stroked upward, across the nub at the top. Words left her, the only sound from her, a keening moan. When Martin sucked at her nipple, his fingers still moving between her legs, Dorothea moaned again.

In. Out. Her eyes closed, her hands grasping at the sheets. The swirl of his tongue around one nipple, then the other, causing tension to build in her body. Below, his hands continued worrying at her cleft, spreading moisture to provide more friction as he stroked. Her hips moved of their own accord, pushing against his hand, vaguely aware when one finger became two thrusting rhythmically into her, his thumb rubbing over the nub.

Muscles tightened, driving her higher, harder, until she tumbled into a wave of pleasure. Gasping, she started to come back to herself. For a moment, she let her eyes stay closed, then opened them to find Martin propped on one elbow, his other hand describing circles on her belly. "Did—did I cry out 'yes'?"

He grinned. "Quite a few times. I think I'm properly reassured you agreed to this."

"But—" Dorothea caught some air into her lungs. "Isn't there more?"

"Quite a bit more. But I think you're better prepared now. More … relaxed."

He let his hand drift lower once more, causing her to shiver as he stroked between her legs. Now, though, she was aware of a heat and hardness against her. "Is that it?"

When he looked at her curiously, she shifted, moving her hand to catch his hardness. Martin made a noise, and she couldn't help smiling. "That is it."

Dorothea drew her hand along his length, exploring. She wasn't completely ignorant as to anatomy, but she also knew seeing a stallion ready for a mare was different from a man. It was still a little nervous to think Martin's hard length would slip inside her with any ease.

But her body craved him, especially as he reached for her again, sliding his fingers into her cleft once more. She shifted onto her back, but this time he came with her, moving to settle himself between her legs. Dorothea still had hold of him, and as he stroked, so did she. Her hands moved gently, unsure how much pressure to use.

He leaned down and kissed her, demanding and hungry, as his fingers stoked the fires within her once more. As he touched, she found her hand move more boldly, fingers caressing each ridge beneath the skin.

Raising his head, Martin sucked in a deep breath. "I can't wait for you any longer, Dorothea. I need you."

No one had ever needed her. They'd needed her talents, her brain, her ability to get things done, but no one had ever needed *her*. But Martin did. At this moment, in this place, there was a connection between them. "I agree," she whispered, afraid anything louder might break the spell.

He stroked her cleft once, twice, three times, and when she found herself squirming beneath his hand, he removed it and brushed her hand aside. His erection took his hand's place, hot and hard against her. He shifted, rubbed and she gasped. "This may hurt," he warned, "but I'll try to be careful."

"Brandy." The word sputtered ridiculously from her lips, causing him to still.

"You need brandy to get through this?" Martin sounded unsure.

"No. After. Aunt Honoria said. If it hurts. Ask for brandy." She took a deep breath and shuddered as her body connected with his in just the right place. "Martin, don't stop. I didn't agree to be left hanging."

"As my lady commands." He shifted then slid inside her a bit before pulling back. She moaned in pleasure as he moved again, deeper this time. Another withdrawal, another thrust, and this time she felt a pressure. It must have shown on her face because he asked, "Does it hurt?"

"Not exactly. Can you move again?"

Martin did. This time there was a brief discomfort as the pressure released. He moved again, and the discomfort faded, replaced by warmth, the tightening of muscles and heightened sensations. She shifted her hips, changing the angle and …

Dorothea's back arched as she moaned. This was what Lady Wilmont spoke of, this delicious pleasure.

Martin stopped. "Brandy after, I promise."

"To hell with the brandy," she spit back. "Don't stop moving."

He looked surprised, then laughed, moving again. She strained upward to kiss him, wrapping her arms around him as he fervently responded. His hand gripped her hips, thrusting deeper and deeper into her, winding the spring tight. Finally, she could take no more, her world exploding in waves of pleasure which had her crying out for him. A moment later, he stiffened, and a different type of warmth flowed into her.

Spent, Martin collapsed atop her. Dorothea couldn't help her involuntary, "Oof."

"Did I hurt you?"

"No," Dorothea pushed at him. "But you're heavy."

Laughing, he shifted. "One of the most romantic things a lady has ever said to me. Come here."

She settled into his arms. "Do you need a brandy?" he asked as they lay under the covers.

"Will you have to move to get it?"

"Yes."

"Then, no, I don't need it."

He chuckled against her hair, his body began to relax. Soon, the slow rise and fall of his chest told her he'd drifted off to sleep. She should as well; the day had been long, awaking early to begin preparations. But there was also no tasks planned for tomorrow, save spending time getting to know this man who lay by her side.

As Dorothea shifted, Martin mumbled under his breath, tightening his arms about her but not waking. Smiling to herself, she settled and let her eyes drift closed. Perhaps there'd been no fervent declarations of love, but she hadn't repulsed him. Perhaps it was enough to build upon.

❧

The sun streaming through the window combined with an unholy racket from outside pulled Martin from slumber. Drayton Manor, wedding yesterday, he turned his head to find Dorothea stirring next to him. *Rogers said something about the locals serenading us.*

With a groan, he threw back the covers, retrieving his dressing gown from the foot of the bed. Wrapping it close about him, he padded across the floor to retrieve Dorothea's nightdress and robe from where they'd been discarded the night before. "What is that noise?" he heard Dorothea ask from behind him.

Turning, he found Dorothea sitting up in bed, the covers wrapped around her more for warmth than modesty. "The tenants have come to serenade us. It's a local custom. They serenade in the morning, so you pay them in ale to go away."

"And we must make an appearance, looking fresh from bed?" She held out her hand to take her garments. "There is a similar custom in Buxdale. They bring the new couple a strong bowl to fortify them so they'll return to bed."

She pulled the nightdress over her head, then scrambled out of bed as she pulled her robe about her. "But the couple's also expected to offer food and drink in return. Shows their household will be welcoming to guests."

Thank goodness she didn't act missish about the idea; he liked the interruption no better than she, but he understood the importance of observing the customs. Striding to the door, he called for his valet. Moments later, both Barker and Mercer appeared. "Mercer, your lady needs to dress. Barker—"

"Knowing of the custom, I laid out something simple for you to wear. No cravat, I think."

"Excellent." He took a deep breath. "Now, I think we need to make an appearance at the window."

He offered his hand to Dorothea and she took it, allowing him to lead her to the window. Outside, a group of musicians were gathered, who might well have been celebrating before their arrival. The crowd with them carried holly, a symbol of hope for fertility. A ragged cheer went up when Martin opened the window, pulling Dorothea in close to join him. A new song was struck up, something about health and happiness. The words were a bit unintelligible, but the sentiment heartfelt.

When they were done, Martin leaned forward. "Lady Abernathy and I thank you for your warm wishes on such a cold morning. If you'll return to the front, Rogers has some refreshments waiting. We will join you shortly."

Another ragged cheer and the crowd began to disperse generally in the direction indicated. Pulling his head back inside, he closed the window, "Ready for your first appearance as Lady Abernathy?"

"Better your tenants than the Ton," she said. "Your tenants don't bite."

"You haven't met them." He gave her a brief kiss. "Get dressed, but remember this is casual. We're all going to pretend we tumbled out of bed and threw something on so we're decent."

He headed back to his room, trailed by Barker. When he was nearly dressed, Martin realized how comfortable he'd felt with Dorothea. He had expected some awkwardness, but there'd been none. He wasn't quite certain what to make of this knowledge.

Dressed as befitted a gentleman wakened from his marriage bed, he returned to Dorothea's room to find her maid fastening her gown. "You're ready?"

"We don't want to keep them waiting, do we? No, my hair is fine. I think tousled is better than brushed fully out."

So she did not linger over her toilette when the occasion warranted some speed. Good to know.

She laid her hand in his when offered, and together they headed down the stairs. Rogers waited in the entry hall, a mug of ale on the tray he held. "Custom dictates you offer this to the musicians, my lady."

"Thank you, Rogers. I wouldn't want to slight them." Taking the mug, she looked up at Martin. "Shall we?"

A cheer went up at their appearance, followed by another as Dorothea stepped forward to offer the mug to the musicians' leader. "To thank you for your serenade and your welcome."

The man took the mug with a bow, then lifted it in the air to cheers from the crowd. "The best of luck to you, my lord and lady. Here's to a fruitful union."

The mug passed between the musicians before being returned to Martin for him to drink as well. Only a little was left, but he swallowed all. "The only thing I can add to my wife's words," he said when he was done, "is my hearty thanks."

Rogers took the tankard from him as the drum began to beat. The crowd took up the rhythm, their faces expectant. "We're supposed to kiss," Martin told Dorothea.

"All part of the ritual," she said, but he sensed no hesitation as she stepped into his arms.

His intention had been for a reasonably chaste kiss, but she relaxed against him, the kiss deepening. Vaguely, He was aware of cheers from the crowds, but his attention stayed with Dorothea. No, no hardship in marrying her. Not when she was warm against him.

Pulling away, he found himself blinking down at her. Dorothea's cheeks flushed, not from the cold. Her eyes were bright as well, full of promises.

He wanted to be away from here, back to peace and seclusion where only the two of them dwelled. Turning to the crowd, he said, "We thank you for your company, but if you will excuse us …"

Ribald laughter met his words, but Martin didn't care. He happily pulled Dorothea back inside the manor. "Upstairs," he said, his voice rough in his ears.

Her response was to follow eagerly where he led. Up into her bedroom once more, the door shut firm behind them. They tumbled into the bed in a heap, kissing passionately. "How long do we have again?" she asked.

"Not long enough," he replied, wishing there weren't other responsibilities waiting for him in London.

She reached out a hand to stroke his cheek. "Let's make the most of it."

Martin couldn't argue.

CHAPTER 15

As the country gave way to the outskirts of London, Dorothea sighed, leaning her head against Martin's shoulder. "Can I confess I'm not eager to be back in the city?"

She felt his chuckle rumble in his chest. "If not for the king's illness ..."

He trailed off and Dorothea shifted her head to better see him. "Will you need to go to Parliament tonight?"

"Hopefully not, but I will likely have visitors to discuss where we are."

"I don't enjoy the experience your mother does, but if I can help—"

"You'll be busy settling into the house, paying the calls newly married ladies are supposed to make," Martin said. "I want you to become familiar with our acquaintances."

Which sidestepped the question, but she decided against arguing. She understood the importance of meeting her husband's circle, but her stomach still twisted at the idea of so much time in Lady Abernathy's company.

Closer to the townhouse, Martin helped replace her bonnet, tying the ribbon to one side of her chin. "Perhaps not as expert as Mercer," he teased, "but I think you look lovely.

Dorothea hoped so. Martin appeared annoyingly pulled together as he handed her down, nothing to betray some of the joys they'd indulged in during their travels. She wagered Lady Abernathy would notice every wrinkle in her gown.

The door opened before they finished climbing the steps, the butler bowing low as he ushered them in. "Welcome home, my lord, my lady."

"Thank you, Farthing. It's good to be back." Martin handed off his things. "I assume my mother and sister are around here somewhere."

"In the drawing room. They did not receive callers this afternoon so they would be ready when you and young Lady Abernathy arrived home."

Martin flashed a smile at Dorothea as she removed her hat. "Young Lady Abernathy. I like that."

Dorothea smiled back, though she didn't find herself fond of the appellation. Something about nagged at the back of her neck.

Farthing cleared his throat. "The staff are ready to greet you and your bride at your command. Her ladyship worried it might be too taxing for her young ladyship after the rigors of travel, but I thought your lordship might wish otherwise."

The message was unmistakable: *This is my home, not yours.*

Martin frowned. "Gather everyone before supper.

With that, he led Dorothea toward the drawing room. Cecilia was seated at the piano, while Lady Abernathy was in a chair by the window to catch the best light for her needlework. She was on her feet the moment Martin walked through the door. "You're home!"

While she wrapped him in an embrace, Cecilia rose. "Welcome back," she told Dorothea as she offered a kiss to the cheek.

Dorothea accepted the gesture, still uncertain where she stood. There'd been little opportunity to get to know Martin's family beyond the formal visits before the wedding. If not for the wedding, it was unlikely she would know them at all.

"We've received quite a pile of invitations," Lady Abernathy said, turning to offer Dorothea a brief and formal kiss. "I accepted a few because I knew Martin would want to attend, but you'll need advice on the others."

"Dorothea and I will go over them later." Martin smiled at her. "I want to introduce her to our friends as soon as possible."

"Of course. After all, she is a Drayton now." She turned back to Dorothea. "You must think my manners are terrible to keep you standing here. Martin, did you think to feed this child on the road?"

"Oh, we ate," Martin replied with a wolfish grin that could be interpreted as something else.

"Behave. Come along, Dorothea. I imagine Mercer is upstairs unpacking."

She led Dorothea from the room and towards the stairs. "The Wilmonts had your trunks sent over, and my maid saw to those. We must visit the modiste, my dear. The day dresses will do for now, I suppose, but your evening gowns are not acceptable. One looks as if a bottle of ink had been upended over it."

"Which one?" Dorothea asked.

"Pale gold with a touch of green, I think. Did suit your coloring, I recall, so we should find you another in that shade. Fischer says she will do everything she can, but she fears the gown may be ruined."

The one Lady Wilmont took from Alyssa to outfit Dorothea for her first event after the engagement. "There must have been an accident while packing," she said, her voice a bit flat.

Lady Abernathy did not appear to believe the excuse, but didn't press. "Speaking of maids, do you not think someone who understands the way of our household might be better?"

Someone Lady Abernathy would approve of. "We're still early days, but I think Mercer is working out quite well."

"Hmm. Let me know if you change your mind."

They did not speak again until they reached the rooms set aside for the viscount's wife. The sitting room and bedroom were decorated in bold golds and white, much like the dressing table at Drayton Manor. "So many happy memories in this room," Lady Abernathy said with a sigh.

Dorothea stayed silent, deciding it best to let her mother-in-law move from this topic to the next at her own pace. A moment more, then she was back to briskness. "You'll want to redecorate as this is your room now. Martin's suite is through that door." She indicated a door in one wall.

Mercer entered, carrying garments from Dorothea's trunk. She curtseyed before proceeding to the wardrobe. Lady Abernathy watched the maid as she worked, her gaze weighing and measuring. "If we are not entertaining or going out, dinner is at seven. We dress, of course."

She paused, mouth pursed. "I will leave you to settle in," she said at last. "Martin will be up to check on you soon."

Only when left alone did Dorothea realized her arms were rigid by her sides, fists clenched tight. It was nothing said, but something in Lady's Abernathy's manner put her teeth on edge. The condescending niceness extended to a poor relation that would disappear the first time she broke an unspoken rule.

Dorothea might be married to the current title holder, but the Dowager Viscountess Abernathy still ruled this roost.

◈

Martin rapped on Dorothea's door shortly before dinner. "How are you settling in?" he asked.

"Mercer is done with the unpacking," she said, rising from her chair. "Your mother wants to take me to the modiste. She doesn't think my evening wardrobe is sufficient."

"I'm not surprised. You must admit most of your wardrobe is simple." He reached out to take her hands. "Buy what you think you need, and don't let her bully you."

She pulled a face which had him wondering if there might be something else he should know. "Shall we go down? We shouldn't keep the staff waiting."

He offered her his arm and together they descended the stairs. The staff, assembled as requested, looked upwards, regarding Dorothea with curiosity. "We're ready to begin, Farthing?"

The butler bowed. "We are, but her ladyship sent word she would appreciate if we waited for her to arrive."

Martin didn't feel like waiting, and Dorothea would likely be more comfortable if she could meet the staff without his mother weighing every gesture. But if he ignored his mother's request, she would be difficult, and he didn't want to cast a pall over their first evening back. "We will wait for formal introductions, but I wish to introduce her to Mrs. Richards now."

Farthing agreed with a nod of his head and gestured for the housekeeper to come forward. Mrs. Richards dropped a formal curtsey. "Welcome, your ladyship. Allow me to offer my felicitations on your marriage."

The words were correct, but reserved, an attitude which warned Mrs. Richard's loyalty remained with his mother. Only to be expected, he supposed. Given time, the power would shift from Lady Abernathy, and the London staff would come to accept Dorothea's presence.

Dorothea's voice was warm in contrast. "Thank you, Mrs. Richards. I will be relying on you as I learn the ways of the house. After all, a lady may issue commands, but the housekeeper is the heart of any establishment."

The coolness of Mrs. Richards' reserve melted a touch. "I'm glad to hear that, your ladyship. Lady Abernathy said you should direct any questions to her, but, well, we will talk."

Of course his mother had directed Mrs. Richards to send Dorothea to her. Not surprising, but he couldn't help being a touch annoyed.

"I had hoped you would wait for me."

Everyone turned to find Lady Abernathy descending the stairs, Cecilia trailing behind. "We did," Martin said, "but I thought Dorothea should at least meet Mrs. Richards."

He earned a cool look, but she did not reply, instead nodding to Farthing as a signal he could begin. As introductions were made, she stood one step behind Dorothea, suggesting they continue when Dorothea paused to exchange a word with the cook or any others. By the end of the introductions, Dorothea still wore a smile, but Martin noticed a hint of strain.

Introductions done, Lady Abernathy swept the family into the dining room. One end of the long table was set for the four of them, near the fire burning in the hearth. "Martin, you should take your usual place. Dorothea, you sit next to Cecilia."

Lady Abernathy settled herself in the seat to Martin's right, looking expectantly at the others. Cecilia indicated Dorothea should take the place at Martin's left hand, the seat which had been hers up to now. *Thank you*, Martin mouthed as he escorted Dorothea to her seat before taking his own place at the head of the table. He didn't miss the frown on his mother's face. She hadn't counted on her daughter ceding the higher place to her new sister-in-law without being asked.

Power plays everywhere. He saw it in Parliament and now here.

With the meal served, Lady Abernathy led the conversation. "Tomorrow, we need to go through the cards left for you and decide which ones you wish to return. Martin, this would be an excellent moment to consider your acquaintances and decide which ones you wish to continue. Not all your friends are suitable for a married man."

"Several of those you would deem 'not suitable' are gentlemen I need because of Parliament, especially now," Martin said. "I will go through the cards, I promise."

Lady Abernathy offered a reluctant agreement this might be the best way, while Dorothea offered a much more enthusiastic response. Not that she was allowed any meaningful part in the conversation, given how firmly Lady Abernathy directed everything. Martin tried to include her, but he had only marginal success. Cecilia didn't even try, giving most of her attention to her plate.

Meal done, Lady Abernathy stood to lead them from the table to the drawing room. She and Cecilia picked up their embroidery and settled in close to the lamps, but Martin said. "I'm going to show Dorothea the study."

Lady Abernathy lifted a skeptical eyebrow, but said nothing as Martin pulled Dorothea from the room. Once inside the study, Dorothea asked, "Is this what I'm supposed to expect every meal? Snides and barbs designed to remind me of my previous circumstances and how our marriage came about?"

She pitched her voice so it wouldn't carry beyond the room, but the fury in her eyes warned at her anger. "I'd hoped Mother would accept the situation and would try to make the best of things. I'm not defending her," he said, holding up his hand to forestall her response. "You shouldn't have to put up with such behavior."

She shook her head. "She doesn't want me here. I'm just a pawn in this ridiculous feud or a spy sent to trouble her."

Dorothea turned away, shoulders hunched as she wrapped her arms around herself. Martin closed the distance between them and moved in front of her. "You're my wife. You have every right to be here, every right to express an opinion. I'm pleased you didn't rise to the bait, but I understand you can't be expected to endure forever. She just … she needs a little time."

Her expression was skeptical, and Martin couldn't blame her. "She needs to adjust to the idea she's now the dowager, and you are the current Lady Abernathy. In theory, she should cede the reins of the house to you."

A snort. "With her dying breath."

All too likely a possibility, though Martin decided not to voice agreement. "Think of it this way: not even a month has passed since your aunt's ball. She hasn't had time to get used to the idea of me being married, much less married to you. All her grand plans went into a cocked hat and she's going to harbor resentment."

"Which she will take out on me."

"Which she's going to take out on you," he agreed. "She shouldn't, but she will, until the moment she accepts you're here and you're not going anywhere. I know it's hard, but can I ask you to bend? At least for the next few weeks? I'll try to talk to her, but she's unlikely to soften until the hurt fades."

Martin reached out to run his hands along her arms. "I don't want us fighting over this. If nothing else, Mother would enjoy that."

Dorothea considered this for a moment. "She wants you to send me off to the country. And, no, no one told me she said such a thing," she added as he opened his mouth. "Embarrassments are always sent to the country so they're out of sight."

"Wouldn't do much to calm the scandal if I shipped you off as soon as we married," Martin countered. "She understands. Which means you won't have to worry about her misbehaving in front of others."

"You're forgetting some of what I've seen." Dorothea sighed. "But you're right. If we're on visits, Lady Abernathy will want everything to appear correct."

"You shouldn't call her Lady Abernathy. Call her 'Mother'."

The words sounded wrong the moment they left his mouth and Dorothea's expression only confirmed it. "Maybe not," he said. "Perhaps 'Mother Abernathy'?"

Her face showed what she thought of that suggestion, but he shrugged. "The choice is not unexpected. She'll get used to it."

Dorothea sighed. "Couldn't we go back to Drayton Manor?"

The words were wistful, but her face showed she understood they couldn't. "Once this issue of the king is settled," Martin said, moving closer to run his hands down her arm, "we will go away on a proper wedding trip. I promise."

The words coaxed a smile from her as she drew closer. Surprising how comfortable he found himself with Dorothea. He'd expected some awkwardness, but those feelings had disappeared quicker than expected, as if a missing piece had somehow, all unnoticed, slid into place.

He slid his arms around her, and bent his head to hers. After only a few seconds, though, a knock came at the study door. With reluctance, Martin extracted himself. "I fear this may be someone from Parliament," he said.

Farthing stepped in with a bow at Martin's call. "Sir Roger Phipps, Lord Blair, and the Earl of Newlyn, my lord. They apologize, but say it is urgent they speak with you."

"Should I not wait up for you?" Dorothea said.

"Most likely not. If I wasn't needed in Lords, they would have let me be. Show them in, Farthing."

The three men entered, looking a bit surprised to find Dorothea as well as Martin. A few words of social niceties, and she excused herself, closing the door behind her. "I fear we may put you in the soup with your lady, Abernathy," Newlyn said.

"I warned her; she understands. What is the word?"

"We're voting tonight, both chambers, on whether or not Parliament should discuss a Regency Bill." Roger offered up a rueful smile. "Close enough for you to be needed."

"The Prince will offer both his apologies and his thanks when he hears of your sacrifice on behalf of England," Blair joked. "Be prepared for a few rude comments. Some hope you're still too caught up with your new wife to pay attention to such things."

"Then let's give them a surprise."

The gentlemen lingered in the hall as Martin crossed to the Drawing Room. "I must go to Parliament tonight. The vote on whether or not we'll pursue a regency bill is happening," he announced.

"Won't your wife be disappointed at being left alone so soon after your wedding?" Lady Abernathy asked, not bothering to glance at Dorothea, who'd take up a position by the fireplace.

"Dorothea understands," he said, his tone a touch sharp. "She knows how important this is."

He crossed the room to embrace Dorothea. "Don't wait up," he told her. "I'll see you in the morning."

He kissed her and whispered, "Don't let Mother bully you."

She smiled at him. "I think I may retire early. I have a touch of a headache, most likely from the carriage ride."

Martin doubted that, but he suspected the words were for his mother, not him. Dorothea reached out and picked a small piece of lint from his collar. Martin caught her hand and kissed it. "Until morning."

A quick kiss of his mother's cheek, a squeeze of Cecilia's hand, and back into the hall, slipping into the coat Farthing had waiting. "Shall we, gentlemen?"

As he made his way to the waiting carriage, Martin couldn't help the sense he and Dorothea both faced lions.

CHAPTER 16

Dorothea woke and reached for Martin, disconcerted to his place empty, not even a warm spot to indicate his presence. *I've slept alone all my life. How did sharing a bed with him become natural so quickly?*

Martin next to her when she woke might not feel foreign, but this room did. Perhaps because she found herself alone. Perhaps because the decor mirrored Lady Abernathy's taste, not hers. Perhaps because her mother-in-law thought her an unwelcome interloper.

She was doing herself no favors by lying in bed and brooding, she decided and rang for Mercer. The maid appeared a few minutes later, carrying a tray with a cup of chocolate and a few slices of toast accompanied by a small jam pot. "Good morning, my lady. Mrs. Richards thought you might appreciate something to break your fast before you go downstairs, but you are expected to join the family for their meal at ten."

She caught a whiff of chocolate and her stomach growled in response. "Thank Mrs. Richards for her kindness."

Toast devoured and dressed in her best day dress, she relaxed with a volume from Hookham's Lady Wilmont included with her things. *I knew you would want to finish this,* read a note slipped in beside the strip of leather to mark her place. *Don't let That Woman try to convince you an account at a lending library is unnecessary.*

She found the words kind, though the tone less than helpful, and added 'library subscription' to the growing list in her notebook. When Mercer warned her it was near ten, she began to slip the notebook into her petticoat pocket by habit, but stopped. She doubted taking notes at the breakfast table would be viewed as acceptable.

Downstairs, she realized she didn't know if the family took breakfast in the dining room or somewhere else. She felt a bit foolish asking a footman for directions, but was escorted to a room at the back of the house, overlooking the garden. At the small round table, four places were laid, the morning's first post waiting beside three. She took the seat with no mail.

The footman stepped forward to pour tea when Cecilia appeared. "Did you sleep well?" she asked. "Is your headache is gone?"

"A bit of overtiredness," Dorothea said. "The last week has been a bit unsettled."

"Things should be quiet today. Be warned, though, Mother's holding an open house tomorrow to celebrate the New Year, so guests will be here most of the afternoon. And we stay up until midnight tonight, welcome the year in."

Which meant family customs Dorothea was unfamiliar with. "I'm not sure what I'm supposed to do this evening."

Cecilia frowned. "Not much, I think. Just family, the chief servants and some of the others come in to watch the year turn. Your maid should join, but Mrs. Richards will tell her when."

"Tell her when for what?" Martin asked as he entered. He greeted Dorothea with a kiss, then took his place.

"The plans for tonight," Cecilia said.

"You mean standing in the hall, waiting for the clock to strike and me having to open the door to a blast of freezing air so I can usher the new year in and the old year out?" He took his seat and nodded to the footman, who came forward to fill Martin's cup with coffee. "Charming custom. I look forward to it every year. I warn you, madam, my feet will be ice when we retire."

Dorothea smiled at his assumption they would be retiring together. "We'll find a remedy. How did things go last night?'

"Both houses voted we should—and are compelled by necessity to —sit and consider a bill of regency as His Majesty shows no sign of recovery. After the evidence produced in mid-December, steps must be taken to ensure proper authority is in place for the safety of the country. Now the fun begins."

He rolled his eyes, provoking some smiles and chuckles from both women. "I'm glad everyone is in a fine humor this morning," Lady Abernathy said as she entered.

She moved to her place, regarding Dorothea with a bit of surprise. "So glad you could join us. I know in some households, married women take their breakfast in their chambers. I think such indulgence only encourages sloth."

"I'm used to early hours," Dorothea replied, choosing to ignore the implied insult. "I often write invitations or place cards. Fewer distractions."

"Hmm." Lady Abernathy nodded to the footman, who poured her chocolate, the signal for the others to serve themselves from the plates on the table.

Lady Abernathy inquired about the vote, and Martin gave her a brief summary. "There is hard work ahead," she pronounced. "You will, of course, be of whatever use you can be to His Highness. He will, in the end, be grateful for your efforts."

She turned her attention back to the morning mail. *I should have brought my notebook,* Dorothea couldn't help thinking as Lady Abernathy announced which items she deemed worthy of attention and attendance. Martin engrossed himself in his own correspondence, while Cecilia appeared torn between her mother's letters and her own.

None were prepared for the explosion which accompanied one of the letters. "The nerve of that woman! It's bad enough we'll be forced to invite her to Cecilia's ball, but the idea I should be in need of comfort from her is insulting."

The footman circulating with the chocolate pot froze in place, surprised by this outburst. Dorothea fell back on instinct, caught his eye, and waved a dismissal. He stared at her for a moment, then remembered his training and returned to his place against the wall.

"Mother, what are you talking about?" Martin asked.

"Lady Wilmont, of course.' Lady Abernathy dropped the sheets as if they might bite. "She writes she intends to pay a call today 'to ensure all is well' and offer what support and comfort she can. I won't have her in the house, do I make myself clear?"

Dorothea's eyes were fixed on the letter, wondering if pointing out Lady Abernathy was likely not the intended recipient would lessen the explosion, or provoke a greater one.

Martin had no such hesitation. "Mother, who is the letter addressed to?" he asked, his tone annoyed.

"To 'Viscountess Abernathy', of course. Who else would it be addressed to?"

Martin leaned forward. "Perhaps the letter is meant for Dorothea. After all, she is addressed as Lady Abernathy now."

He kept his voice quiet, but there was a decided edge as he emphasized Dorothea's new title. "I believe your correspondence should be addressed 'The Dowager Viscountess Abernathy.' That is the correct form."

Which meant the invitations Lady Abernathy had been reading out were likely addressed to Dorothea as "the lady of the house."

Lady Abernathy stared at her son for a long moment, then summoned the footman with a gesture. She handed him half the pile, including Lady Wilmont's letter, then waved in Dorothea's general direction. "We still need to meet on the other invitations," she said, her voice laced with ice. "Some would not be advantageous to accept.

Accepting the letters from the footman, Dorothea did her best to be gracious. "Of course. You are more familiar with your circle than I am."

Lady Abernathy sniffed and turned her attention to her next letter. Across from Dorothea, Cecilia exchanged a glance with her brother. It didn't take a genius to realize they both saw trouble ahead.

Dorothea turned her attention to what Lady Wilmont's letter, eyes running over the crabbed but florid hand. Lady Abernathy had not read beyond the first paragraph, or the explosion would have been much worse. Lady Wilmont did write of her plans to call and offer Dorothea what support she could. She also referred to Lady Abernathy as a she-wolf.

She also said she might need Dorothea's help in getting permission for Alyssa to waltz at Almack's. There'd be trouble if Lady Abernathy heard.

She refolded the letter and placed it next to her plate on the side away from Lady Abernathy. "Lady Wilmont and Alyssa are coming to call at two," she said.

"We will not be home for them" Lady Abernathy said. "I'll give Farthing the instructions."

Dorothea sighed. "I will see them. You do not have to."

"I. Do. Not. Want. That. Woman. In. My. House. Do I make myself clear?"

Her glare transferred from Dorothea to her son when Martin spoke. "Be reasonable. The Wilmonts are Dorothea's family. It is natural to wish to see how she is settling into her new home."

"Dorothea should be doing a number of things to support her new position," Lady Abernathy said. "Instead, she must play hostess to a boring old hypocrite who is laughed at from behind the hand of every respectable person in London. The Sudleys did not invite her to their rout despite her best efforts to win them to her side, and yet she appeared, part of Lord Hatchard's party. Lady Sudley showed tremendous restraint in not having them escorted to the door at once."

Having met Lady Sudley, Dorothea also knew if the lady allowed supposed gatecrashers to stay, there must be more to the story. It also told her what she could expect every time her family was mentioned. And what was likely said about her behind closed doors.

"I'll make no apologies for my aunt's behavior," she said. "But I think I should be able to receive my family in my home from time to time." A pause. "Mother Abernathy."

Lady Abernathy's head jerked back toward her at the words. No, she didn't like it. "I think Aunt Honoria will understand if you are not present, but I intend to leave instructions with Farthing they are to be admitted."

"Martin—"

"I think Dorothea's being reasonable, mother. I would ask you to be as well. As she said, she's not asking you to be present."

Mother and son stared at one another across the table. Lady Abernathy broke the contact first. "Very well. This time. I must insist, however, you change into one of your better dresses before they arrive. I'll not see the family embarrassed by you not being dressed appropriately for your station."

"I thought I could lend Dorothea a short jacket and chemisette," Cecilia said. "My burgundy velvet you don't think is appropriate in London for an unmarried woman."

Lady Abernathy sniffed. "You may change after we finish. The invitations need to be discussed, and both of you should be ready in case we have callers." She glanced toward Dorothea. "If others are here when Lady Wilmont arrives, she will be shown to a separate room and you may excuse yourself."

"I understand." A victory of sorts, which did nothing to endear her to her mother-in-law. "Thank you."

The politeness only earned her a glare. Somehow, they managed to get through the rest of the meal, and Cecilia stole Dorothea away. "Thank you," Dorothea said as they climbed the stairs.

"Your dress is fine," Cecilia replied. "Mother just—she doesn't like being crossed or bested."

"I guessed that."

They entered Cecilia's room and she headed straight for her trunk. "I'm glad you did, though. Maybe she'll realize people need to live their own lives."

She gave Dorothea a smile. "Maybe you and Martin can convince her."

Dorothea returned the smile, though she sensed Martin's sister had her own agenda.

⬥

Dorothea paused just long enough before the large looking glass in the front hall to ensure her borrowed feathers were in place. Mercer had

141

assured her she was more than presentable, but Dorothea felt the need to double-check before greeting her guests.

She assumed it would be more than one guest, though she harbored a hope Lady Wilmont wouldn't bring Alyssa along. They could enjoy a pleasant coze and Dorothea might be a bit more honest. Not that she would mention a word about Lady Abernathy's behavior. Lady Wilmont would leap to those conclusions on her own.

She started to push the drawing room door open, but years of habit kicked in and she stopped at a mere crack, straining to catch the conversation inside. "Do you think she's had a chance to speak with the patronesses yet? I wonder if they'll pay her any mind. Who is she, after all?"

No missing the sneer in Alyssa's tone, as there was no missing the annoyance in Lady Wilmont's response. "She's a married woman with a title, which is more than you, miss. Your little tricks won't wash now. If you want any favors from her, best mend your ways."

It was the type of conversation Dorothea used to back away from, waiting until Lady Wilmont emerged or Alyssa moved on to another topic. Looking down, she realized her hand had drawn back, ready to retreat.

No. They were not in the Wilmont townhouse, Dorothea no longer the relation who survived on the charity of the second cousin twice removed she called "aunt." She was Lady Abernathy, with a butler, a maid, and a position in society.

The stray thought she also possessed footmen to put Alyssa out if she overstepped her bounds put a smile on Dorothea's face and she pushed open both doors.

Lady Wilmont's senses were also well trained, her scolding of Alyssa ceasing the moment Dorothea entered. She held open her arms. "Dorothea, my dear child. You are looking wonderful!"

A warm embrace, then she stepped to cast a critical eye over Dorothea's appearance. "Turn about. Is the spencer new? I don't recognize it from before."

Dorothea did as bid. "The jacket and chemisette are borrowed from Martin's sister."

"How kind of her. When you go shopping, you should consider a walking dress in in that shade."

Before Dorothea could respond, Alyssa said, "He hasn't let you go yet? How parsimonious of him."

"Dorothea just returned from her wedding journey. Come make your curtsey."

Alyssa's eyes narrowed at the reminder social rules dictated Dorothea must now be curtseyed to by an unmarried woman. Sullenly, she moved forward two steps and dropped the barest curtsey acceptable before stepping back. Lady Wilmont glared at her daughter, but Dorothea caught her eye and shook her head. The issue was not worth a cloud hanging over the rest of the visit. At least, not where Dorothea had to hear.

She led the way to sofa, sitting at one end while Lady Wilmont took the other Alyssa perching on a chair. Glancing about the room, Lady Wilmont asked, "Isn't Lady Abernathy—I mean, the Dowager Viscountess—joining us?"

Lady Abernathy was Not At Home to Lady Wilmont, but Dorothea saw no use in the social lie. "No, and I'll confess I'm glad. I don't imagine you were looking forward to seeing her."

"I suppose we still must to be polite to one another when we meet in public. At least, I feel we should be. I can't speak for her behavior."

The invitation for Dorothea to opine on her treatment since her arrival last night was clear. She declined. "One advantage," she said, leaning in. "If you wish to stay beyond the usual allotted time, there's no one to say no."

Lady Wilmont chuckled. "True. I imagine your response to any cards left for you went out this afternoon, so it's unlikely visits will be paid today. With the flurry over the vote to discuss a Regency Bill, I imagine the gentlemen won't be flocking for Miss Drayton, either."

She cocked her head to one side. "Yes, the color suits you. Kind of Miss Drayton to lend it to you. You should make use of being allowed stronger colors. You may dress as fashionably as you please, with no worry of what Mr. Shipley or his parishioners might. think."

"What a relief," Dorothea said. "I think I'll be more inclined to think charitably of the vicar's wife in Martin's parish."

They shared a laugh. "Are you going to ask her about the ball, Mama?" Alyssa sat straight, perched on the edge of her chair, looking ready to depart at the first opportunity. "You said you would."

A glare, cast in Alyssa's direction, but Lady Wilmont sighed. "I don't suppose the Dowager Viscountess has given you details of her ball."

Dorothea shrugged. "Martin and I arrived home yesterday evening late. Today, I was touring the house, so, no, the ball hasn't been discussed."

"You will ensure we're on the guest list?" Lady Wilmont asked. "I don't want any confusion. We had an … incident at the Sudleys." Lady Wilmont waved her hand. "Nothing serious, only a misunderstanding. But That Woman would have no hesitation in leaving us off the list. If you cannot sway her, I would appreciate knowing so we do not appear where we are not wanted."

The look Lady Wilmont cast Alyssa showed there was more to the Sudley story. "I will write the invitation myself," Dorothea said. "I have no plans to upset Lady Abernathy's preparations, but I do think I am allowed to ensure my guests are invited."

"Hmm. By rights, she should cede the duties of hostess to you. Given how short a time since you were married, though, best not to demand your rights as Lord Abernathy's wife. Yet. It will be understood by all this will be her farewell. You must ensure she doesn't linger and usurp your place for too long, or there will be talk. Within another month after the event, you'll need to take your rightful place, or she will never allow you too."

Dorothea imagined how Lady Wilmont would act with her son holding the title and a new wife who wanted to assume her duties. Little possibility the transition would be pleasant or easy.

There was also a ring of truth in the words, Dorothea knowing the struggle would come sooner or later. Her aunt's words, though, brought to mind something else. "You might not wish to discuss this, but I would like to know. What caused such bad blood between you and Lady Abernathy?"

Lady Wilmont drew herself up, opened her mouth, then deflated. "I don't know. I did steal some suitors from her during our season, so perhaps that might have something to do with it. She acted cold and rude when your Uncle Richard and I returned to Town the next year. Not that we ever got along."

What a disturbing thought. "Uncle Richard was courting—"

"Dear lord, no." Lady Wilmont let forth a peal of laughter. "Your uncle Richard never courted Lady Jane Dunn, third daughter of the Earl of Lutton. She believed herself too high and mighty for the likes of the mere heir to a barony. I'm surprised she lowered herself to marry a viscount."

More chuckles and a shake of her head. "I suppose she thought Abernathy the best offer. She didn't accept him until her second season. Once the betrothal was announced, she made a point to remind me she stood higher than I in precedence. She's an earl's daughter, my father was a baron, she always stood higher, even after I married."

Lady Wilmont shrugged. "I didn't come to London much after the children came, so I suppose everything laid fallow until now."

Dorothea would wager her aunt was not as innocent as she portrayed. She could see parallels playing out, with Cecilia taking on the role of her mother whether she wanted to or not. "Will I get to dance with the Prince of Wales?" Alyssa asked, dragging the conversation back to herself. "Do arrange it, Dorothea. Everyone I know would be so jealous."

"I'm afraid the decision is up to His Highness," Dorothea said. "I don't believe he dances with unmarried ladies. He might dance with Cecilia, but only because the ball is in her home. If he does, it will likely be a promenade or something similar. He will, of course, dance first with Lady Abernathy."

Lady Wilmont fixed Dorothea with a firm gaze, all softness vanished. "He should open the ball with you. Your husband is the current title holder." She reached out to pat her hand. "Don't worry. I'll help you take control."

With a sinking feeling, Dorothea realized this marriage could make things worse rather than better if Lady Wilmont had her way, no matter her intentions.

CHAPTER 17

"Mother says you did your best to save me money when you went shopping," Martin said a few days later. He lounged where Dorothea could catch his reflection in her mirror as Mercer put the final few touches to her toilette for the evening. "Says she was forced to twist your arm to order the minimum number of items she thought you needed."

"I think your mother's idea of what's needed and my idea are quite different." Mercer stepped back and Dorothea nodded her approval of the maid's work after a brief consideration in the mirror.

"Don't get me wrong. I won't be upset if you don't follow Mother's habit of overspending her allowance every quarter. Still, you are allowed to spend some money and outfit yourself as needed." He tilted his head to one side. "I like the dress, by the way."

The compliment warmed her. The unfinished gown had been an impulsive purchase when the modiste told her the original client cancelled the order. Lady Abernathy had expressed doubts, but Dorothea liked it well enough and the idea the dress could be ready within a day after minor alterations had been enough for her. "I think I'm ready. Thank you, Mercer."

Mercer took the hint, leaving them alone. "I see you wore the headband I sent over" Martin said, rising from his chair to move closer to the dressing table.

Dorothea lifted her hand to touch the diamond and emerald headpiece woven into her hair. "I feel a bit silly with no necklace. I thought about my pearls, but --"

"I told Mercer to ensure you didn't put on a necklace." He brought forth a box from behind his back, "because I wanted you to wear this."

He was close enough she didn't rise to take the box from him. She flipped it open and the contents caught her breath. She wasn't prepared for the emeralds accented by diamonds sparkling in the candlelight.

"They are part of the family jewels worn by the Viscountess Abernathy, passing from one generation to the next. Mother told me one of your new dresses would be complimented by this."

"Martin, I—I don't know what to say."

"Thank you might be appropriate."

She stared at the jewels for a moment longer, knowing she had never held such a beautiful thing before in her life. Looking up, she found one corner of his mouth quirked up in a slight smile. "Thank you," she said, unable to add any more.

He reached for the box. "Let me put it on you."

Extracting the necklace and tossing the box on to her dressing table, he moved behind her. The metal lay cool against her skin as he settled the jewels about her neck, the stones glowing with an inner fire. Dorothea followed his movement in the mirror, his slight frown of concentration as he worked the clasp. "There's a tiara as well," he said, "but it's far too formal for this gathering. Thus, the headband."

Having clasped the necklace, Martin straightened, gazing at the effect in the mirror. "Suits you quite admirably."

He leaned down and planted a kiss on the back of her neck, lingering over the area. Dorothea closed her eyes and began to relax, trusting his hands on her shoulders would keep her from falling. In the past weeks, she found herself hungering for his touch, ever ready to lose herself in the delicious sensations he aroused in her. This was, she admitted, a rather delicious way to live her life.

From her neck, Martin proceeded to her mouth, showing his thoughts were not on the evening's entertainment, but something much more delightful and intimate. Dorothea did not object to such a diversion, and when a knock came at the door, she whispered in his ear. "Tell them to go away."

For a moment she thought he might, but then he straightened. "Mother and Cecilia are waiting downstairs." He stepped back and held out his hand. "Besides, this is your first event as Lady Abernathy. We don't want to disappoint everyone, do we?"

With a sigh, she placed her hand in his and rose. After the last few days, she wouldn't mind disappointing everyone. There'd been a round of calls, being introduced and observed as if she was some unusual, potentially dangerous, creature. Unfortunately, her and Martin's absence would only raise more gossip, and a further round of calls wondering if she was well or, if not, what the reason was.

"I thought we might need to send one of the servants to retrieve you," Lady Abernathy said as they descended. "We're going to be late."

Disapproval colored her words, a sound becoming all too familiar, as was the critical eye she cast over Dorothea's gown. Before she could ask Dorothea to turn for further inspection, Martin said, "If we're in danger of being late, we should go. The carriage is waiting?"

"I just want to see if—"

"I think Dorothea looks lovely. Don't you think so, Cecilia?"

Cecilia agreed but Lady Abernathy pursed her lips and moved toward the door. Dorothea told Cecilia it was wonderful to be allowed more than pale colors, but didn't take her eye from her mother-in-law, knowing more battles lay ahead.

Their trip to the Hastings Townhouse felt familiar, with Lady Abernathy issuing a string of instructions as the carriage drew near their destination, just as Lady Wilmont always did. "Cecilia, I don't know if the Duke of Stockwood will be present. Rumor is he's somewhat hurt by something Lord Hastings said. If he is, you are to obtain two dances with him." She paused. "If he asks for a third, you're not to say no."

A third request would be tantamount to a public statement of intent. Cecilia didn't appear happy, but she also didn't argue. "Martin, you're to stay by Dorothea's side as much as possible. She hasn't attended an event like this and will need your guidance."

After several days of petty slights, this was too much. "I know how to behave myself in a ballroom." Dorothea said tartly. "Mother Abernathy."

A muscle in Lady Abernathy's right cheek twitched at the appellation. Martin had been right; his mother didn't care for the term. She thought he was wrong Lady Abernathy would come to accept it, so Dorothea had been careful in her usage, but at this moment, she didn't care.

Lady Abernathy fixed her with a level gaze. "It is one thing to attend as a poor relation to fetch and carry and take notes on what your aunt might want. Another thing entirely to be a guest in your own right, a viscountess on whom every eye will be focused. They will be focused on you, Dorothea, waiting for you to make a mistake and prove the gossips right."

"Enough, Mother," Martin snapped. "You'll not speak to my wife thusly."

Lady Abernathy considered Dorothea for a moment, then turned her head to face Martin. "No, I suppose I shouldn't. You did all this work to protect our family name and I would be wrong to put everything to flame. None of that means I must enjoy or approve of the fact, even if a word does not pass my lips in public. Unlike Dorothea's relations, I understand the value in keeping my opinions to myself if they might hurt the family."

She glanced back to Dorothea. "Comport yourself in a way which doesn't shame us all if you can. If you can't, there will be consequences."

Dorothea said nothing. Her hands curled into fists, and the urge to do something to embarrass the family was almost overwhelming. After all, the gossips would enjoy a field day if the Dowager Viscountess Abernathy were to arrive with the imprint of Dorothea's hand across her face.

Martin looked as if he wanted to say something, but he kept his mouth closed, instead reaching out to wrap one hand around

Dorothea's closed fist. He didn't try to uncurl her fingers, but let his hand stay there, looking at her with eyes which ordered her not to explode.

Yes, they were off to a lovely start.

Dorothea was near quivering with rage as they entered the connected salons serving as the Hastings' ballroom and Martin did not blame her. His mother's disapproval colored every word she spoke, but tonight had been an open declaration no quarter would be offered in their struggle.

All this boded ill for the future. Not just London and the season, but after, when Dorothea would be expected to take up the reins of control at his main seat and village. Dorothea had said she did not intend to challenge his mother's supremacy over the ball in February. They would host other events, though, and if Lady Abernathy refused to allow those responsibilities to shift in any way, tongues would wag. Too much wagging and all he'd done to cool the feud and keep them out of scandal would be for naught.

Though, if Dorothea slapped his mother as he feared she wanted to, all bets were off.

"We're not late," he said as they found a place along the wall, hoping the cheer in his voice didn't sound too false. "The dancing has not yet begun."

"Yes, but this is hardly the best vantage point," Lady Abernathy complained.

Martin opened his mouth to ask her not to sulk, but shut it as Lady Knowle descended. "There you are! I wondered when you would get here. No difficulties, I trust?"

Instantly, Lady Abernathy's face was serene. "Why are you concerned? We're not late; the dancing hasn't begun."

"True, but you know everyone wants to see the new Viscountess Abernathy." She turned to Dorothea. "You are looking lovely, child. You cleaned up very nicely."

Martin's mother possessed the ability to turn the charm on and off, never giving a hint of what lay below the surface, but Dorothea was an unknown quantity. She always appeared to keep a level head in public dealing with whatever Lady Wilmont threw at her, he had never witnessed insults. She might not publicly show her anger at Lady Abernathy, but nothing prevented her from unleashing on Lady Knowle. Which would almost be worse. Almost.

Lady Abernathy watched as well, her shoulders tense. Dorothea lifted her chin to meet Lady Knowle's gaze. "I was just telling Cecilia what a difference it makes when one is able to put strong colors in one's wardrobe. I think having the choice is beneficial to any woman."

Her voice was pleasant, her gaze unflinching, dared Lady Knowle to make further references to her origins. The woman did not reply for a moment, taking Dorothea's measure. "Did you enjoy your wedding trip?" she asked at last, moving on to the trivialities one might ask any bride.

Martin wanted to embrace Dorothea as she answered the questions, a polite expression on her face. He waited, though, until Lady Knowle tired of the game and turned to Lady Abernathy to discuss some other gossip. "Well done," he said, taking her hand.

She smiled at him, but cast a rather annoyed glance at Lady Knowle. Or was it his mother? Or both? Whichever, he cautioned, "Don't."

"May I at least think about it?"

"That I will allow. Gotten me through more than one evening. Don't worry; the dancing will start soon. You'll be out on the floor and won't need to speak with Mother."

"I'll hold you to that," she warned.

The room had begun to fill, giving all the signs of a crush. Gentleman appeared to inquire as to Cecilia's availability for a dance, and a few asking if Dorothea might be willing to partner them. Her smile as she agreed without the caveats offered before her marriage warmed Martin's heart. She was blossoming, becoming more comfortable in her new role, They needed to give a dinner soon where Dorothea would act as host. Lady Abernathy would offer a hundred reasons against the idea, but Martin put her objections down to unhappiness at having Dorothea under her roof.

No, under *his* roof. His mother held a life tenancy, but it was his home and Dorothea would need to take her rightful place. He didn't fancy the fight when she did.

His attention was caught by Lady Knowle gesturing for someone to join them. Then he realized Lady Knowle gestured to Lord Manville.

"You were terribly difficult to find," Manville said as he approached, kissing Lady Knowle on each cheek. "I had to search everywhere for you." Turning to Lady Abernathy, he made a deep bow. "So lovely to see you again, my dear Lady Abernathy. Rather, I should say *Ladies* Abernathy, as young Lady Abernathy is with us."

He bowed to Dorothea as well, looking for all the world as if paying her the proper respect, but Martin couldn't help thinking there had to be more. If anyone waited for something to happen, it was Manville and Knowle.

What they waited for became apparent when Manville turned and called, "I found you a place as I told you I would."

Even before Lady Wilmont came into view, Martin knew what the man hoped for. No one believed the feud between Lady Wilmont and Lady Abernathy was done, only simmering for the moment due to their need to present something resembling a united front. Manville wanted to add fuel to the fire.

Lady Wilmont stopped when she realized the destination. "We can find accommodation elsewhere," she said.

"I don't know what you might find wrong," Manville said, his voice all sweetness. "Unless, of course, you object to the company?"

Martin's hands flexed as he resisted the urge to strangle Manville, but his mother rose to the occasion. "Lady Wilmont, this is quite a crush and I doubt you'll be able to find an inch elsewhere. A space is free next to my daughter-in-law."

There was the mother he knew. With one hand, she showed solidarity in the face of gossips while also offering a bit of a backhanded insult by describing Dorothea as her daughter-in-law rather than acknowledging the connection to Lady Wilmont.

Lady Wilmont must have also found not giving Manville and Lady Knowle what they wanted worth enduring her enemy's company.

"You are too kind, Lady Abernathy," Lady Wilmont said, giving Manville a slight side-eye. "I can talk to my niece. It's been almost a week since we've had a chance to visit."

Lovely. Now Dorothea was a toy for the two of them to fight over. Little to be done for it as Lady Wilmont joined Dorothea and her daughter took up her place behind, next to Cecilia. He didn't miss that Cecilia took a slight step away, putting a bit of distance between the two girls.

Lady Abernathy turned back to Lady Knowle, continuing their conversation as if nothing had happened, while Lady Wilmont engaged Dorothea. She appeared pleased at Dorothea's appearance, but she also asked how Dorothea was being treated. Vexing because Dorothea might answer honestly. Martin didn't want her to be honest, not here and not now. If Lady Wilmont heard how Dorothea had been insulted, she would be offended, and Martin wouldn't blame her.

The musicians struck a chord, signaling the start of the dancing. More young men appeared, begging for the hand of both Alyssa and Cecilia. Roger Phipps managed to get to Cecilia first, while Matthew Henry beat out Lord Tinley for Alyssa by a hair. "I don't like how he's been sniffing about her," Lady Wilmont said to Dorothea. "I'm worried. Do you think you might —?"

Before Lady Wilmont could make the request, Martin held out his hand to Dorothea. "Please excuse us, Lady Wilmont, I think I'm going to enjoy the opportunity to dance with my wife."

Martin noticed Dorothea didn't hesitate in letting him lead her to the floor. "One near disaster averted," she said when they took their places. "Your mother would throw a fit hearing me asked to do something for Aunt Honoria."

"Would you have done what she asked?" he found himself asking, earning a sharp glance from Dorothea.

"She's my aunt, and if what she wants is something simple, I will try to help, no matter what your mother might think. They're my family. I'm not going to cut off all relation to them because your mother doesn't like Aunt Honoria."

He felt a flash of annoyance. Lady Wilmont had done little but cause misery since the season began, but his wife wanted to keep contact?

He caught himself. She was right. Ties of blood were not so easily severed. Given Dorothea appeared to enjoy a warm relationship with her aunt, not surprising she would want to continue the relationship, in spite of—or even because of—his mother's objections. The little curl of annoyance lingered, though, as the orchestra began to play. He pushed it down, focusing instead on the woman front of him.

After all, he could deal with such things later.

CHAPTER 18

"Everything's horrible," Cecilia said as she and Roger made their way through the figures. "Mother takes any opportunity to put Lady Wilmont down whenever Dorothea's in the room. So far, she's managed to control herself, but after tonight …"

She shook her head, and Roger squeezed her hand. "I think she still resents your brother chose to marry Miss Hindley—Lady Abernathy. She would be happier if he had chosen to ride the scandal out."

"What Mother wants is Martin to ship her back to the country where she won't be seen. If she gets pregnant, Mother might get her way. She might let her come back to town for my wedding, but I doubt it. Mother would like her out of sight, out of mind, but still produce the heir, of course."

The movements of the dance took them away from one another, but when they circled back, she said, "Mother's getting more insistent about the Duke of Stockwood. I know he's had an appointment with Martin on at least two occasions, but he's never said anything to me, thank goodness."

"Your brother might have refused him."

Cecilia shook her head. "No. His Grace would say something. Perhaps he's trying to buy a horse or some land. It'd be like Martin not to tell Mother. But the meetings give Mother hope His Grace will appear on our doorstep, declare his undying love, and I'll say yes, despite previous protests to the contrary."

Her face turned serious. "Have you had a chance to talk to Martin yet?"

Roger shook his head. "Not yet, but he's been focused on settling into married life and I don't have the license yet. He did leave a card at my residence after I left mine, so at least I'm still in good odor."

Cecilia laughed. "Of course you are. The two of you have been friends forever. I can't imagine what could come between the two of you."

"Politics. Martin and I could find ourselves on different sides of the Regency issue. He's ambitious, may not wish to align himself with someone who's not completely supportive of the Prince."

"All the more reason to ask him now," Cecilia insisted. "Even if he doesn't want to speak to us for a while after you make your move, I'll support you."

"Cecilia, you don't know what I might be thinking."

"If it's not treason, and won't hurt Martin too much, I'll stand by you. I love you, Roger. I want to be your wife. I'm tired of waiting. We need to act."

He chuckled. "One of the reasons I love you. You're decisive."

"Despite being overwrought sometimes?" She smiled at him, a smile for which he would gladly sell the world to be honored with every day for the rest of his life. "We best return to the dance before Mother notices we're not there."

With reluctance in every step, he let her lead him back to the figure, falling into the pattern until the music ended. Once their bow and curtsey were made to one another, they had no choice but make their way back towards where Lady Abernathy waited, though they did let their steps linger a touch. As they drew near, he noticed Lady Knowle had disappeared and Lady Abernathy was studiously ignoring Lady Wilmont, which meant she was paying much more attention to events on the floor.

Had she seen them? If she had, what did she think of their behavior? She didn't appear happy, but that could be put down to the proximity to her rival. Whatever the reason, Roger quickened their steps, delivering Cecilia to her mother's care. He lingered a bit, continuing with idle conversation until another gentleman came and claimed Cecilia's hand, Lady Abernathy nodding approval.

He was about to depart when Lady Abernathy said, "Perhaps this is not the most convenient time and place for this discussion, Sir Roger. I think, however, it best we speak sooner rather than later."

She had somehow acquired chairs for the party, and indicated the seat next to her—the one furthest from Lady Wilmont. "Please sit, sir. We can speak, and those who do not need to hear our conversation will find listening more difficult."

She cast a meaningful glance in Lady Wilmont's direction as Roger took the chair. "I have given this considerable thought," she said after a long, pause, "and I believe it would be best if you chose not to call upon Cecilia for a time."

Lady Abernathy spoke as if discussing a menu with her cook. "Am I forbidden the house?" he asked. He'd anticipated this blow was possible, but it still hurt.

"No. For the love I bear your mother and the long friendship between our families, I would ask you not allow things to come to such a place. I am *requesting* you do not offer attentions to Cecilia. Were some legitimate business to bring you to our home, you would be welcomed as an old friend of the family."

She turned dark, cold eyes to meet his. "But nothing more. Do I make myself clear?"

"Perfectly," Roger replied, the word clipped. "I would ask for an explanation, however."

Her answer did not come directly, eyes turning toward the floor where Cecilia was dancing, then toward one of the entrances where the Duke of Stockwood had appeared with several of his fellow club members. Perhaps the duke found forgiving the insult worth an evening's entertainment. "No surprise an affinity has grown up between the two of you," she said at last. "You have known one another all your lives. I am not certain such an affinity is the best reason to rush into a marriage. I want my daughter to know something of the world before she makes her choice."

"Makes her choice? You mean, chooses the man you want." Roger's voice dripped with contempt. "There are others I would not be surprised to find sacrificing their daughters on the altar of ambition, but you? It makes me sick."

He rose, unable to sit still any longer and listen to her words. "Do you care nothing for her happiness? Would you see her married to a man so unsuited for her so you can triumph in a petty battle over social standing? I was brought up to think better of you."

Lady Wilmont's head turned as his voice rose, but part of him no longer cared. Not after weeks of stolen moments with Cecilia while her mother paraded her before a silly ass whose only recommendation was the title he bore.

"Sit down," Lady Abernathy hissed, "or I will forbid Cecilia from ever seeing you again."

He balked, tired of obeying her commands. He could ignore her, go find Martin and beg a word with him. All Martin needed to do was say yes or no, but if he forced a fight between Martin and his mother at this moment, Roger knew he might well come out on the losing side.

With ill humor, he sat again, flipping the tails of his coat out of the way with an annoyed gesture. Silent, he chose not to speak, leaving the next move to her. She was agitated, though only someone who knew her well would recognize the signs in the smooth surface.

A deep breath, then she turned to Roger and said in a steady voice, "I want what is best for Cecilia. I worry she turns to you because you are comfortable and familiar. While she might find that acceptable now, will she still find it so in ten or twenty years? Will she be content with life as the wife of a simple baronet or yearn for something more? I want her to consider other gentlemen before her mind is so settled as to accept no other alternative."

She met his eyes, her expression somber. "Do I make myself clear?"

He realized what excuse would be given to Martin, all concern and worry Cecilia might be cutting herself off from something better. "In more ways than one." He rose and bowed. "I suppose you would prefer I did not linger."

Lady Abernathy smiled and nodded her head graciously. "I'm glad we understand each other."

Roger's fists clenched in anger as he walked away. A quick survey of the floor found Cecilia deep in the dance, a smile on her face. The sight of her warmed him, but he would much rather be out there with her himself.

There'd be no further chance for tonight. Claiming Cecilia for a second dance would push Lady Abernathy to more public action, for which he would not be forgiven. "Praise in public, punish in private," was an aphorism Lady Abernathy had uttered to his mother more than once. Woe betide him if he forced her to break the dictum.

No, the timing wasn't right. He would get Cecilia word somehow. He just needed to figure out how.

❧

Dorothea wasn't surprised to discover a note n Lady Wilmont's quick, spikey hand among the letters waiting for her at breakfast the next morning. A quick glance showed a plea to assist with something regarding Alyssa. Deciding such was best dealt with later, away from the rest of the family, Dorothea folded the paper up, sliding it under the other items awaiting her attention.

"Invitations?" Lady Abernathy asked, as she did every morning. Dorothea was expected to detail them all and allow her mother-in-law to render judgement.

"Some," Dorothea said, opening the next envelope. "An invitation to dine next week with the Forbreaths."

"You mean, Sir William wants to bend my ear about the Regency Bill," Martin said. "He thinks the pill will go down better if he invites you along."

"Sir William's against restrictions, isn't he?" Dorothea asked, "But also for letting His Majesty's household stay in the Queen's hands, is he not?"

Martin blinked in surprise. "Yes, he is. A difficult needle to thread and he'll need to jump one way or the other eventually."

"You hope to retain him on the Prince's side."

Martin chuckled. "You have been paying attention."

Dorothea shrugged. "As much as I can. I was in the habit so I could note who would serve Lady Wilmont's needs."

Lady Abernathy pulled a sour expression. "I suppose Lady Wilmont misses your expertise. A surprise she's not here every day to beg your assistance."

The dig was relatively mild compared to others, but Dorothea still didn't like it. "I think Lady Wilmont can manage her dinners quite well."

A small snort was the only comment offered. "The other invitation?"

So she had seen Dorothea put the note away. "Not an invitation. A note from a distant relative." A white lie, but one she was more than happy to utter if Lady Abernathy stopped bothering her.

"I thought you didn't have any relatives beside the Wilmonts," Cecilia asked in all innocence.

"No relatives beside the Wilmonts who were willing to do their duty by a member of the family in need," Lady Abernathy said. "I ascribe that to Lord Wilmont. He is a kind and charitable soul."

Dorothea ignored the jibe. "They heard of the wedding, and since they have a daughter coming out next year …"

She let the words trail off, allowing Lady Abernathy to draw her own conclusions. More fibs, but Dorothea supposed she could live with those. Discussion turned again to the invitations, Lady Abernathy issuing her dictums despite the fact the invitations were technically in Dorothea's purview. This would be a long campaign, with many hard-fought battles and Dorothea knew she would see losses along with the victories.

Somehow, they managed to get through breakfast. Dorothea scooped up the letters, ostensibly to write responses, but in truth for a chance to read what had been written in some type of privacy. Then Martin said, "I think I may need to give a dinner."

Dorothea's mind went over the what she knew of the family schedule. The Abernathy ball was scheduled for the eighth of February, less than a month away. "Soon, I suppose."

Lady Abernathy glared at her. "There will be thirty guests for the dinner before the ball," she reminded Martin. "I don't believe we have room for anymore."

"I'm talking something not so formal. A political gathering. Something where I can invite gentlemen whose votes we will need in Commons and Lords. The idea is to gently try to steer them in the right direction. It would make His Highness happy if I could help in the votes."

He looked down the table at his mother. "Next week, I think. I want Dorothea to play hostess. Time she's seen to take her place in small ways, at least. I think she would be a help."

Lady Abernathy pursed her lips. "Shall I endeavor to find an invitation elsewhere for myself and Cecilia?"

"Since I'm not planning to invite the wives, yes. One thing for Dorothea to be at the table, but Cecilia, no. I need to figure out who I need to invite, though. We're going to be ten or fifteen, so whatever you can do to start planning would be appreciated."

He rose, and leaned down kiss Dorothea on the cheek. "I'm off to my club. Time for me to do what I can to support the Prince."

Once he was gone, Lady Abernathy turned to Dorothea. "I'll tell Farthing and Mrs. Richards you are in charge of this dinner."

"A little difficult to plan when we don't know who is coming or the exact date," Dorothea pointed out.

"Consult a calendar, then review the linen and china. Mrs. Richards can tell you how many folk the table can comfortably sit. Come, Cecilia. We need to leave for calls."

Pausing at the door, Lady Abernathy added, "Of course, if there are any concerns you cannot answer, they can come to me."

Cecilia offered a sympathetic glance as she followed her mother out. Rather than heading for her desk as originally intended, Dorothea stewed. Why should she be surprised Lady Abernathy would not hand over the reins of control to her willingly, even for a small dinner party? She wouldn't do something obvious to scuttle the event. Oh, no. Simply put Dorothea in a position where she had to ask for help, the price for which would be turning over all control.

At last, she pulled Lady Wilmont's note from the pile.

I would not be surprised to discover you are under orders not to receive me. I understand, but we still expect an invitation to the Abernathy Ball. She cannot deny you the privilege of your own guests. Or does she keep all within her control, using the excuse of your recent marriage? Do not trust her, for she will make your life a misery if you let her. At the same time, you must also be careful to do nothing to allow her to drive a wedge between yourself and Lord Abernathy. When husband and wife are divided in such a manner, there will *be trouble. Remember, you hold the key to the future of the Abernathy line, but she will always hate you because you were not her choice.*

Dorothea let the letter drop the table. Nothing here she didn't know and while Lady Wilmont gave what she thought was sound advice, it only served to help aggravate all the unhappiness Dorothea felt at the moment.

With a sigh, she picked up the letter again, deciding she should finish. More ranting against Lady Abernathy, but close to the bottom, the tone changed. *You are sorely missed, my dear Dorothea, especially when I write out invitations. I remember our conversations, how we'd discuss what various gentlemen were up to. Now, I am forced to rely on Alyssa for assistance and companionship. I find little joy on either count. She shows no head for this work, and I fear once she marries, she will endure a difficult time, for she thinks little of the effort. Therein lies a regret, but one I can do little about now.*

There is something you can help me with if you are able. If Lord Tilney is on the guest list for the ball, please see if you can remove him. Alyssa unfortunately believes he is where her attention should lie. I'd almost rather she chase Stockwood, though the duke appears quite firm in his turn against her. Tilney will do nothing but lead her into disaster. He was the one who swept us into Lord Hatchard's party and to the Sudleys, knowing full well we had not been extended an invitation. I was obliged to apologize most profusely to Lady Sudley and beg her indulgence until I could extract Alyssa. Lady Sudley showed great kindness by allowing me to do so. I keep a watchful eye, but you know what Alyssa is like when she grows determined; telling her "no" only encourages her.

The letter ended with a postscript. *Please do not expend any effort towards Almack's on Alyssa's behalf. I should not have asked in the first place as I doubt the patronesses will find her suitable, no matter who might champion her.*

Not an outrageous request, but Tilney was in the Prince's circle, almost certain to be on the guest list. It'd be difficult to get Lady Abernathy to remove him. More likely would be the suggestion the

Wilmonts stay away if they had such concern about the man sullying Alyssa's honor.

She would be caught in the middle of this damn feud forever, or at least until the end of the season. If she could keep her head about her that long.

CHAPTER 19

The next few days were busy, leaving Dorothea little time to worry over the feud. They would host fourteen gentlemen, with her and Martin making sixteen. She quizzed him on the debates, keeping a list of items to use if conversation flagged.

On Thursday, she and Cecilia were in the middle of deciding between two sets of china when Farthing entered the drawing room. "Sir Roger Phipps is here, your ladyship."

"Show him in," Dorothea said, noting how Cecilia brightened. At the moment, only the two of them were downstairs, Martin out on business and Lady Abernathy in her room until the first of the afternoon visitors arrived.

Roger entered, bowing first to Dorothea, but when his attention turned to Cecilia, it did not take a trained eye to realize whom he was glad to see. "Martin is not here?"

"I'm afraid he's at his club. If you wish to depart, I will understand, but you are also welcome to stay a few minutes. We've not seen enough of you of late."

He hesitated, then smiled. "I suppose a few moments would not be amiss, Lady Abernathy. How are you settling in? We didn't find a chance to speak the other evening."

Roger's conversation was innocuous as they sat, all the while he and Cecilia devouring one another with their eyes. Had Cecilia's mother realized the pair were falling for one another?

Feeling very much the third wheel, Dorothea rose. "Sir Roger, I'm going to be rude and beg your indulgence. We are planning a dinner with a number of tasks to complete. I would appreciate if you kept Cecilia company while I work at my desk. She must be desperate for the chance to speak with someone about something other than the number of teaspoons we possess."

"Do you think you can manage without me?" Cecilia asked, a catch in her voice.

"For a few minutes at least. Sir Roger?"

Roger looked as if he had been handed the greatest gift in the world. "I would be honored to do such a thing for you, Lady Abernathy."

Dorothea nodded, making her way back to her desk, while Cecilia and Roger both sat down upon the sofa. She saw no harm in giving the two a bit of privacy under a chaperone's eye. Much better than having them seek out some furtive rendezvous.

She picked up her pen and set to work, making certain they were well within her sight.

✦

"I didn't expect that," Roger said, dropping his voice so the words would not carry.

"Dorothea is kind, and does her best to think of others." Cecilia shifted towards him. "A quality I admire."

"I'm glad she doesn't feel as your mother does." He hesitated, wondering how to deliver his news. "Your mother asked me to stay away from you."

"What?!"

Dorothea's head rose from her work at the exclamation. Quickly, Cecilia cleared her throat, doing her best to act as if everything was fine. "When did this happen?" she asked, ensuring her voice remained quiet.

"The other night. She said she wanted you to have knowledge of the world before you made any decisions on a husband."

"You mean, before she can maneuver me into being betrothed to the Duke of Stockwood."

"I need to speak with Martin, to force the issue. The worst he can do is say no."

"I can't imagine he would." She reached out to grasp his hand. "When he says yes, I will be the happiest woman in the world."

He wanted to respond with how happy her happiness would make him, but Lady Abernathy's voice cut through the room. "What, may I ask, is going on here?"

Roger shifted back in reflex, dropping Cecilia's hand. He rose to offer a formal bow. "Good afternoon, Lady Abernathy."

Her eyes were cold as she came forward. "Don't 'good afternoon' me, young man. I think I'm justified in asking again what is going on here."

Cecilia rose to her feet. "Sir Roger came looking for Martin, Mama. Dorothea invited him to stay for a few minutes."

"If Dorothea invited him, why is she at her desk?" She turned her head toward her daughter-in-law. "How long has Sir Roger been here?"

"Not above ten minutes," Dorothea said without hesitation.

"How long did you leave them alone?"

"They're not alone. I was here."

"I think you, of all people, would be cognizant of how a young lady's reputation can be lost if the wrong impression is given. Please ring for Farthing."

The butler appeared in the doorway in answer to the summons. "Farthing, what time did Sir Roger arrive?" Lady Abernathy asked, her eyes never leaving Roger.

The butler frowned. "Perhaps ten minutes, my lady. He asked for Lord Abernathy, then inquired after the young mistress."

"Thank you, Farthing. Sir Roger will be leaving now."

It was a dismissal. Moreover, it was an eviction. Which meant the next time he called, Roger would be informed the family was Not At Home to him.

With nothing to do but accept the defeat, Roger turned back to Cecilia. "I will see you soon," he promised. He bowed to Lady Abernathy and moved toward the door. Before he departed, he turned back to offer Dorothea a bow. "Lady Abernathy, allow me to thank you for your hospitality. I am sorry if I took advantage of your generosity."

He left, one thing on his mind. He needed to find Martin before he spoke to his mother.

With the door closed, Lady Abernathy let her cool exterior drop to reveal the fury beneath. "How could you do this? How could you let Cecilia indulge in an assignation?"

Dorothea took a deep breath replying. Be calm. "I do not think Roger and Cecilia sitting on sofa while I am watching them is an assignation. Better than them trying to sneak away during a dance."

"So you don't care a fig for her reputation or her future."

"Mother!" Cecilia inserted herself between Dorothea and her mother. "Stop being ridiculous."

"You are not going to marry Roger Phipps," Lady Abernathy snapped. "You have an opportunity to become an important member of society. I won't allow you to throw yourself away on a penniless farmer."

"He's not penniless," Cecilia shot back. "He's a member of Parliament and a baronet. His family has been important in the county long before our family arrived."

"The issue is not up for discussion Go to your room."

Cecilia's expression was rebellious. She turned toward Dorothea, but Dorothea shook her head. "Not now. Later, yes. Now, no."

A stubborn expression crossed her face, but she did she was told, leaving Dorothea and Lady Abernathy to face one another. "I thought you would have sense not to leave her alone with a gentleman. Though, given the way Lady Wilmont lets her daughter fling herself at every man in London, hardly surprising you would think nothing of such liberties."

"I was not more than five feet away," Dorothea protested.

"Engrossed in your lists." Lady Abernathy strode across the floor to the writing desk. "Are you satisfied with what we possess?"

She glanced down and reached out to take hold of Lady Wilmont's latest note, lying half open. "What's this?" she demanded.

Dorothea held out her hand. "Please give it back."

Lady Abernathy moved away. "*You must force her to hand over the reins, though she will resist,*" she read.

Her face flushed and she demanded, "How often does Lady Wilmont write to you like this?"

"My aunt does not like you. Are you surprised any advice she gives me is colored by how she feels about you?" Dorothea held out her hand. "May I please have my letter back?"

"How. Often?"

"Since Martin and I returned to London. I don't mention it because every time you hear her name, an argument begins."

"If not for Martin's insistence refusing them an invitation would be an insult to you, I would not allow that woman and her wretched daughter in this house. I promise you, once the ball is done, I fully intend to give instructions she is not to be admitted, whether I am here or no. You may visit her in her home to reap the 'benefits' of this advice she offers you. I have had enough of the both of you disrupting this household."

She crumpled the letter, dropping it to the floor. "I'm certain you intend to try wrapping Martin about your little finger when he returns, but you must fight me if you keep associating with Lady Wilmont. This is still my home and I am still in charge here, even if you are Martin's wife."

Without another word, Lady Abernathy marched from the room. Dorothea realized her hands were clenched in fists, nails digging into her palms. She took a deep breath and unfurled her fingers, noting the crescent-shaped impressions left in the skin.

Calm. She needed to be calm. The thought crossed her mind she should try to make amends, but she doubted any efforts would enjoy much success. Even if she gave in, cut the Wilmonts from her life and let Lady Abernathy have her way with everything, she doubted those actions would be enough.

Self-effacement was not in Dorothea's nature. Not when she had other options. For the first time in her life, she might.

Moving to the bell cord once more, she tugged a bit harder than necessary, then settled herself at her desk, trying to cultivate a calm demeanor. When Farthing appeared, she said, "Please tell Lord Abernathy I would appreciate the opportunity to speak with him as soon as he arrives home. Before he speaks with his mother."

Instructions delivered, Dorothea picked up her pen once more, though she watched the butler out of the corner of her eye. He hesitated, bowed and departed. There was another burr that itched, for undoubtedly her instructions would be reported to Lady Abernathy.

⚜

Martin frowned at the note from his mother, asking he speak with her as soon as he returned, preferably before he spoke with his wife. The note worried him, as it'd been sent in reply to his own note to Dorothea letting her know he would be dining at his club. With luck, the two women wouldn't kill one another before he returned.

Part of him wondered if his life would be easier if he had married one of the young women his mother tried to steer him toward. With someone willing to take a back seat to Lady Abernathy, Martin doubted he would find happiness. With a bride who wouldn't, he would find himself in the same position at some point or another. His mother would not give up control unless forced. Hell, she still didn't always want to acknowledge his rights as the current title holder.

He had finished his meal when Roger appeared in the dining room entrance. In the need for some sensible company and taking the temperature of Commons before the evening debates began, Martin lifted a hand in greeting. "If I knew you were going to be here," he said as Roger joined him, "I would have waited."

"I'm not certain you would find me pleasant company," Roger said, looking none too happy.

"What's wrong? Troubling news from home? Your mother is well?"

"Mother is fine. I—"

He leaned forward. "Are you seriously considering the Duke of Stockwood as a possible husband for Cecilia?"

The question caused Martin to laugh involuntarily, choking on his wine. "Damn it," he managed at last. "Will you give a man some warning when you tell a joke?"

"Your mother isn't joking."

"My mother has some fantasy Stockwood will come up to snuff any day now. He hasn't asked and I don't think he's going to. Sometimes I think the only way any woman is going to get that man to the altar is to trap him."

He paused, his glass halfway to his lips. "I'm sorry. The joke was in poor taste. I'm touched you worry about Cecilia. I know she's fond of you."

Before Roger could say anything else, Martin leaned forward. "Now, rumor has it some firebrands will be speaking in Commons tonight."

Roger hesitated, looking for all the world as if he didn't want to tell Martin. "There will be wrangling over clauses. Mr. Herbert of Kerry is threatening to rise and say the Prince of Wales is unfit to be Regent."

Martin grimaced. "Can't we get this damn thing done? The king is ill and unable to govern, nor is he likely to recover soon, if at all. We cannot let things float along. Someone must be at the helm."

"With the Prince of Wales, flawed as he is, is the most natural candidate." Roger nodded. "On that, at least, we can agree."

"Some are determined to treat him as if he were a naughty child."

"Because he behaves like a naughty child," Roger said.

"Are you voting in favor of additional restrictions?" Martin asked, unsure he had heard correctly.

"That's not what I said, nor is it what I want to speak to you about."

Perhaps it was the stress of the last few days, but Martin found himself vexed more than he should be. "You know how hard I work to support the Prince's cause. I thought you stood with us."

"I do, but not as uncritically as you appear at times. Before you say I didn't give you a hint, I tried. You've been so locked in this damn feud of your mother's, not paying attention to almost anything else. I agree the prince should be regent because we cannot continue in limbo. He also spends wildly, elevates his friends whenever possible, and surrounds himself with toadies who seek nothing but their own advancement."

"Might I remind you His Highness calls upon me for advice?" Martin said, his voice frosty.

Roger sighed. "I don't mean you. I mean men such as Tilney. He does nothing but encourage the Prince to spend money. Perceval says His Highness' debts are something close to half a million pounds."

Martin feared Roger's might well be right. "A prince is expected to live as a prince."

"There's living as a prince and being a wastrel. His Highness often is the latter." Roger paused. "Commons will balk at paying those debts. You know we're going to be asked to."

"We can't send him to debtor's prison."

"That. Is. Not. The. Point." Frustration crept into Roger's words. "Commons agrees there should be some restrictions to prevent him from emptying the treasury. Yet, we still receive addresses from his brothers, along with the mayor and aldermen of London, asking us to let him serve without any."

Roger took a deep breath, then leaned forward. "I'm changing the subject. What if Cecilia wanted to marry someone who supported the Tories more than the Whigs in this matter? Who might be considering crossing the aisle to join them when the division comes?"

The words provoked a snort. "Who? Cecilia doesn't favor anyone in particular. Certainly not someone with Tory leanings."

Roger remained silent as the truth began to sink in. "I tried to talk to you for well over a month," he said after a moment. "Your mind was taken up with the feud, your marriage, or this damn bill, leaving room for little else. I should tell you Lady Abernathy is absolutely opposed. In fact, she had me removed from the house this afternoon."

Was this what his mother wanted to speak to him about? "What happened?"

"She found Cecilia and I talking. Dorothea was with us, but at her desk, where she withdrew to give us some privacy. Your mother came in and made herself quite clear I was not part of any plans for Cecilia. Then she called Farthing and asked him to escort me out the door." He snorted. "You may have married, but she still rules."

There had to be more to the story, but the dining room had begun to clear as gentleman departed for either Commons or the Strangers' Gallery. If Martin wanted a seat to view the proceedings, he must move soon. "The Prince likes you. Supporting the Tories will wound him."

"The Prince enjoys drinking and dicing with me. That I'm not adverse to loaning him small sums, same as you, doesn't hurt." A bitter note colored his voice. "I imagine I won't be doing more of that if I speak tonight. I own no real position save as a member of commons, with no title to guarantee me a seat at the table. You possess standing where I do not. Another reason for your mother to oppose a betrothal with Cecilia."

He leaned forward. "Your efforts are to convince members to vote against the restrictions. Let me try to convince you to vote for them when the bill comes to Lords. Think of the prince with all the power and no check. We've got a war to fund, which isn't going well, if we're honest. Do you think we're going to be able to find the money to prevail against Napoleon if the Prince of Wales is spending it all on his pavilion?"

Martin had no good answer to the charge, much to his shame. "You never told me why you support him so blindly in this," Roger said. "Is ambition so important? What could he promise you to make you consider endangering your country for his favor?"

The words stung with a grain of truth. " I'll thank you to not impugn my honor."

"I suppose you're not going to smile on my request for the Fair Cecilia's hand?"

The words were a mimic of what Stockwood called her, close enough to make Martin wince. "Not if you're going to annoy the man who holds the key to any advancement you might hope for. Or if you're going to suggest I'm doing what I'm doing for selfish motives."

Roger nodded in acceptance. "We've been friends a long time, Martin," he said as he rose. "I hope we can put this behind us at some point."

The idea of finding himself at odds with one of his oldest friends hurt more than Martin wanted to admit. It made him angry as well. "Perhaps. Not today, though. You'll understand if I allow my mother's request you not present yourself at our home to stand."

Roger stood and offered a deep, formal bow, an acknowledgement of the gulf that now lay between them before joining the general exodus.

Martin stayed where he was, stewing. Yes, he was angry. At Roger and at himself as well, for not seeing the signs before. That was his fault, though he would be more than happy to blame Roger for the storm awaiting him at home. At least now he wouldn't go in blind.

He managed to secure a place in the gallery, fairly packed with those who wanted to watch. Much of the debates fell along predicted lines. Commons appeared balanced between those who were for restrictions and those in favor of even more restrictions. A defection one way or another could be the decision.

The hour was late when the Speaker recognized Roger. "It may surprise some to find I am now leaning to support the restrictions. I am a loyal servant of the king, but also a friend to the prince, drinking and gambling with him. Because of this, my honorable friends, I must support the restrictions, as I know how he can rack up debts."

His mouth twisted in a smile. "I have a call on those debts. During more than one evening, I had the pleasure of loaning His Highness a pound or two which I have not seen again."

His words provoked a roar of laughter from the Tory side and Martin's heart sank. No, Roger was cutting himself off for the foreseeable future. The prince did not take kindly to being made ridiculous.

Martin would be forced to break the news to Cecilia. Perhaps he should go drinking after this, delay his return home until he was certain both his mother and his wife were asleep. It might be the only peace he would see for a while.

CHAPTER 20

Dorothea waited outside the door to Martin's study, trying to convince herself she wasn't eavesdropping. He'd not slept in her room the night before, arriving home long after the rest of the house had been asleep. Now, he was in his study early, seeing neither her nor Lady Abernathy, sending for Cecilia before breakfast.

Lady Abernathy passed through the hall for the fifteenth time, stopping when she saw Dorothea. "They're still in there?"

Dorothea nodded. They were in an uneasy state of truce at the moment, both curious. Had Roger found him the night before to explain the situation? Was Martin giving Cecilia his answer to Roger's request?

The door opened, and Dorothea stepped back, narrowly avoiding a collision with Cecilia as she hurried for the stairs. Lady Abernathy called after her, but she didn't respond. Her face, though, had been wet with tears.

Martin emerged, looking somber. "Roger Phipps," he announced, "publicly broke with the Prince of Wales last night. He is supporting restrictions on the Regency bill."

"How publicly?" Dorothea asked, knowing it must be bad.

"He told Commons he thinks His Highness is irresponsible when it comes to spending. He said he knew this because he lent money to the prince on more than one occasion, never seen it again."

"His poor mother," Lady Abernathy murmured. "She had such hopes for him."

Martin nodded unhappily. "I had to tell Cecilia I couldn't consider Roger as a potential husband."

"Why?" Dorothea asked. "He's of good family. You said so yourself often enough."

He turned toward her. "He insulted me, implied I supported the prince solely for personal gain. We … argued. His words were not temperate, and he made more than one enemy yesterday. I'll not see my sister marry a man with no future."

He glanced from one to another. "He told me what happened when he came to visit. I want to speak to you both. At the same time. I'm in no mood for one of you to try working your way around the other."

With a sweep of his hand, he indicated the study, allowing them to proceed him into the room. Once the door was closed, he took his place behind his desk. "I understand Roger called on you yesterday, Dorothea, and you allowed him private conversation with Cecilia."

"With me sitting not five feet away." She didn't want to rehash this again.

"Not paying attention," Lady Abernathy snapped. "You, of all people should know better."

Martin turned to his mother. "Did Roger behave in a manner in any way disrespectful or forward toward Cecilia?"

"No, but the idea—"

"We had no callers beside him, so who is to know Dorothea allowed this. They've sat in close conversation before, with you in the room."

Lady Abernathy pursed her lips. "He knew I didn't want him calling."

This was news to Dorothea. News to Martin as well, given the expression on his face. "When did this happen?"

"At the Hastings affair. I told him I thought it best if he didn't call on Cecilia. He was welcome to call on you if business required. He decided to flout my request."

Martin turned to Dorothea. "Did Roger come for you or me?"

"He said he wanted to speak with you," Dorothea said. "I told him you were at your club. I also invited him to stay for a moment, as I felt both Cecilia and I needed a brief break. I was being polite."

"So, you willfully flouted my instructions, despite my not wanting him to call on Cecilia."

"It might have been useful to tell me if you have such instructions," Dorothea snapped back. "Had I known, I would not have extended the invitation, though I think you are wrong."

"So you would quarrel with me on who I think my daughter should associate with?"

"You didn't tell me, Mother." Martin wrested control of the conversation again. "Did you stop to think that until last night, I counted Roger as an ally in Parliament, and he might have reason to visit this home?"

"I said he could call on you," Lady Abernathy replied.

"By doing so, you told him he is unwelcome except for political necessity. Thank you, Mother. You made things *so* much easier."

He turned toward Dorothea. "Why did you decide to let Roger and Cecilia to speak, knowing my mother favored another match?"

"Because I know you don't approve of her choice. I've seen the way they look at one another, even if your mother desires something else," she replied. "I thought it better they speak with a chaperone present rather than seek stolen assignations on the dance floor."

Martin glanced from one to another. "Both of you wanted to speak to me to tell me the other was wrong. Both of you left instructions with Farthing I should speak to you first."

His expression warned he was annoyed with both of them. This would not be the last time. "Sir Roger is now officially banned from the house, I suppose," she said.

"You are correct," Martin said, "Though not for your reasons, Mother. Things are ill between he and I. Until such time as they are not, no, he is not welcome here. I would, however, ask if you want to bar someone from the house, you communicate the information to

Dorothea. If you don't, I don't want you crying to me she's disobeyed you."

He turned to Dorothea. "I'm asking you to abide by Mother's wishes where possible. If you have an issue, speak with me; I will speak with her. I don't want any more of this trying to put me between the two of you. Do I make myself clear?"

"Completely," Dorothea said, her response a little colder than intended.

"Does this mean you'll not invite Lady Wilmont and that dreadful daughter of hers here again?"

Dorothea turned to Lady Abernathy, fully ready to give her a piece of her mind, but Martin intervened. "Mother, please remember these are Dorothea's relations. Stop making such comments in her presence; you're not helping."

His expression softened as he turned back to Dorothea. "Would you go up and check on Cecilia?" Martin asked. "I think she may need a shoulder to cry on."

As Dorothea began to move, Lady Abernathy said, "Comforting a daughter is a mother's responsibility."

"In this case, I think Dorothea would be better suited. Given I just told her I won't agree to her marrying Roger, I doubt she'll be happy to see you. I also don't want you trying to shove her into Stockwood's arms."

Lady Abernathy's expression said she might try, which did not bode well for Cecilia. Dorothea could not remedy that now, so she did as Martin asked, leaving mother and son to say whatever they had to say to one another.

🙚🙘

Martin didn't speak when Dorothea left them, but stood before the window, hands clasped behind his back as he gathered his thoughts.

Lady Abernathy broke the silence first. "I must admit I'm not surprised about Roger; he's always been a bit of a wild one. "

Feeling a slow burn of anger, Martin turned toward her. "If not for the argument between Roger and myself, I would happily give my blessing to his request."

"Cecilia's your only sister. Don't you want her to marry well?"

"I want her to be happy, which appears to be different from what you're interested in."

He began to pace, filled with restless energy. "My decision may please you, but it does not please me. Roger has been a friend to this family since we were children, but he's been treated him somewhat shabbily of late. I put him off several times. I should have realized his position had shifted. I took his support for granted, and it cost me."

"Are you saying you would consider a man with little no future in politics, no title, and only a small fortune as a possible husband for your sister when she could have almost any peer in the realm?"

"If I could be assured of her happiness, yes. Not now, though. Not after this. Do not take this as a sign the path is clear for Stockwood. Why are you so set on him, Mother? How many times must Cecilia tell you she doesn't want to marry him? She doesn't need to marry for money."

"I'm thinking of the future of the family," Lady Abernathy replied. "The two of you prattle on about 'happiness' and 'love', never realizing those things are ephemeral. When I was Cecilia's age, I fell in love. He betrayed me, let himself be lured away by another woman. My heart broke and I was certain my life was over."

She drifted toward the globe which stood in one corner an anniversary gift from her to Martin's father. "My mother sensibly let me mourn, then reminded me the purpose of marriage is to gain advantage for my family. I would make connections to help not only my children, but my nieces and nephews, as they, in turn would help us. The Earl of Chalton is an ally not only because you share politics, but also because you are cousins through me."

Her hand rested briefly on the surface of the globe before she turned back to him, face set, gaze determined. "You threw away your chance to make a match which would bring value to this family. Your wife possesses some small talents, I'll allow, but what else does she bring? Ties to an undistinguished family teetering on the edge of scandal. If connections are to be made in this generation, Cecilia must make them. No, His Grace is not exciting, but he brings with him connections to the royal family."

She paused. "He will respect and be kind to her, which is more important than you can imagine."

Martin had no reply and she drew herself up. "You've made your position clear. Now, if you'll excuse me, there are other household matters I need to attend to since you asked your wife to take care of my daughter."

She strode from the room, not waiting to hear if he had anything else to say. Martin realized there was little use pursuing the conversation.

Weary, he sank into a chair. How had he come to this point? A close friend opposed to him politically. His sister was upstairs crying her eyes out because she loved the boy she grew up with. He didn't really know his wife, his mother hated her, and the duke his mother wanted for his sister was a fool.

What the hell should he do?

"Go away."

The sullen growl in response to Dorothea's knock did not come as a surprise. "Martin asked me to come up," she said.

Her words provoked no response telling her to enter, but neither was there another call for her to go away. Cautiously, she opened the door, peering inside to find Cecilia curled in a ball on the bed, weeping. Closing the door behind her, Dorothea crept forward. "He wanted to know how you were."

Cecilia sat upright, face red and streaked with tears, eyes angry. "How does he think I am? He's told me he won't let me marry the man I love because of some stupid political fight. My mother is celebrating because she never wanted me to marry Roger. Now she's free to shove me at the Duke of Stockwood."

"Martin again told her he's not going to give his permission, unless you agree. If you don't want to marry Stockwood, he'll support you," Dorothea offered.

"If I don't marry His Grace, it'll be someone else with wealth and a title. Mother's determined, and usually gets her way. She doesn't give a fig about anyone else's feelings."

Harsh words, and, Dorothea suspected, not unjustified. "I suspect she's doing what she thinks is best for you."

"Marriage to a man I don't love is what she thinks best for me? Not as if he'd bring Martin any political advantage. I could almost —*almost*—understand. I think this is pure social one-upmanship. She wants me to have the greatest catch of the season so she can shove it in Lady Wilmont's face."

This was not pretty, gentle crying, but the kind to make Cecilia's face red and blotchy, her nose beginning to run. Dorothea fetched a handkerchief from the dressing table, passing it to Cecilia without a word. Cecilia blew her nose even as the tears splashed the bodice of her dress. *At least she's wearing wool, not silk.*

Cecilia wiped at her eyes before blowing her nose again. "Why should you care? You seem happy enough with your husband."

There was bitterness in her voice, another thing not unjustified. "For a long time, I didn't think I would ever marry. I was the poor cousin, standing on the edge of the party but never invited to participate. Lady Wilmont decided she would find a husband for me, our local vicar." Dorothea sighed. "Believe me, the Reverend Shipley is not what I wanted in a husband, but it was him or spinsterhood, living on someone else's charity. I understand how hollow you can feel inside, like your heart's going to burst from unhappiness."

"Are you suggesting I soldier bravely on because you managed to? Or perhaps I should try to ensure Roger and I are caught in a compromising position so honor demands we be wed or risk scandal?"

Dorothea winced, the arrow striking home. "No one is suggesting such a thing. I know you're hurting, but there must be a way we can salvage this."

"How?" The word came out almost as a howl.

"Patience. No, hear me out. This happened suddenly; we shouldn't be surprised Martin acted the way he did. He's hurt and feeling betrayed by Roger's actions. Plus, it appears Roger said some things in his speech the Prince might take offense at. Your engagement to Roger being announced at this moment could rebound on your brother."

Cecilia considered her words. "How long must I be patient?" she asked at last.

"At least until the Regency Bill is passed. Once that happens, I'll do what I can to help them reconcile. If they can put this argument behind them, Martin might be more amenable to the idea of your betrothal. Remember, if he agrees, he'll have a fight on his hands with your mother. All you need to do in the meantime is play by your mother's rules and avoid a proposal from the Duke of Stockwood." Dorothea grinned. "How long has your mother been waiting for his proposal?"

The question coaxed a small smile from Cecilia. "Over a year. He's called on Martin at least twice."

She patted Cecilia's hand. "I think he's a pleasant man who enjoys your company because you are not trying to trap him into wedlock."

Again silence as Cecilia pondered her words. "You're right. I won't let Mother see how upset I am now. With luck, she'll be lulled into a false sense of security."

Something about the phrasing bothered Dorothea, but she hoped things would work out. It was all she could do at the moment.

CHAPTER 21

By the time the day of the dinner arrived, the question was no longer whether or not there would be restrictions on the Regency, but how many and for how long. The faintest whisper of a chance existed Commons might vote in favor of full freedom, but as one gentleman said, "What is the harm in a year? The time will pass quickly, give him time to settle into the role, understand he can't pursue pleasure willy-nilly."

Down the table, Dorothea listened to Mr. Henry explain some point. She responded with questions which appeared to intrigue the gentleman. While the dinner wasn't going to accomplish what Martin had hoped, the failure was not hers. This boded well for the future. About the only thing which did at this point.

His mother acted more frantic about preparations for the ball than he could remember, all the while ignoring Dorothea whenever possible. For her part, Dorothea appeared to be biting her tongue with uncomfortable frequency. Cecilia was quiet, smiles emerging only when she encountered those from outside the family, but those were not as bright as they used to be.

And he couldn't complain to Roger, because he and Roger weren't speaking.

Dorothea rose when last of the plates were cleared away. "Gentlemen, I will leave you to your drinks and discussions. I thank you for your patience with my questions and bid you good night."

She left the room, pausing briefly when Martin caught her hand to place a kiss on it. In some areas, they were still in harmony, but the wall between them grew during the day.

"You've done well, Lord Abernathy," Mr. Henry said when she was gone. "Your wife is a clever woman. I should think you for seating me near her. Most entertaining."

"Not a surprise," another guest said. "She always was the brightest of the lot when I dined with the Wilmonts. Limited education, quite naturally, but picks things up quickly. I understand why you fell for her."

Martin relaxed as the sentiment caused general agreement around the table. With luck, talk around the circumstances around his marriage was beginning to die down. With a nod to Farthing to begin serving the port, he said, "I hope she pled the Prince's cause well, sir. I have no doubt you know why you were invited: to discuss the matter of restrictions upon the Prince of Wales when he is made Regent and how far they should extend."

The conversation began to dive into the various weeds of the matter. Where there should be restrictions, and for how long. Should the queen have care of only the king's person or would she also control the offices which came such responsibility? Should such be given to His Highness? Doing his best to guide and shape the conversation, Martin thought they might ensure the Regency was not entirely hobbled.

In the midst of the discussion, Farthing entered with a small silver tray, offering it to Martin with a bow. Martin took the note which lay there, glancing at the bottom to see the signature. *Stockwood.*

Struggling to suppress a groan, he read through the few lines. *Abernathy: Was wondering if I could call on you tomorrow to discuss some matters. Say, 1 PM? This is private, between you and me.*

Wonderful. His mother would be thrilled and Cecilia would hate him a little more. "A reply is requested, my lord," Farthing said.

Martin wanted to put him off, but didn't have a reason to. "Tell the messenger I'll expect His Grace at one."

Farthing bowed before departing. Martin tried to focus his attention back to the conversation, for all the good it would do.

❦

"But fly-fishing is a real art. Out there, all alone with nature."

Martin sighed. Stockwood had been talking drivel for twenty minutes and gotten nowhere. If this interview followed the course of the previous three, the duke would continue on for another ten minutes before begging his leave.

Deciding enough was enough, Martin leaned forward. "Your Grace, while all this is fascinating, isn't there something else you wanted to speak with me about?"

Stockwood stopped, blinking twice. How could his mother consider this man as a potential son-in-law? After a long pause, Stockwood said, "Funny thing, that. Been trying to screw up the courage to ask you for the fair Cecilia's hand in matrimony. Been trying to each time I talk to you."

"But …?" Martin asked, the word hanging in the air.

Wodehouse shifted in his seat. "Every time I've tried, I stopped on the brink, and we end up talking about fly-fishing or something. Just haven't been able to bring myself to do it."

"Any particular reason?" The question was not necessary, Stockwood unable to bring himself to the point was reason enough to let the matter drop. The man acted with no guile, leaving Martin more than a little curious.

"Don't know. Well, I do know, but you'll find it silly. I enjoy Miss Drayton's company and I think she might enjoy mine. I can't help the feeling her heart's located somewhere else. A bit disheartening for a chap. I'm not passionately in love with her -- not like you are with young Lady A. I respect her and I suppose I must marry at some point to provide an heir. She treats me well, so why not her? Would make your mother happy."

"It would make my mother extremely happy, but you wouldn't be marrying my mother."

Stockwood looked shocked. "I should say not!"

Martin took a deep breath. "I'm not going to give you an answer now. I want to talk to Cecilia first. My main concern is if she'll be happy."

"Of course! Wouldn't want the fair maiden to feel she's being bundled off like a sack of grain. Decided I should make certain you won't chuck me out of the house on my backside if I had the audacity to ask."

Martin assured the duke several times he had no intention of chucking him out of the house, then took that as the excuse to usher him out of the study. *At least one of us is in a cheerful mood.*

Once Stockwood was safely gone, he turned away from the door, only to find his mother, his sister, and his wife all waiting for him. "Did he ask this time?" Lady Abernathy said, cutting to the heart of the matter.

"Not exactly. He wanted to make certain I wouldn't chuck him out of the house for daring to ask."

Lady Abernathy smiled broadly. "At last! We can start planning the wedding. The banns must be cried, of course, Cecilia's trousseau—"

Martin held up a hand. "I told him Cecilia needed to give her consent before I gave permission."

Cecilia's face wore an expression of relief as Dorothea moved to her side. "Before you complain, Mother, I might add His Grace was very understanding. There's no love, but some affection. I wonder if it is enough to make a marriage."

"Love, affection, what ridiculous modern notions," Lady Abernathy waved the words away. "In my day, we understood marriage was for the betterment of the family. Your father didn't make protestations of love when he offered for my hand. He thought my background suitable and I would make a proper mother for his heir."

All heads turned toward her. "You always told me you had your pick of men during your season," Cecilia said.

"I did, except for the one man I wanted. He had his head turned by a venal, hateful woman who wanted to take him away because he belonged to me. Let that be a warning to you."

Before Martin could explore this fascinating avenue any further, Lady Abernathy said, "Come, Cecilia. I want you to understand what an opportunity this is for you."

He expected Cecilia to resist, but she meekly said, "Yes, Mother," and let Lady Abernathy lead her away.

"I think she's trying to avoid a fight," Dorothea observed.

"I have no intention of letting Mother bully Cecilia into an unhappy marriage for the sake of a social standing. She should be satisfied she's managed to get the proposal. Sort of. I think Stockwood is getting tired of being chased by almost every eligible woman in London. He's retreating somewhere he believes will be safe." He shrugged. "It wouldn't be a bad match. He'd be kind, let Cecilia manage him, and better off for it."

"What does Cecilia get out of the match when her heart is elsewhere?"

"I am *not* going to give permission for her to marry Roger Phipps," he snapped. "He's proven to be no true friend."

"Perhaps when some time passes."

"I'm not discussing this, madam, and that is my final word."

Dorothea stared at him for a moment, then dropped a slight curtsey. "As you wish, my lord. Please excuse me."

He had an urge to call after her as she left the hall, but didn't. His pride felt hurt again. He knew, though, his refusal was another brick in the growing wall between them.

❦

It was four days later when Cecilia found herself at an event with Roger also in attendance and she might seize an opportunity to speak with him. What she needed was an excuse.

A clearing of the throat, caused Cecilia to remember her manners, turning back to the Duke of Stockwood. "So, shall we do the country set?" he asked.

Cecilia shook her head. "I'd rather rest during this one, if you don't mind, Your Grace. Perhaps the supper dance?"

Far from being disappointed, Stockwood's face lit up. "I say, that would be capital, Miss Drayton. We can enjoy a pleasant conversation during the break."

He bowed then moved away, as hoped. A glanced towards her mother found her holding forth about something to Lady Knowle, neither glancing in her direction. Carefully, Cecilia moved away and about the edge of the room toward Roger. He must have been watching because he started toward her.

They met in a secluded corner, hidden from the room by both a pillar and a potted plant. Roger brought her hand to his lips, placing a lingering kiss upon her glove. "It's been too long," he whispered.

"I hoped you'd come," she whispered in return. "Everything's been awful. The Duke of Stockwood asked Martin for my hand."

Roger grimaced. "What did Martin say?"

"He won't give permission unless I agree. But you know Mother. She's insistent this is the right thing, marshalling all sorts of arguments. She's not going to give up, Roger. She's going to keep at me until I'm worn down enough I'll agree."

She tried to ensure her face showed her intent. "Take me away, Roger. I want to be gone from this place; I want to be with you."

Roger frowned. "You don't know what you're saying."

"Yes, I do. Elopement and social embarrassment seems the only way we can be together."

Roger shook his head. "Don't you realize this could mean an irrevocable break from your family? Look at Lady Eastleigh. His family still hasn't accepted her after almost twenty years. Martin moved heaven and earth to avoid one scandal. He won't forgive you for another. Better for me to try patching things up with him first."

He glanced around. "Being seen speaking like this isn't going to help. You should go back."

"But what if you can't patch things up?" Cecilia asked. "What if Mother keeps pushing on Martin to convince him this is the right thing to do. She's determined, no matter my feelings."

He seemed to be weighing her words. "Do you want to marry me so much?" he asked. "I mean, with all your heart?"

"Yes," Cecilia breathed, almost trembling as she waited for his next words. Had he come to the same conclusion?

"You're willing to risk a break with your family for this?"

"They'll come around eventually," Cecilia assured him. "Martin's known you forever. I can't see him wanting to stay mad at you."

Another pause as he glanced about. "I have an idea. I'll send a letter when everything is arranged. But I am going to try to reconcile with Martin first."

She moved closer toward him. "Roger——"

He caught her hands. "We must be careful. If we're seen——"

"If you're seen doing what?" Martin said, his voice a harsh whisper.

Turning, Cecilia found they were discovered. Martin stood behind her, Dorothea hovering at his side. She thought of saying something glib, but decided she would only make matters worse. "I love him, Martin."

"Not the point. You're hiding behind a frond to steal a kiss." His gaze turned toward Roger. "I did not think you would violate my trust in this way."

"Your mother has forbidden me the house," Roger said, his tone flat. "You made yourself quite clear you no longer wish my company. The only way I can speak with Cecilia is at events such as these."

Martin kept his gaze fixed on Roger. "Dorothea, would please take Cecilia back to Mother."

"Martin——"

"Don't argue with me."

Dorothea reached for Cecilia's hand, pulling her away. "Your mother hasn't seen any of this," she whispered as they moved. "She's been too involved watching my cousin make a fool of herself."

Reluctantly looking toward the floor, Cecilia found Alyssa Wilmont in the steps of the country dance, moving closer to her partner than polite, leaning forward so her breasts almost touched his chest. Along the wall, the matrons and chaperones leaned their heads together, whispering at the sight, her mother among them.

Cecilia turned back to where Roger had stood. He was gone,

being escorted from the room by Martin. She tried to follow, but Dorothea caught her arm. "No, you don't"

"I thought you said you supported me," Cecilia near spit at her.

"I counseled patience, not stolen moments. What we need is to find you a nice safe partner before anyone notices what's happening."

❧

Martin burned with fury as he and Roger made their way into the foyer. "How dare you embarrass my sister."

"Miss Drayton did not act embarrassed when we spoke, but glad to see me," Roger replied.

"I saw how glad. You're lucky I didn't want to raise a fuss, or you would find yourself on the floor."

"Kisses are often stolen at a ball with little harm done to the lady's reputation."

"Or great harm." Martin clenched his fists. "Do you remember what happened to me?"

The words lay between them for a long moment. "I'm sorry," Roger said at last.

"A little late for that. I am asking you act as a gentleman. Otherwise, I must give instructions you or your mother are not to be admitted at Abernathy Hall as well as London."

A harsh statement, but Martin felt he no longer had any choice.

Roger gave him a wounded, expression, then his face hardened. "I cry you pardon, Lord Abernathy. I shall not trouble you again."

Roger turned on his heels and marched toward the door. Not until he left did Martin turn away, unhappy how this had turned out.

Returning to the ballroom, he made an effort to keep his face pleasant, chatting with other guests as he tried to locate Cecilia and Dorothea. Both were on the floor, making their way through a measure, but behaving as if all were well. Unlike the Wilmont ball, where news of his indiscretion spread like wildfire, he saw no gossips making their way toward Lady Abernathy with knowing looks. With luck, disaster at large might be averted—but he held no hopes for the moment when he could speak to Cecilia without their mother present.

CHAPTER 22

The first traces of dawn were on the horizon when they arrived home. Dorothea had been on tenterhooks all evening, wondering if Lady Abernathy had seen something, or someone else mentioned it. Disaster appeared to have been be averted, her mother-in-law all smiles when Stockwood claimed the supper dance with Cecilia. "I am for bed," Lady Abernathy said, stifling a yawn as she headed toward the stairs. "Don't linger too long."

They all said their goodnights, everything pleasant, but the moment Lady Abernathy was out of sight, Martin said, "Cecilia, I want to speak to you and Dorothea."

Cecilia's face lost the smile she had worn most of the evening. "Couldn't this wait until we've slept?" she asked.

"I don't think so. Let's go into the study. I don't want us overheard by Mother."

No one sat when they entered the room. Cecilia hovered near the fireplace, while Dorothea took up a position near Martin's desk, placing her out of the direct line of fire. Martin started to pace, hands clasped behind his back. After a long, strained minute, he said, "You are not to speak with Roger Phipps again. This comes from me, not Mother."

"Why?" Cecilia shot back. "He's been our friend all our lives, but suddenly he's not good enough?"

"Because, after being told not to go near you," Martin replied, his voicing rising to match his sister's. "He decided to ignore the request."

"Roger didn't seek me out. I'm the one who came to him."

"That only makes it worse!" Martin brought his fist down on the desk with a crash and Dorothea flinched. "Do you have any idea how much shame you might bring on this family with your actions? Do you have any conception of the consequences?"

Cecilia turned to Dorothea. "You talk to him. You understand. You said so."

Martin turned toward Dorothea, anger simmering in his eyes. His fury was for Cecilia, but she knew it could be directed toward her if she wasn't careful. "I counseled patience," she said, each word careful. "You wanted advice on how to change Martin's mind; I said not to push the issue."

"You encouraged her?" Martin asked, his voice tight.

"I suggested her best course was to be patient. To wait for the quarrel between you and him to repair itself before she raised the subject again. I did *not* suggest she undertake a clandestine assignation with half of society about."

"The quarrel's unlikely to be repaired now." He rounded back on his sister. "Even if you were the one to initiate the contact, Roger should know better. He allowed you to put yourself in a position where you could become a target of shame and mockery. I can no longer trust him."

"Why? Because he's going to embarrass you in your quest for political power? What am I supposed to do now? Marry some man you deem will bring *you* advantage, no matter my feelings?"

"Stop it, both of you!" Dorothea moved to insert herself between brother and sister. "This isn't solving anything. Besides, if you get much louder, your mother will hear the fuss. Do you want her to ask questions in the morning, if she doesn't come down now?"

They stopped, but neither appeared happy. Having quieted them, Dorothea turned to Martin. "I doubt Roger intended to seduce

Cecilia. Most likely, he wanted to make some explanation or say his farewells."

"They were trying to hide. Which makes me to believe there was something on his mind other than mere explanations."

"Moments of stress can cause people to forget themselves."

Martin fixed Dorothea with a steady gaze. "One near-scandal in the family is enough, thank you."

His words cut through her like a knife. Worse was her realization he meant those words to hurt. A lingering resentment or did he feel trapped in a situation his honor forced him into despite his protestations otherwise? She didn't want to consider the thought. Deliberately, she turned toward Cecilia, somehow managing to speak in a calm voice. "You're lucky your mother did not see you. It is in your best interest for her not to learn of this, so I suggest you do not continue to antagonize your brother."

"Who will tell Mama everything at breakfast." Cecilia's voice was angry, dripping with resentment.

"And listen to her crow triumphantly how she was right to want him banned from the house in the first place?" Martin snorted. "I get enough grief from her these days without adding to it."

Again, their voices rose and again Dorothea attempted to stop them. This time was more difficult, however, the siblings continuing to argue over her best efforts to quiet them. In the end, Cecilia stomped toward the door, pausing just long enough to fling a final insult at Dorothea. "I shouldn't be surprised you changed your tune. I wonder whose side you're really on."

Once she was gone, Martin said, "We need to watch her. She's angry enough to do something stupid."

Dorothea sighed. This was like being at the Wilmont's, dealing with the upset over one of Alyssa's fits. "Too close and she's more likely to try something. Besides, if you start keeping an obviously close eye on Cecilia, your mother's going to suspect something. I thought you didn't want—"

"I know how to handle my own sister, thank you very much."

His tone was snappish, his expression angry. He began to pace again, his movements that of a caged animal. "When I asked you to check on her, I didn't think you would fill her head with some nonsense about how she could convince me to let her marry Roger. I never said she could marry him."

"I tried to give her some comfort, calm her down."

"You did a fine job there. Next time, leave my family to me or Mother. Clearly you don't understand how we do things. Goodnight, madam.

He strode from the room. Dorothea wondered if she had been a fool these last weeks. She thought there was something growing between them, that he cared more than mere physical passion. They shared laughter and secrets, but all felt like ashes now.

He couldn't be rid of her. They were married, tied to one another for the rest of their lives. Divorce was possible for those in the upper class with money and influence to pursue it, then survive the scandal. Given Martin had been unwilling to ride out the gossip surrounding their discovery together, she doubted he'd take the larger step. For better or worse, they were stuck in this marriage. The only question now was whether or not they would be able to find a common ground to live on.

Martin stared down at his breakfast plate with no real appetite. For several days, there'd been tension between himself, Dorothea and Cecilia. True to his word, nothing was said about the incident with Roger or the argument following. Thankfully, Lady Abernathy gave no sign she had any knowledge, and no gossip arrived at the house bearing news which might alert her.

One problem averted, but that still left him with the issue of Cecilia. He couldn't restrict her comings and goings, not without raising suspicions. He was certain his mother kept some kind of watch, unless Lady Abernathy trusted Roger to stay away per her request. Which he doubted after she asked him to leave.

Cecilia was still angry with him for siding with their mother, not seemingly giving a fig how her behavior might reflect on the family. There was also tension between himself and Dorothea. She had to realize his mother would not react well to the idea of another, less titled suitor, and still provided Cecilia with encouragement in the form of comfort. Did she not suspect her actions would encourage Cecilia to do something rash?

He didn't know if he could trust those nearest and dearest to him these days.

Both Cecilia and Dorothea were quiet, sorting through the letters set beside their places. One Dorothea put aside, likely the daily missive from Lady Wilmont. His mother was unreasonable to demand she cut all communications, but he had to confess the flow of advice surrounded by an ongoing diatribe didn't make him happy either. Not sharing the messages was best for continued peace, but it didn't mean he cared for her receiving them.

Lady Abernathy had just finished sharing a tidbit from an old friend when Cecilia said, "Mrs. Porter's publisher is releasing a new novel from her."

Martin grimaced at the name of the gothic novelist. "I thought you despised Mrs. Porter's works."

"They're horrible," Cecilia admitted cheerfully. "Full of looming gothic castles and brooding lords with deep secrets. I adore them. Mrs. Radcliffe takes herself so seriously. Mrs. Porter writes as if she knows she's over the top, which is all part of the fun."

Lady Abernathy sniffed. "I wouldn't be surprised if 'Mrs. Porter' is some grubby little man in rented rooms in Clerkenwell. No decently born lady would willingly put her name on such trash. I don't know what young people are coming to."

"I think I may go to Dutton's and fetch a copy. Helen Ryan says she's going to go, and we could take tea together while we start reading. She'll likely be there with her mama, so we'll be properly chaperoned."

Lady Abernathy stared at her daughter. "If this book is the sensation you think it is, then there will be a terrible crush. No fit place for a young lady in those circumstances."

"I could take my maid," Cecilia said, her voice perilously close to a whine.

"I said no, and that is my final word on the subject."

"I'll be happy to take Cecilia," Dorothea said. "I need to set up my subscription with Dutton's, so Cecilia may write ahead to request a volume be put aside for her. If we're only fetching a package, we should not be so bothered by the crush."

Martin almost objected on the grounds Dorothea being so accommodating might raise Lady Abernathy's hackles, but Cecilia glared at her sister-in-law, all suspicion. Which meant this wasn't some scheme the women had cooked up together.

"I don't want you there, either," Lady Abernathy said. "My son has a position to think of, and you should consider it as well. Being seen buying a piece of trash is hardly an action to serve him well."

You may have married, but she still rules. Roger's words rang mockingly in Martin's ears. "My wife is welcome to go if she so wishes," Martin said with more than a touch of annoyance. "Her behavior is under my dictates, Mother, not yours. I would thank you to remember such."

"As long as she is living in my house," Lady Abernathy retorted, "I believe she should conform to what I think is appropriate behavior, just as I expect Cecilia to do."

Martin braced for the sharp remark from Dorothea at the idea she should be governed by her mother-in-law more than her husband. Her jaw tensed and her lips pressed tightly together, but she stayed silent, developing an intense interest in her plate. "This is *my* house," he said at last. "Which means Dorothea is under my direction, not yours. If she wishes to visit Dutton's on the day a popular novelist releases a new book, I say she is welcome to do so unless I decide circumstances dictate otherwise."

Dead silence fell over the table as Martin silently wished all the women in his life to perdition for putting him in this position. Having taken the stand, though, he was damned if he would cede the field without a fight.

Lady Abernathy raised her cup, took a sip, then set it down. Slowly, she removed her napkin from her lap and placed it on the table next to her plate. "Perhaps Cecilia and I should leave for home so your wife may step into her ... proper place. Once we settle the business with the Duke of Stockwood, of course."

The expected response was, of course, "You can't leave Mother. I bow to your wishes," or words to that effect. He did not feel in the mood to play the game this morning. One look at Cecilia's face revealed the business would not be settled as his mother hoped. "No earlier than the end of next week," Martin said, his voice firm. "After all we wouldn't want to deprive Cecilia of her chance to obtain Mrs. Porter's new novel, would we?"

A little thing, but Martin couldn't resist. "If you think best," Lady Abernathy said, rising from her place. "Now, if you'll excuse me, I must see to some things I must do if I'm to effect a transition within this house."

She sailed out of the room without a backward glance. "I hope you're happy, Cecilia," Martin said as he tossed his napkin down. "She's going to be impossible to live with."

"She's been impossible since before we got to London," Cecilia replied. "At least we didn't hear another round of veiled insults against Lady Wilmont."

"Mother's going to play the martyr. She's going to resent every action Dorothea takes, more than she does now."

"I'm not the one who reminded her it's not her house."

Martin took a deep breath and counted to ten before speaking. "What was I supposed to do? Sit by and let her tell my wife how she's supposed to behave?"

He turned toward Dorothea. "You're unusually quiet. Don't you have anything to say for yourself?"

Dorothea looked up from her plate, her eyes calm. "No, my lord. You made yourself clear the other evening my comments on family matters were not welcome."

Cecilia stood. "I think I should get ready for visitors."

Martin waited until the door closed, leaving him and Dorothea alone, before asking "And what do you mean?"

She shrugged. "I take my cue from you. You resented my interference between you and your sister, so I thought the best course would be to keep quiet while you fought with your mother as my input would not be welcome from either of you."

"My mother is ready to quit London, hand control of the house over to you, and that is all you can say?"

Despite his best intentions, Martin felt himself grow angrier. The calm, collected way Dorothea regarded him did not help. "I do not believe your mother intends to quit London or relinquish power any more than you do. She will use your sister's refusal to marry Stockwood as an excuse to remain, all the while playing the martyr."

She picked up her knife and fork once more. "If she should, much to my surprise, decide to leave, I will do my best to perform the job satisfactorily and not prove an embarrassment. I realize I'm not exactly what you wished for in a wife, but I hope, with time, you will cease to regret this situation you find yourself forced into."

Her words stung. Where could she have noticed he resented the match? Yes, he resented the way she seemed determined to meddle in family business, but he tried to tell himself such was to be expected of any bride, and nothing more.

With no good way to respond, Martin fell back on formality. "I will hold you to that, madam. Pray excuse me, there is business for me to attend to."

Walking out of the room, he couldn't help feeling despite the apparent victory, he'd lost. Badly.

CHAPTER 23

As predicted, there was a crush at Dutton's, with both men and women vying for those copies of Mrs. Porter's novel not already spoken for. The staff happily assisted Dorothea with her new account, but she regretted the impulse which had caused her to volunteer for this expedition. Especially since she had lost track of Cecilia.

"Enjoying the crowd, Lady Abernathy?"

Dorothea discovered Lord Blair in the press next to her. "It's terrible," she replied. "I don't know why Cecilia insisted on coming today, even if she asked a copy be put aside for her."

Blair seemed surprised. "I can understand my sister wanting a copy—the only reason I'm here—but I can't picture Miss Drayton reading such twaddle."

Dorothea shrugged. "She says she and her friends enjoy them because they're awful. I volunteered to chaperone."

"No accounting for taste, I suppose. Bravo to you for being the sacrificial lamb." The crowd shifted and he inched closer to the counter. "Lord, what a mess. I wonder if all these ladies are truly interested in the Porter trash or if some hit on the idea of using this to cover an assignation. It'd be easy to slip away in this crowd and not be noticed. Yes, you, sir. I'm next."

Blair touched his hat to her as he moved closer to the counter. The comment was an idle one, but Dorothea felt a touch of panic at his words. Cecilia had been accepting of the situation since the blow up —*too* accepting. Had she used the event to arrange an assignation with Roger Phipps?

She began to hunt for Cecilia in earnest, impeded not only by the crowd, but her attempt to ensure she didn't alert others something was wrong. Too many people who knew the Abernathy family were present. One hint and the news would spread across London.

"Dorothea! I am surprised to find you here today of all days."

She did not need Lady Wilmont today, but Dorothea forced herself to smile and accept her aunt's greeting. "You don't have an account at Dutton's, Aunt Honoria."

Lady Wilmont kissed the air formally beside' Dorothea cheek. "Opened one when I heard about Mrs. Porter's latest. Took forever for Hookham's to obtain a copy. Why not a second account somewhere I can expect to receive the book at a reasonable time?" She sighed. "I suppose we won't be borrowing quite as many now, though, not with you gone."

"I'm sure you and Uncle Henry will read enough between you." She wanted to get away, but she also wished to avoid comments she was "acting strangely." "I checked the guest list for the ball," she said, grasping at straws. "I'm afraid Lord Tilney is in the Prince of Wales' party. We can't disinvite him."

Lady Wilmont offered a resigned sigh. "At least you tried, my dear, and I appreciate that." Jostled, she glared over her shoulder at the offender. "This is no place to talk. Come to visit tomorrow, since I imagine Lady Abernathy will throw a fit if you allow me within the Sacred Precincts."

She paused before adding, "I'm taking Alyssa to Bath after your ball. For the waters. She needs a break from London."

Lady Wilmont appeared as if she needed the break. "Of course, we could go earlier, though we would miss your ball." She gave a hopeful smile. "Would you like to come along?"

The idea was tempting, even she would be forced to deal with

Alyssa. Then Lady Wilmont laughed. "I know you can't, my dear. Come tomorrow. I have missed you."

Dorothea promised she would, knowing she would offer what support she could. Released, she searched again, then took up a position to watch the central desk. Cecilia would most likely be looking for her, so best to stay in one place until she returned.

Several minutes passed and the crowd began to thin. Dorothea made one last search. Growing desperate, she stepped outside.

No sign of Cecilia, though their footman waited patiently, ready to dispatch one of the urchins hanging about to send word to the coachman. Before Dorothea could ask him if Cecilia had been outside, one of those urchins raced up. "You be Lady Abernathy?" the lad inquired in a squeaky voice.

"Here, off with you," the footman said. "Don't be bothering your betters."

Dorothea gestured for the man to back away and let the boy approach. "I'm Lady Abernathy."

He held out a note, carefully folded. "Another lady asked me to give this to you," As Dorothea reached out, he pulled back. "Said you'd give me half a crown."

Dorothea managed to pull a crown from her reticule and shoved it into the urchin's hand, not caring she'd doubled his promised fee. The lad's eyes grew big and he thrust the note at her, racing away with his prize. With trembling fingers, she unfolded the parchment to reveal Cecilia's neat writing. *My dear Dorothea,* the note began.

It is unkind of me to lay this burden on you, but I have eloped with Sir Roger Phipps. Mrs. Porter was an excuse. Assure everyone I will come to no harm with Roger to protect me, and I will communicate once the deed is done. I know they will be angry, but they must understand my love for Roger is as great as my love for them, and I will not endure our parting, nor consider marriage to another. I only hope they can find it in their hearts to forgive what I know my mother, at least, will consider a betrayal. God keep you safe and well, and I pray he sends you and Martin half the love I feel for Roger.

Your loving sister, Cecilia.

P.S. Also, if you can, please spare a kind word to His Grace, the Duke of Stockwood. I'm flattered he thought enough of me to ask for my hand, and for understanding it couldn't be given by Martin's fiat. He can be a dear fool and I hope, one day soon, we can still be friends.

P.P.S. I know Martin will attempt to come after us. Please try to convince him not to chase after us on the North Road, for he will not catch us there.

For a moment, Dorothea thought she would collapse, so loudly did the blood pound in her ears. She called for the carriage, knowing she needed to return home.

❧

Martin sighed at the sound of raised voices penetrating the quiet of his study. *What now?* Setting his pen aside, he emerged to see what new disaster awaited him, and was surprised to find Dorothea there, still in her bonnet, speaking to Lady Abernathy, who stood halfway down the stairs. "I came home once I realized," she said. "We may already be too late, though."

"What's the problem here?"

Dorothea spun toward him, eyes wide. "Thank goodness you're here. There is no time to lose."

Before he could ask what was wrong, Lady Abernathy descended. "Let us go into the drawing room," she said, taking hold of Dorothea.

As she settled Dorothea on the sofa, Martin fetched a small brandy. When he held out the glass to Dorothea, though, she pushed it away. "We have no time."

He stared at her for a moment, puzzled. Slowly, the missing piece became clear. "Where's Cecilia?"

"Gone." She offered him a somewhat mangled piece of paper.

Martin took it and scanned the lines, words leaping out at him: *… unkind of me to lay this burden upon you … I have eloped …*

"What do you mean she's eloped with Roger Phipps?" he roared.

"What?" Lady Abernathy looked up, her attention now on him. "Give me that letter."

She snatched it from his hand, her eyes racing over the lines. Martin turned his attention back to Dorothea. "How did this happen?"

Dorothea breathed more calmly now, but still visibly shaken. "I lost sight of her in the crush at Dutton's. I searched and waited, then stepped outside to see if she left word with the footman. A street boy brought me this note." She frowned. "I paid him a crown, and Cecilia had promised him only half a crown."

"This is not the time to worry over the size of a coin. You saw no sign or her? Or of Roger?"

She shook her head. "I might have missed him. The crush was as bad as your mother predicted. I think Cecilia counted on the crowd."

Lady Abernathy finished the letter and let forth a howl. "How could she do this to me?"

Turning on Dorothea, she raised an accusing finger. "You've done nothing but bring trouble to this family. Do you tell Lady Wilmont all about your mischief, do you laugh together?"

"Me?" Dorothea replied. "I'm as surprised by this as you."

"I'm sure you are. Isn't that why you continued such close contact with Lady Wilmont, all those little notes you try to keep from us? Were the two of you planning this, helping Cecilia elope to clear the field for her daughter? I doubt your efforts will yield results; even a fool like Stockwood has more sense than to marry that little trollop, unless your next step is to ensure she traps him in a compromising position, just like you trapped my son!"

"Mother, calm yourself." Martin didn't want to admit how much of her words echoed thoughts which had whispered in his mind of late. Not when things were spiraling out of control.

"I. Didn't. Trap. Him." The words were uttered through gritted teeth as Dorothea rose. "But you would rather believe the gossips over your own son because they suit your view and damn the facts."

The last words were practically spat out as Dorothea advanced on Lady Abernathy. "Cecilia originally wanted to take her maid, remember? Someone she might take with her or send with word of this disaster. I volunteered because I decided it would be a nice gesture on my part, something to bridge the gap between her and I. She accepted, knowing she was going to elope with Roger. So who's the one who's been used here?"

Dorothea stepped close enough Lady Abernathy took a step back. "What's more important? Arguing about a petty, stupid feud which should have been buried two decades ago? Or sending Martin to try and catch them before there is too much damage?"

Lady Abernathy opened her mouth, then closed it again. She turned to Martin seeking support. "Given how sympathetic you were to Cecilia and Roger, after Roger had been barred from the house," Martin said, doing his best to keep his own temper, "you should forgive us for having doubts."

"I'm not the one trying to force Cecilia into a marriage she doesn't want."

"We've been nursing a viper in our bosom, Martin!" Lady Abernathy found her voice again. "How many times has she taken the Wilmont's side, or tried to drive away some of Cecilia's suitors."

"Do you hear yourself?" Dorothea's voice dripped with contempt. "I am tired of this feud, which landed us here. I am tired of your insults and slights, acting as if I was something to be tolerated. I didn't ask for this marriage, and was foolish to think it might be something warm and loving. You don't want to give me a chance."

She rounded on Martin. "You say Cecilia could do worse than Stockwood for a husband. Would you rather she marry him than Roger?"

Stung, Martin responded, "The duke would be kind to Cecilia, and do his best to keep her safe and secure."

"So Cecilia's feelings don't factor into this, despite everything you said previously?"

"They didn't factor into my decision to marry."

He regretted the words the moment he said them, even if they had whispered in his mind at moments when he felt low. The way Dorothea looked at him, he knew he'd made a mistake which would take a long time to repair, if ever. "I told you I didn't want charity," she said. "You claimed that wasn't what drove you, how you thought this wouldn't be a bad marriage. Were you lying to me ... or to yourself?"

He didn't have an answer. After a moment, she drew herself up and took a deep breath. "If you want to go after Cecilia, I'll tell the cook to wrap something for you to take. You'll likely want the phaeton as well. It will move faster than their carriage."

She walked out, her head held high. "Are you going to let her speak to me that way?" Lady Abernathy demanded.

"Why not?" he replied bitterly. "She's right. Now we're shackled to one another for life, and nothing you have done since she arrived makes this situation more bearable."

"I meant her rudeness."

He cut her off. "I need to get on the road and try to bring Cecilia home, or you can kiss any idea of a family reputation goodbye."

He stalked toward the door but couldn't resist turning back for one final word. "Dorothea's right about another thing. You seem more invested in your damn feud than your children's happiness."

Martin didn't wait for an answer.

CHAPTER 24

A storm blew in as the sun set. Even with his greatcoat and the cover of his vehicle, Martin found himself drenched as he urged the phaeton along the North Road.

There'd been little luck finding any trace of Roger and Cecilia, or of anyone who'd seen their carriage. Despite a two-hour start or more, Martin's lighter, faster conveyance should have caught up with them. The only hope was, while changing horses at a coaching inn in Hatfield, one of the ostlers said a hired coach with a man and a woman had come through earlier. With a coin or two pressed into hand, he added the coachman spoke of stopping in Stanborough due to the weather. Martin gave the man a final coin, then pushed on.

There were three coaching inns in Stanborough. When he reached the third, Martin admitted it was best he stop for the night as a shivering boy took the horses' head when he climbed down from the phaeton's seat. "Get them out of this weather," he called as he made a dash for the door.

Inside, the inn was snug and warm, a fire crackling in the hearth, the common room crowded. Not surprisingly, travelers declined to venture out on such a night if they had any choice. A few patrons glanced up as Martin entered, but most kept their attention on their meals or their companions.

The landlord came forward with his best professional smile. "Good evening, me lord. What may I do for you?"

Martin was certain the salutation a best guess, based most likely on the quality of his clothes. "First," he said, drawing off his wet gloves, "I need a room for the night and some supper."

The landlord frowned. "I'm afraid all the rooms that would suit a gentleman of quality are taken, me lord. What's left …"

"Will do me fine, as long as there is a bed." He scanned the room. "I can dine here as well as in a private parlor. The requisite is the food be hot."

"Me wife makes an excellent stew, and she'd be honored to spoon some up for yer lordship. It's not fine fare, but tasty and hearty." The landlord craned his neck, as if checking to make certain no one else came through the door. "Did yer lordship bring a manservant with him?"

"Only myself. The second thing is to ask if you had a private coach come through with a young man and woman."

The landlord began to shift from one foot to another. "Any particular reason yer lordship might inquire after such a coach?"

Martin would prefer not to be blunt, but he didn't see the use wasting time cross-examining the landlord. "The young lady is my sister. I wish to fetch her back before the cad she's with can whisk her away to Gretna Green."

Roger must have spent a fair amount of gold, given the way the landlord shifted nervously. He didn't speak, but kept looking toward a door which led off the common room. "You'll be rewarded for this," Martin said.

Without waiting for further confirmation, Martin strode across the floor to fling open the door.

The young lady sitting on the gentleman's knee let out a squeal as he strode into the room. Unfortunately, she was not Cecilia, nor was the gentleman Roger. Which meant he was on the wrong trail. "Lord Aldus?" Martin said in surprise as he recognized the fifth son of the

Marquis of Hampton. He recognized the young lady as well. "Miss Hickinbotham?"

Lord Aldus reached for Miss Hickinbotham's hand. "You weren't sent by my father, were you? Or Miss Hickinbotham's father? My father thinks I should marry a Cit's daughter with a fortune, perhaps become involved indirectly with trade."

"Mama wants me to marry the Duke of Stockwood, because she doesn't think Aldus—Lord Aldus—is grand enough," Miss Hickinbotham sniffed. She was very pretty, with blond hair and large blue eyes gazing up at Martin. That they were about to overflow with tears didn't hurt her cause. "You won't stop us, will you?"

Did every infernal matchmaking mama in London want their daughter to marry Stockwood? Martin felt a surge of pity for the man. "You can't believe I'm going to countenance the two of you running away and bringing shame to your family. Landlord!"

The landlord appeared in the doorway, wiping his hands nervously on a towel. His wife hovered behind him, also with a worried expression on her face. "Are these two the only couple in a coach who stopped here?"

"Aye, my lord. The only other folk were on the mail coach." He hesitated. "This is not yer sister?"

"No, but the young lady is not wed to the gentleman. I can't stand by and allow them to elope, so I must crave your indulgence and ask your wife take Miss Hickinbotham in hand this evening. Tomorrow morning, we'll see about arranging her return to London separate from Lord Aldus."

"But, Lord Abernathy!"

Martin turned around. "No buts from you, young man. If I stood by, your father would never forgive me, and I need his vote in Lords. Back to London with the pair of you."

He turned back to the landlord, jingling some coins in his pocket. "I would like to show my gratitude to you and your good wife for whatever discomfort this situation causes. The gentleman will share the room you arrange for me."

With the coins pressed into his palm, the landlord smiled. "I reckon my missus can watch the young lady for the evening. Will, ah, will you be joining the couple for supper?"

Martin glanced back at the table with little enthusiasm or appetite, aware of the mournful looks given him by the two lovebirds. "I'm afraid so."

After giving orders to the cook for the packet of food and word the phaeton needed to be readied, Dorothea retreated to her room. She didn't need to be in the middle of whatever conversation mother and son were having.

She heard the bustle at the front of the house as Martin left, marked by his voice barking orders she couldn't quite make out. After that, she waited for at least another half hour before deciding to venture downstairs, feeling restless. Her needlework was in the drawing room, and if she was going to immure herself in her room, best to have it with her.

Halfway down the stairs, she remembered Mercer could be sent to fetch the work bag without risk of Dorothea facing Lady Abernathy. With a sigh, she rationalized they must meet again at some point. If they were going to screech at one another like alley cats, better to do so while Martin was gone.

The drawing room was empty, and Dorothea hesitated. Should she count herself lucky, grab the bag and retreat, or try to determine the older woman's location? A discreet cough behind her indicated she was not alone. "Lady Abernathy is in her room," Farthing said as she turned, "Supper will be sent up on a tray. She has asked she not be disturbed."

Which meant she didn't want to see Dorothea. "She was distressed?"

"Quite, madam."

A certain frostiness colored the butler's words and she wondered if he, too, thought her the architect of their current troubles. "Thank you, Farthing. I think it best, considering the circumstances, we are Not At Home to anyone. Tell any who inquire Lady Abernathy is suffering from an ague. We will continue to say so until we receive word from Lord Abernathy."

Farthing lifted an eyebrow in surprise, but he did not quarrel with her orders. "I will also need some notes delivered," she continued. "Please have the footmen ready."

Farthing bowed and departed, leaving her alone again. At her desk, Dorothea considered the stack of invitations awaiting replies. If Martin couldn't find Cecilia, these would likely be withdrawn because the family would be hanging their heads in shame. They had weathered one scandal this season; foolish to think they could weather two.

She dashed off a few lines to their hostess for the evening, apologizing for the lateness of the missive. Lady Abernathy had acquired a cold, and it was thought best she rests. Then, she pulled another sheet of paper toward her to write a second note, this one to Lady Wilmont. *I know we agreed I would visit, but Lady Abernathy has a slight cold and I do not want to risk the possibility of carrying infection. Pray forgive me for putting you off as I know you have things to discuss. Once she is well, I promise I will visit.*

With both notes sealed, she rang for Farthing. "These are to be delivered to Lady Ross and Lady Wilmont," she told him. "No reply is expected on either."

Farthing regarded the note addressed to Lady Wilmont with some suspicion. "Yes, madam."

"I doubt we will hear from Lord Abernathy tonight, but if a message arrives, please bring it to me directly. Also, if Miss Cecilia appears, with or without Sir Roger, show them in to me."

"With all due respect, madam, I think Lady Abernathy should be consulted on these decisions."

There it was. Challenges she must take from Lady Abernathy, but she would not put up with such from the butler, or she would never be more than an unwelcome guest in this house. Dorothea said, in as firm a voice as she could manage, "*I* am Lady Abernathy, Farthing. I will consult with the Dowager Viscountess when she is well enough to speak with me. Until then, please either follow my instructions or let me know you are unable to do so, and I will make arrangements with someone who can. Do I make myself clear?"

Farthing stiffened. "Perfectly, madam."

With a bow, he turned to go. Just before he reached the door, she said, "One more thing, Farthing."

He turned, face schooled, but a wariness to his eyes. "Yes, madam?"

"The proper form of address for a viscountess is 'my lady.' Please don't make me remind you again."

More stiffening, enough so she wondered if he might break. "Yes, my lady."

She had not made a friend, but Dorothea didn't care at this moment. For better or worse, she was a fact of life in this household. Lady Abernathy might wish her to perdition, and Martin tolerate her because his honor demanded, but if she couldn't enjoy love or affection in her marriage, she was damn well going to be treated with respect by the servants. If she could not achieve that, she was there on sufferance, like so much of her life. This time, with prettier clothes and pocket money.

Hardly the life she wanted, but it was the one she had.

Martin wondered if Miss Hickinbotham knew how much Lord Aldus snored. Lying in the bed found for them, he supposed he should be grateful the mattress was clean and reasonably comfortable. Otherwise, he would be forced to strangle the lad.

It wouldn't bother Miss Hickinbotham, as she believed her swain the most gallant, wonderful man in the world. If it did, well-bred couples often slept in separate rooms and come together only for procreation or physical need.

He had slept in his own bed quite a bit of late, he realized. Not only that, he hadn't bothered to seek Dorothea out for the pleasures they enjoyed on their honeymoon. How had he reached that state?

That's not your only problem, nor your most urgent.

No, the urgency now was Roger and Cecilia. In the summer months, the North Road was the easiest, swiftest trail to Scotland. In the depths of January, it was the only viable option. Roger didn't keep a carriage in town, so one would be hired, and a hired carriage was unlikely to be faster than his phaeton. They had to stop at one of the inns along the route, if only to change horses. Instead, they had vanished off the face of the earth.

Still nagging at his mind was the question of why. All too easy to believe Cecilia would agree to an elopement; he would be blind to miss how on edge she had been. No, her seeming acquiescence of late masked her plans to escape. His mother might think otherwise, but the last person Cecilia would confide in would be Dorothea. He suspected Dorothea made the offer to accompany Cecilia to Dutton's to annoy his mother.

This plot lay between his sister and Roger. Martin had decided against her letters being checked before they were handed to her, because he couldn't see submitting his sister to such an indignity. Not to mention such an order would alert his mother something was afoot. The letter to Cecilia from Miss Ryan was likely from Roger himself, giving her instructions for the rendezvous.

Why would Roger put himself in such a position? Martin influenced, if not controlled, his seat in Parliament. He had to know such action would ensure Martin sought elsewhere for a man to represent the borough. Of course, given the harshness of the words between him, no doubt Roger assumed Martin would want another man to stand for the seat. There were always boroughs in need of a member. He might be finished with the Whigs, but his friends among the Tories would happily bring him to their side. Many would bet Martin would forgive his sister and her new husband, despite Lady Abernathy remaining stiff-necked.

He shifted to get more comfortable, which provoked a particularly loud snore. Martin imagined Roger's younger brother would have something to say about the action. After all, it did not reflect well on a cleric in such an exalted position of the Archbishop of Canterbury's chaplain—one of them, at least.

The Archbishop of Canterbury.

Martin sat straight up in bed, causing Lord Aldus to flop on his side, the snoring growing worse. Thomas Phipps was on the Archbishop's staff; he remembered the party the Phipps threw to celebrate the appointment. A man so highly placed might easily obtain a special license if needed by a close relation, and the Reverend Mr. Phipps was another of Cecilia's old playmates.

Don't have Martin search for us on the North Road. Cecilia gave him the clue in her letter, but it'd been ignored in their haste, assuming the pair headed North because almost everyone who eloped tried for Gretna. He spent the afternoon getting soaked, while she and Roger had been most likely been comfortably wed in a church with proper witnesses. Wedded and bedded by now, so there'd be little he could do to dissolve the match. God, his sister was a clever girl.

Flopping back onto the mattress, Martin stared up at the ceiling. The next step would be to return to London, track down Thomas Phipps, and wrangle the truth out of him. Then figure out how to deal with this mess. Dorothea would have some ideas; she had a deft hand at smoothing things over, a skill learned of necessity under Lady Wilmont.

If Dorothea was willing to help him. He'd sided with his mother too often, cast her as the outsider who didn't understand, when all the while, she urged him to realize a problem was brewing. He shut her out, buying into the suggestion her actions were nothing but an attempt to cause trouble. He remembered the anger in her eyes and wondered how badly the bridge between them was broken.

The question now was whether or not he could make amends with his wife or live as strangers all their lives. He wanted to make amends. Would she?

That kept him staring into the darkness for some time.

CHAPTER 25

Martin availed himself of some hot broth in the parlor, having decided against risking the coffee after a whiff of the landlady's brew. A paper of some kind to read would have been pleasant, but one couldn't expect such luxuries when on the road. At least he would be back in London by nightfall and able to sleep under his own roof.

He took comfort in the thought, and leaned back, propping his feet on the table. He still needed to track down Roger and Cecilia, but with the probability they were wed, a certain urgency was now lacking. His immediate problem for the morning involved Lord Aldus and Miss Hickinbotham.

On cue, Lord Aldus entered the parlor, looking as if he had not rested for all he snored the night away. "I hope you slept well at least, Lord Abernathy."

Sullen resentment colored the young man's tone, hardly a surprise. "Well enough, given the circumstances. I'm trying to decide exactly what to do with you."

"Let us proceed on our way?" Aldus replied. At Martin's raised eyebrow, his shoulders drooped. "I though you decided you're going to drag Miss Hickinbotham back to London to stop our elopement. Love doesn't matter to you at all, does it?"

The words echoed those Dorothea had thrown at him. "Why does everyone keep bringing up love to me?" Martin demanded. "When did that become the chief consideration in a marriage?"

Aldus appeared confused. "You loved a penniless poor relation and married her despite the objections of your family. Why should you speak to me of family obligations when you put your happiness before social or financial considerations?"

That cover story would follow him the rest of his life, he realized. "I would point out my wife is of a good family," he began, hoping to twist this in some way to satisfy the lad.

His words only served to puff Aldus up more. "As is Miss Hickinbotham," he said. "Her ancestors entertained Queen Elizabeth in their home, the very one she will one day inherit."

"So she's an heiress."

"Yes, my lord. Five hundred acres in Dorset and a thriving farm. Her aunt's Lady Kilmane, you know. Lady Kilmane is supposed to help her catch a titled husband."

Martin pondered the situation, discarding the fact the Old Queen never made it as far as Dorset on her progresses. A thriving farm might be a fine start for the fifth son of a marquis. Lord Aldus never showed an interest in politics, the army, the church, or any of the other traditional pursuits of younger sons of peers. Nor did he have a reputation as a gambler or spendthrift. In Martin's opinion, the lad always seemed a bit plodding and thick when they happened upon one another.

Yet, Miss Hickinbotham loved him, plain to see in the way she gazed up at Lord Aldus. She thought him the strongest, handsomest, wisest man in the world. What he wouldn't give to have a woman gaze up at him in such a way.

One had. Before things went sour, Dorothea looked at him just that way when they were on the dance floor. When he held her in his arms. Beneath him, her hair spread wildly out upon her pillow.

The last time they spoke, her eyes had been cold and angry, tired of the insults she suffered. He could guess what waited for him: his mother wanted Dorothea sent away and wouldn't allow peace in the house until he agreed. Lady Abernathy might claim she would hand over the reins of control, but he wouldn't take the bet. Dorothea was an outsider who dared to challenge the established order, so must either be brought to heel or expelled.

"Farming's not easy work," Martin said, trying not to let himself drown in unpleasant thoughts.

"I'm not afraid," Lord Aldus said. "I quite like being out on my father's lands. I help bring in the harvest, which he doesn't really approve of me doing. To work the land, watch it thrive? I can't think of a better life, save having the woman I love at my side."

The young man was possessed of firm conviction, a surety Martin himself lacked. This marriage was not the "right" one for either Lord Aldus or Miss Hickinbotham, but in their hearts, it was right. Because sometimes seeds grew even if planted in rocky soil.

He needed some of that surety back, and here was one way to help. Rising to his feet, he strode toward the door, clapping Lord Aldus on the shoulder. "Let's see if Miss Hickinbotham is awake and make our plans for the return. I'll talk to your father, help plead your cause."

Perhaps by pleading yours, I'll find a way to plead my own.

Dorothea paced the drawing room. Up and dressed earlier than was fashionable, she felt trapped. Even if she had somewhere to go, doing so would negate the illusion they were mired up because of some slight illness.

She started at the tap on the door, trying to calm herself as Farthing entered, carrying a note. "From Lady Wilmont, my lady," said, dashing all her hopes of other news. "There was a container as well. I left it in the hall. It … sloshed."

Frowning, she opened the note. *"I am sorry to learn of the illness in your house and I must commend Lady Abernathy's decision to stay in rather than risking it turn to something worse. Sadly, as we grow older, what could be shrugged off when young can become something more serious.*

I also thank you for not wishing to expose Alyssa to the possibility of such an ague. She is not taking the care of herself as she should. I now must keep constant watch for fear she will expose herself in such a manner as to take ill. If she had her way, I don't doubt she would follow the scandalous French fashion of dampening her gown to cling to her body. Your uncle put his foot down at the merest suggestion of such a thing.

I do miss your presence. Only once you were gone did I realize how much you helped mitigate the tension with her. I know I counseled you should assert your authority with Lady Abernathy, but perhaps I was wrong. Better if you woo her to your side so she comes to rely on you as much as I did. If you can, you will come into your power without the conflict which marks my relationship with her.

In hopes you yourself will not take ill, I had Cook prepare some bone broth such as we use at home. Get Lady Abernathy to have some as well, if you can. I hold the recipe for this dear, but I wrote it out so you may instruct your cook. Think of this as a gift to warm your house and keep you and your new family well.

Yours, Honoria, Lady Wilmont

Dorothea sighed. *Now she suggests I try to get along with Lady Abernathy?* "Farthing, please take the container to the kitchen. Ask the cook to warm a bowl for me. I would also like some sent up to Lady Abernathy on her morning tray. Please also tell the Cook I will share the recipe with her when we speak on the menu later."

Farthing did as commanded, though Dorothea wagered he found the offering somewhat distasteful. She remembered the soup well, remembered its comforting taste those times she was ill. It was a kindness from her aunt, especially to share the recipe.

The broth filled her stomach until breakfast was presented as she sat alone at the table. A pile of letters waited, and she sorted through them half-heartedly. She could do nothing at this point as she couldn't make any answers until they knew the situation.

She was still at the table when there came a distant knocking, indicating a caller or message. Instinctively, she rose, but hesitated before entering the front hall, relaxing only when Farthing appeared with the silver tray. "An answer is requested, my lady," he said. "I believe this is Miss Cecilia's handwriting. It's addressed to his lordship, but I thought best you should see it as soon as possible."

"Is the weather still foul out?" she asked as she took the note. "Invite the messenger to wait in the kitchen. This may take a bit."

In the morning room, she noted the lamps had been lit, though the drapes were drawn back. The sky was still gray outside, and she wondered if the rain of yesterday would turn to snow. Settling herself near a lamp, she angled the page and began to read.

Dearest brother,

I beg your pardon for the difficulty which I undoubtedly put you all through, but I want you to understand I am certain it was for the best. I am well and safe, having the honor of now being Lady Phipps. Roger and I were married yesterday afternoon by the special license his brother Thomas procured for us when we thought you might agree to the match. He performed the ceremony himself in the presence of no less than eight witnesses, several being other clerics and members of Parliament whom Roger asked to attend.

Again, I beg your pardon and will do so in person if you will receive us. We wish to call at your convenience, in the hopes whatever fury I aroused will have abated. I hope you will let us explain why we were forced to such desperate actions. I suspect you understand some of the reasons why.

Your loving sister,

Cecilia Phipps

So they were married, and Martin was out on the road searching for them. She wondered if she might get a message to him, let him know he needed to return. She still didn't understand why Cecilia had done what she had. The girl was hardly a dewy-eyed miss who believed the idea eloping 'romantic.' She had to realize there would be shame and scandal to deal with.

Dorothea was also past trying to understand why any of this family did what they did. Why did Lady Abernathy so insist on a man her daughter didn't want to marry and her son seemed disinclined to favor? Why did Martin refuse to give his consent for the match with Stockwood, then insist Cecilia might want to consider him given changing circumstances?

"Was that Martin at the door?" Lady Abernathy asked as she entered the room, causing Dorothea to turn. "I thought I heard something."

Even on a morning with no guests expected, Dorothea had always seen Lady Abernathy ready to receive company. This morning, though, both hair and garb were simple, more suited to the country than the city or not sleeping well.

"A messenger with a note from Cecilia," Dorothea said, holding out the paper. "I opened it in my eagerness despite it being addressed to Martin. I don't think he would mind if you read it."

Lady Abernathy hesitated, then fairly snatched the paper from Dorothea's hands. "Forced?" she exclaimed at last. "I only wanted the best for her."

"I think she believed Roger Phipps was best for her and felt backed into a corner where she had no choice but to marry the duke or take drastic action."

"Easy for you to suggest I allow my daughter to marry a lowly baronet when you have done so well for yourself."

"I did not expect to marry well," Dorothea said, doing her best to keep her temper, yet let her voice be firm. "I expected to marry a country vicar, if at all. This is about Cecilia, not about how Martin and I came to be."

"What do you care about Cecilia's happiness? You have been a trial to this family since Martin met you. If not for the fact it'd be a scandal, I'd turn you out of the house this very moment."

"I think Martin has a say," Dorothea said.

"Martin and I understand one another. He's come to realize this marriage between the two of you was a mistake. Once he returns, he'll agree to pack you off to the country where you can do less trouble. With luck, you're already with child, so you can do your duty by the family you've worked so hard to destroy."

In the space following Lady Abernathy's words, Farthing cleared his throat. "A letter from Lord Abernathy," he said, looking as if he would rather be anywhere than in this room.

Lady Abernathy held out her hand, but Farthing shook his head. "The courier was told to deliver it to young Lady Abernathy, not the dowager viscountess, my lady. He's an express rider and is to wait for a reply."

Lady Abernathy's hand dropped, but her face grew red, seething with anger. Farthing brought the note to Dorothea, circling as far from Lady Abernathy as possible. Dorothea opened it, scanning the words quickly. "Martin says he got further than Cecilia and Roger could, and he now suspects Roger's brother helped arrange a special license.

He is, however, rescuing another eloping couple, and will share the story when he returns. He believes he'll be back some time this evening. He must ensure the pair are returned home and speak with the parents for some reason."

She glanced up to find Lady Abernathy staring at her with an expression which wished her dead. Taking a deep breath, she continued. "He wonders if I have had word from either Roger or Cecilia. I'm to send a reply via the courier, whom Martin is paying extra for the message brought back to him along the road."

There was more, but Dorothea chose not to read the words aloud. *I had time to think during this wretched journey and I hope we can speak on more amiable terms than when we parted. There is much we need to say to one another for I think we both have been less than honest, and that is no foundation for a marriage. If you are willing, let us try to rebuild in hopes our lives will be closer to what we enjoyed together before we married.*

Your husband, Martin.

Dorothea smiled at the closing, more intimate than the formal "Abernathy" she had expected. "I will write a reply to tell him what we've learned," she said, folding the note back up. "I would like to ask Roger and Cecilia to join us tomorrow."

"Do you think I wish to entertain the man who convinced Cecilia to break so cruelly with her family? I am willing to see her, but I'll not allow Roger Phipps in my house."

Time to take a stand. "I'm inviting them both. I would like to hear what explanation they offer and I think Martin will as well. Breakfast is better than an afternoon call as fewer folk will be about, so less chance they'll be noticed arriving."

"You really think you have a say in this, don't you." Lady Abernathy drew herself up indignantly. "Issue your invitations. Just be prepared for the embarrassment of having them revoked when my son returns."

She sailed from the room, head high leaving Dorothea to write her notes. Just a few lines; that was all there was time for. *Martin, you are correct. We received a note from Cecilia and Roger—addressed to you, but I opened it in your absence—saying they were married by Special License with no fewer than eight witnesses. They said they would like to speak with you, so I am asking them to come to breakfast tomorrow, anticipating your return. I enclose Cecilia's words with this note so you can read for yourself.*

With the words written, she hesitated, wondering how much she should tell him, then decided she would not let him walk in blind. *Your mother is not happy with the idea, saying she would prefer to receive only Cecilia. I think it would be best if we received them both and begin to repair this rift. It would also allow us to come up with a plan to present this in society with as little trouble as possible. I warn you, if Roger is present, I do not know if your mother will agree to join us, or if she does, choose to make trouble.*

A bit harsher than she would have liked, but she knew she had to be economical. Which only left one more thing.

As to your request we speak, yes, I would wish that most heartily. I do not like the place we find ourselves in and hope we can discover more mutually agreeable ground. Your presence has been missed.

Your wife, Dorothea

She sealed the letter with a simple blob of wax, and rang the bell for Farthing. "This is for the express courier," she told him. "Please give him at least a crown before he goes. Lord Abernathy promised him more when he returns, but he should receive something for his pains now. A return note to Miss Cecilia will be ready in a minute."

Farthing did not argue, but bowed and departed. The note to Cecilia was easier, setting the time for breakfast and saying both her and Roger were welcome, though her mother was still angry, but Martin would be there.

With both notes sent, she knew all she could do now was wait and hope Martin would hurry home.

CHAPTER 26

Farthing had the door open before Martin had finished climbing the steps of the townhouse. "Welcome home, my lord. Lady Abernathy is in the drawing room, and the Dowager Viscountess upstairs in her room. Shall I let her know you have returned?"

"In a few minutes. I want to speak with my wife first."

As he shed his greatcoat, what the butler had said sank in. Until now, Martin's mother had been "Lady Abernathy" and Dorothea "young Lady Abernathy." Now both were being called by their correct forms of address. What had happened?

Not wanting to deal with that mystery, he headed for the drawing room. Dorothea rose from the couch the moment he entered, took two steps toward him, then hesitated. "You're home."

"After a long and weary goose chase, yes."

"I'm glad," she said.

Her words warmed him, but the fact she hung back still worried. "Did you miss me?" he asked, taking the risk of opening his arms.

A moment's hesitation before she moved, coming close to wrap her arms about him. "Yes, I did," she admitted.

He closed his eyes for a moment, resting his cheek against her hair. Perhaps there was hope here after all. Despite the unkind words, perhaps they could begin again. "I got your note," he said at last. "I think breakfast is an excellent idea, as well as having them both. Only way to get through this mess."

He released her and moved toward the couch. "I need to sit on something padded. I would not wish such a journey on anyone."

They both sat, facing one another. "Tell me about this eloping couple you found. Your letter hinted at quite a tale."

Not where Martin wanted to begin their conversation, but the story had the advantage of lacking the baggage which surrounded them. She laughed several times during the tale, and Martin relaxed. In her laughter, he once again saw the woman who fascinated him when they met. He had missed her.

As he reached the end, he said, "Miss Hickinbotham who made me think about us."

Dorothea cocked her head to one side, her expression intrigued. "Really?"

"The way she looked at him, he was the center of her world and her life would be bereft without him." He reached out to twine his fingers with hers. "It made me realize you looked at me so at Drayton Manor. I want you to be able to look at me in such a way again."

Her hand began to pull away. His instinct was to hold fast, not let her escape, but he released her, watching as her fingers came to rest close to his thigh. "It's a little difficult when I know you think of this marriage as a bad idea you found yourself trapped into."

He wished he could take those words back, but all he could do was hope they moved forward. "I was angry because of Cecilia. There was this whole thing of Mother being furious because you retained contact with Lady Wilmont. She presented things in the worst light and did her best to turn my anger toward you. Allowing her to influence me was my error."

"I don't think the tone of Aunt Honoria's letters helped. She kept telling me to do what she would do, charge forward and demand my rights."

"Which you did."

She regarded him with a sober gaze. "No, I asked for respect, which I did not receive. There is a difference."

She was right, he had to admit. "Respect includes having your rights as my wife," he pointed out with a smile.

Dorothea smiled back. "I can tell you're a politician."

He almost offered a smart retort, but stopped when her fingers crept forward to touch his. Here was a new start, fragile and tenuous, but there all the same. He cleared his throat. "I assume you came up with a cover story to keep visitors at bay?"

"I pleaded an ague on your mother's part. I was supposed to visit Lady Wilmont today, but I used fear of spreading the infection to Alyssa to put her off." She laughed. "Aunt Honoria thanked me for being so thoughtful. She also sent along some broth she swears by for such things. I had some sent up on a tray to your mother this morning."

"You didn't tell Mother where it came from, did you?"

She smiled. "No, but she consumed it all and asked for more, I'm told. I gave Cook a copy of the recipe."

Martin laughed at the notion, Dorothea joining him. The sound was warm, a sign of hope.

They were still laughing when Lady Abernathy appeared. "Farthing told me you returned. Have you heard?"

"About Roger and Cecilia?" He turned his head to Dorothea. "She warned me, didn't she? I should have realized Roger wouldn't head for Scotland with the Regency Bill still hanging fire. They're too clever by half."

"Is that all you have to say?" Her voice was stern. "The girl runs off, disgraces the family, and all you can do is call her is clever?"

He found himself glad of the warning in Dorothea's note. "I should have been more suspicious of Cecilia's desire to read Mrs. Porter's latest as soon as it was released, even if she enjoys mocking the work."

"You're going to let her waltz back in here with no consequences, as this viper," Lady Abernathy waved her hand at Dorothea, "suggests? I told you, Martin. We need to send her to country before she can do any more damage."

Martin sighed. "Mother, I'm tired of this. I can accept you don't like Dorothea and wish I chose another wife, but must every conversation be an attack?"

"She arranged for Cecilia to meet Roger so they could elope!" The words were nearly shrieked. "You're going to ignore what she did? After everything she's kept secret from you?"

"You mean Lady Wilmont writes to her with what she believes is well-meaning advice?" He snorted. "I'm not surprised Dorothea avoids mentioning the letters given the way you behave."

He glanced toward Dorothea again. "Has Lady Wilmont asked you to do anything for her?"

"See if we might remove Viscount Tilney from the guest list for our assembly," Dorothea said. "My cousin's a bit too fascinated with him."

"You mean she makes herself a scandal."

"This is exactly what I am talking about," Martin said. "You don't want Dorothea keeping secrets? Stop treating her as a blight."

As his mother opened her mouth again, he added. "Dorothea sent me Cecilia's letter, so I know what she wrote. Did you not see her mention the license was procured previously? I think Roger obtained it so they might marry at once if I gave my consent."

"Why would they want to do such a thing?" Lady Abernathy's voice was still harsh, but Martin caught a note of hurt within the words.

"They knew you would try to stop them. How many times did Cecilia say she didn't want to marry Stockwood? You barred Roger from the house because they cared for one another and it didn't suit your plans. You didn't tell anyone, because if I had known, I would have told you to stop being ridiculous."

"Is it ridiculous to want the best for my children? Or help the family better themselves?"

"Not at the expense of happiness or contentment when what you are reaching for offers so little advantage. This is why I will welcome Roger and Cecilia tomorrow. I'm angry with them, but if we don't try to heal, the family will fracture beyond repair. Is that what you want?"

Lady Abernathy sniffled, her eyes beginning to glisten, but the mask slid into place. "It appears what I want doesn't matter." Casting venomous glare at Dorothea, she added, "I shall be out from underfoot as soon as possible, Madam. I cede the field to you."

"She loves her exits," Martin said once his mother had departed in high dudgeon.

"Do you want to go after her?" Dorothea asked.

Martin thought for a moment, then shook his head. "What she wants is me to beg her to stay and agree to her conditions. Cut Cecilia off or try for an annulment. Send you to the country where she can forget about you. I can't."

He turned back to her. "It isn't that I can't. I don't want to."

Stepping closer, he slid his arms around her. "You said we were saddled with one another. I don't want that to be the definition of our marriage, the only reason we're together. I want to build a life with you, so we stand together through good times and bad."

"No more keeping secrets?"

"No more," he said. "For either of us."

She glanced up at him slyly. "So I should tell you what Aunt Honoria says in her letters?"

"Noooo. Those secrets I think you should keep. Unless you think I should know." He tweaked a lock of her hair. "Any other tasks besides asking Tilney be removed from the guest list?"

"Only that she's taking Alyssa to Bath for the waters." Dorothea let her hands rise to rest on his chest. "She may be gone from London the day of the ball since we can't disinvite Tilney. She's worried, Martin. Worried Alyssa will find herself embroiled in a scandal and he'll be at the center of it. She asked if I would like to come along, though she quickly said she was joking."

"Were you tempted?" he asked, wondering why she brought it up.

"Standing in Dutton's, trying to find Cecilia, everything going wrong? I found myself tempted for a moment."

"Why didn't you?"

Dorothea sighed. "I didn't think about it. I was focused on getting away so I could continue the search. But, no I would not. I would spend my time chasing Alyssa around Bath, which is the last thing I want to do. But more, if I did go, it would be admitting this marriage was a failure. I don't want to admit that. I very much want us to succeed." She smiled up at him. "I want to go back to Drayton Manor, if not in fact, then in spirit."

Her words brought a grin to his face, the best news all day. "I want that as well. I want more. I want—"

The words stopped as she stretched up to kiss him, her lips soft against his. His arms tightened about her, pulling her close against him. Some part of his mind cast back to the first kiss, the one which had set them on this path. Without that kiss, she would not be here in his arms now.

They separated reluctantly, moving only as far from one another as was required to breathe. "We aren't expecting anyone, are we?"

"I told Farthing not to admit visitors until I gave the command. I also sent our regrets about this evening."

"Good." He stepped back and caught her hands, tugging her toward the door. "Right now, I would be alone with my wife."

They climbed the stairs hand in hand, their steps growing quicker the closer they came to her room. "That will be all for now," Dorothea told her maid the moment she and Martin came through the door at a near run. "I'll ring when I wish to dress for supper."

Mercer's look of surprise was replaced by one of relief as she dropped a curtsey before departing. "Assuming I let you down for supper," Martin said before the door was closed. Dorothea's response was to laugh and step into his arms. The light was back in her eyes, though it vanished behind closed lids as he lowered his head to hers.

They divested one another of their clothing, eager to touch and stroke. He'd missed her, her skin beneath his fingers, the little hitches to her breath as his hands moved across a sensitive spot. His breath hitched as well when she ran her hands down his chest, nails lightly scraping across his skin.

The bed seemed too far, and they tumbled to the chaise, senses focused on one another. "My sweet," he murmured as he let his lips slide across her breasts and then roam downward. "Not letting you go."

"Don't want. To. Go." Her breath and words came in spurts. "Come. Back here."

Her fingers twined in his hair as he licked and stroked, moving ever closer to that sweetness. "In a moment," he promised, wanting to let the moment stretch as long as possible. Why shouldn't he when she shifted so delightfully under him, punctuating the air with all sorts of delicious noises? Not too long, but just enough so …

When he stroked between her legs, Dorothea's body arched, and she tugged on his hair. Hard. "*Now.*"

"As my lady commands," Martin managed, shifting upwards to kiss her. Hands released from his hair, she let them glide down his back, one dipping low against his thigh, shifting around to wrap her fingers around his length. Now it was his turn to moan against her lips, self-control beginning to slip away. His sense were focused on her, how she felt against him, her taste on his tongue, the touch of her hand on him … *her.*

He shifted between her legs, his tip at her entrance. With gritted teeth, he slid forward a fraction. His reward was a deep, keening moan, followed by a groan of disappointment as he pulled back. Again, he slid forward and withdrew, drawing more moans from her. The third time, as he slid forward, her hips rose to meet him, pulling him in deeper. She looked up at him, pupils dark and wide, her hair starting to tumble from her pins. It was the look Martin feared he would never see again.

She moved beneath him, the shifting of her hips causing an imperative within to move again. His eyes didn't leave her, watching how her skin flushed and her lips, swollen with his kissed, parted. His strokes grew quicker, his hips pushing against her as she pushed back as eagerly as him.

His moans mixed with hers, something which might have tried to be words but emerged only as primal sounds. As her eyes closed and her head arched back, she tightened around him. It was enough to push him over the edge, burying himself as deep as he could.

The pleasure receded and Martin began to come back to himself, more aware of his surroundings. He was most of aware of Dorothea under him, her breathing still quick as her eyes fluttered open. Reaching up a hand, she stroked his cheek. "I did miss you."

He turned his head to place a kiss in her palm. "And I you. I know we still need to—"

Martin stopped as he became aware of where they lay. "Did we," he asked, each word careful, "just make love on my mother's chaise?"

Dorothea stared at him quizzically for a moment, then began to laugh. "It's not funny," he said, untangling himself from her and backing off the chaise lounge as if it might bite him. "I remember being brought to see Mother before tea in this room and her sitting there."

"Here?" She levered herself into a seated position, one arm draped along the back, her naked legs stretched out seductively atop one another. "Where I'm sitting?"

He would be lying if he didn't say she made a delicious image, hair half-tumbled around her shoulders, reaching almost to her full breasts. The breasts which he had so recently been kneading and kissing. His eyes continued to travel down her lush curves, lingering upon …

Martin cleared his throat, doing his best to ignore the stirrings in his groin. "Perhaps you should recover it, choose a different fabric." His mind scrambling to focus on a color that was as far away as possible from the gold-toned fabric Dorothea was stretched out on, watching him with an amused expression. "Maybe something green -- or red,"

"I was thinking," she said after moment, "I should perhaps re-do the entire room. Different colors, re-arrange the furniture."

"You could buy new furniture," he suggested, "Perhaps a new chaise."

No sooner had the words left his mouth than he realized how ridiculous they sounded, and how silly his panic must appear to her. "You may, of course, redecorate however you like. This is *your* room."

The emphasis was more for him than her, a reminder they were to build themselves a new future together. That included not dwelling with the ghosts of the past because his mother had no wish to change.

Dorothea appeared both surprised and skeptical. "However I like? Any color, any style?"

"I will not say no," Martin assured her. "I want you to feel at home."

"Even if I want to keep the chaise?"

He really didn't want her to keep the chaise. "Of course."

She rose in a smooth motion from the surface of that damnable piece of furniture. "Even if I decided to recover it in, say, light puce?"

Martin began to protest at the idea of the brownish lavender, but stopped when he realized she was watching him with a wry expression. "Your choice, but somehow, I don't think it would suit you." He offered a cheeky grin. "Of course, if you want to order up a length and let Mother think you're going to use that color, go ahead. She might object less to what you do choose."

Dorothea laughed, and he joined in, the sound ringing joyfully in his ears.

He could live with the damn chaise.

CHAPTER 27

The table was set for five, but Dorothea suspected they would be only four. The storm clouds on Martin's face as he joined her in the breakfast room confirmed those suspicions. "She's still swearing she'll depart as soon as can be arranged," he told Dorothea in tight, clipped tones. "However, she's making no sign of asking her maid to pack. Not only that, she was giving instructions as to which gown she plans to wear to Lady Sturbridge's musical evening tomorrow night."

Which Martin needed to attend because the danger Sir Philip might vote for the queen's control of the king's household, not just his person. "I think she's hoping you'll flinch," Dorothea said.

"She'll have a long wait." He glanced toward the clock sitting on the side table. "Roger's going to make them late. He always runs behind time."

Distantly, they heard the knock at the front door. "Perhaps Cecilia will be a positive influence on him."

Farthing appeared, formally announcing, "Sir Roger Phipps and Lady Phipps."

Roger and Cecilia hung at the door of the breakfast room, appearing unsure of their reception. "I'm not happy with you, sister for causing so much grief with Mother."

Cecilia brightened a little. "I couldn't think of any other way to get out of the house that morning without you or her."

She turned to Dorothea. "Would you have stopped me if you knew?"

"Of course," Dorothea responded. "Aside from knowing what grief a scandal causes, I would not willingly go through what your mother hurled at me. I know your brother would prefer not to be out on the North Road hunting for you in a storm."

Cecilia rolled her eyes at Martin. "I said not to look for me on the North Road."

"Which I took to mean 'don't try following us'," Martin said. "I took the phaeton and went after you." He turned to Roger. "This is not the way I wish this happened."

"Nor I. Which is why I tried several times to ask you for her hand."

"Then you annoyed the Prince of Wales."

"Did I?" Roger's expression was skeptical. "Did I somehow cause irreparable damage which could never be forgiven? I said His Highness spends too much. I notice no one disputes the fact. You can always claim I was overly conscious of how much a wife might cost since I had mind to marry."

Martin considered. "He does complain about how much Princess Caroline spends."

"Does this mean we're forgiven?" Cecilia asked.

"No," Martin said at the same moment Dorothea said, "Maybe."

They shared a look. "Somewhat," Martin allowed. "There is still much to be settled."

Settling around the table, everyone glanced at the empty place. "Is Mother—"

"She has not forgiven you," Martin said. "In fact, she didn't want to admit Roger to the house and is furious with Dorothea for extending the invitation."

Cecilia smiled weakly at Dorothea. "I didn't mean to cause you so much grief."

"She was already causing me grief," Dorothea replied. "Your actions brought things to the tipping point sooner rather than later."

"You were right about Mother behaving horribly since we arrived in London," Martin said. "She's convinced everything's been ruined and lays the blame at Dorothea's feet. Roger as well."

The footmen entered with the meal, and the four of them fell silent. There was still awkwardness here, things left unsaid which needed to be said before healing began. This meeting wouldn't solve everything, but Dorothea hoped they would make a start.

Once the food was served, she dismissed the servants with a nod. Another thing they needed; privacy to discuss the situation. Martin began with, "Roger, how the hell did you convince your brother to play a part in this mess? I would have thought his concern would be how this would reflect on him."

Roger seemed a bit chagrined. "Thomas is furious. He understood why I wanted the license in the first place, even agreed it was a sound idea. He was less than happy when we appeared, but I told him if he didn't perform the ceremony, I'd find another priest who was less scrupulous.

He reached out to catch Cecilia's hand. "I need to make amends to more than one person, but Cecilia is worth it all."

Cecilia smiled back at Roger, her face alight. Stealing a glance toward Martin, Dorothea saw him watching the pair with a touch of envy. He glanced toward her, and what she saw in his face made her reach out. To enjoy such strength in their relationship was what she wanted, and she believed he wanted it as well.

"Do you think she'll come down?" Cecilia asked as the meal progressed.

"I don't know," Martin said. "She's talking of returning home, how none of us care for her or need her."

Roger raised an eyebrow. "Dramatic, much?"

"It's not funny. She's so lost in old hurts, she's seeing everything through that prism. I think much of this has been buried for years. Lady Wilmont's presence brought to the surface."

"Aunt Honoria's been in London when Mother Abernathy was here more than once," Dorothea said. "I think the trigger was both of them having daughters they were trying to marry off and Alyssa acting much like her mother did in her season. Including, I believe, going after the man Mother Abernathy had marked out as hers."

"You think that is why she was so insistent I marry the Duke of Stockwood?" Cecilia looked more than a little skeptical.

"No, she wanted as much status as she could secure for the betterment of the family. Alyssa wanting His Grace for herself made her focus on getting you wed to him to the exclusion of everything else."

"Your aunt didn't help," Martin pointed out. "She actively pursued Stockwood."

"To annoy your mother by having him at her table. She believed he and Alyssa would not be a successful match, no matter what his title."

"She is a horrible person, so I think you would understand why I don't want anyone related to her under my roof."

They all stood at the sound of Lady Abernathy's voice, turning toward the doorway. The mask was firmly in place this morning, but the anger still simmered below the surface.

Dorothea made the first move. "Thank you for joining us."

Lady Abernathy glared at her, and moved toward the empty place. She paused to give Cecilia a kiss on the cheek, and Dorothea breathed a sigh of relief. At least she didn't order anyone from the house.

They all sat again, though the silence was awkward. "I suppose we need to determine how best to handle this, since we cannot ignore the fact it happened." Lady Abernathy turned to Dorothea. "You're so clever, madam. What solution do you suggest?"

Her voice was cold, dripping contempt. Dorothea chose to ignore the insult. "Did your letters bring you word about the elopement of Miss Henrietta Hickinbotham with the son of the Marquis of Hampton?"

"I don't see what that silliness is to do with us. They departed for Gretna, according to my sources. At least Cecilia and Roger were married with a proper license and witnesses, though we'll be hard pressed to explain why it was done in such a fashion."

"The couple did not wish to make a fuss, especially as the Prince of Wales is annoyed with Roger for his speech in Commons."

Dorothea smiled at Martin. "One on a long list he's annoyed with, from what Martin's said. As his brother is a chaplain for the Archbishop of Canterbury, they decided to take advantage of the route open to them. We don't mention no one in the family was present."

"Do you think that will satisfy anyone," Lady Abernathy said with a sniff.

"Normally, it wouldn't. But Miss Hickinbotham and Lord Aldus were caught and returned. As long as Martin's name is not revealed as the rescuer, no connection will be made between the pair and us."

Roger chuckled. "I think I should be glad you cannot gain a seat in Commons."

Dorothea smiled at Roger. "Which leaves only the question of how to announce the marriage. Your ball is in ten days, Lady Abernathy."

"No. We shall be cancelling as I don't think I wish to endure the humiliation of trying to entertain the Prince of Wales."

"He'll be the Prince Regent by then." Roger looked toward Martin. "The vote in Commons is tomorrow, so the division in Lords should be the day after."

"Which also means," Dorothea said, "unless he chooses to cancel, you will be one of the first, if not the first, hostess to entertain him as Regent."

Anything would cause Lady Abernathy to gain a true advantage over her rival, it would be this. Dorothea could see the struggle. "Cecilia's dreadful marriage …"

Roger bristled, but calmed when Cecilia put her hand on his. "What better place to announce it?" Dorothea countered. "Present Roger and Cecilia to the Prince, if Martin can smooth the way, ensure His Highness was aware what is happening."

She turned to Martin. "Do you think he would agree?"

Martin tapped the table thoughtfully. "He might. He does enjoy intrigue."

"If the Prince Regent smiles upon the marriage, who is going to whisper against it? The Regency bill is an acceptable reason for Roger and Cecilia to not go on a wedding trip, and the ball a reason to delay further."

Nods from Martin, Roger and Cecilia. They all turned toward the head of the table, awaiting Lady Abernathy's reaction. After a long pause, she said, "It is, much to my surprise, an astute suggestion. Why was I not present, if asked?"

"You had an ague. That is the excuse I used. With Roger and Cecilia back, you can continue to use it as the reason for your absence over the past few days. When you have visitors again, hint at a pleasant secret you're not sharing yet. Something which will be announced at the ball. Everyone will wonder, and another reason for folk to not suspect a scandal. If there was one, wouldn't you want to keep it quiet? With something to reveal, and the newly minted Prince Regent, you make your invitations even more prized."

Another long silence, then Lady Abernathy nodded. "Yes, that does sound wise. Fortunately, we don't have many obligations between now and the ball because of preparations."

She turned to Martin. "Do what you can with the Prince. After the ball, though, I still plan to leave since you've made it clear where your loyalties lie."

Her eyes focused on Dorothea. "Do anything to jeopardize this event or my family and I will ensure you regret the day you were born."

Lady Abernathy rose. "Cecilia, I would like to speak with you. Privately."

Cecilia hesitated, but Roger squeezed her hand. "Go on, love. You owe her that much."

The gentlemen stood as the two left. "I think I may forgive you," Martin said. "You'll endure a lot from Mother before she's done."

"We understood we would." Roger dropped his napkin on the table. "Perhaps I should wait in the hall, in case Cecilia wants to depart quickly. Will you be there for the vote tomorrow?"

"Of course." Martin paused for a moment. "Drink before or after?"

That brought a grin. "Before. After, well, I have somewhere to be." Roger turned to Dorothea. "I suppose I can call you sister, now."

She rose to give him a kiss on the cheek. "I'm glad for that. I'll make certain some of Cecilia's things are sent over today. I'll try to talk to her before you leave, but, well …"

"Thank you for everything, Take care of Martin, will you?"

Dorothea promised she would and Roger withdrew, leaving her and Martin alone. "He loves her," Martin said.

"Loves her enough to endure the rage and insults he knows he's going to receive from his mother-in-law." She met his gaze. "I understand how he feels."

He watched her intently for a long moment. "Do you?" he asked

"Understand?" She laughed. "What do you think I've been doing since—"

"Not endure. Love me."

Now it was her turn to hesitate. There'd been something growing within her for some time now. Something which made her willing to agree to his insane plan to cool the feud, not that the plan ever did anything except bring them closer. It'd also been the reason the idea of leaving London had hurt so much and why she'd held such hopes when they wed. The feeling had slumbered over the past week, but it began to stir again. So why could she not put a name on it?

Perhaps because she was afraid he would not feel the same.

They'd said they would try to be honest with one another, though, and best to say the words and learn the truth rather than wonder. "Yes. I love you."

Dorothea braced herself, for a statement of respect and perhaps even affection. Or a promise to make himself worthy of her while avoiding admitting to any such emotion himself. Then he swept her into his arms and kissed her passionately.

She let herself sink into the kiss, then pulled back. "Do you love me? I'm not foolish enough to expect promises of the moon or deep, undying passion. But do you—can you love me?"

"Yes." He spoke without hesitation. "That night, it wasn't only because I felt a responsibility. If I didn't do something, you'd be sent away and I would never see you again. Perhaps I didn't realize it was love, but my family could survive that scandal. I don't know if I could have survived losing you. I know there is one person I want to walk by my side and that's you. I can't promise you an easy or smooth road, but I will be there with you, as I should have been from the start."

Dorothea's response was to kiss him again, unreservedly. No, it wouldn't be easy, but she knew one thing: she was home.

CHAPTER 28

Cecilia's conversation with her mother lasted ten minutes before the shouting began. Three minutes after that, she stormed out of the house, Roger in her wake. Lady Abernathy only offered a curt, "I do not choose to discuss the matter," in response to Martin's query.

Despite this, she proceeded with Dorothea's plan, hinting at grand news to be announced at the ball to all visitors. She also began taking breakfast in her room, leaving Martin and Dorothea alone with the morning repast. Martin didn't mind, happy for the chance to speak with his wife in the morning without drama. It was certainly better than suppers at home, where Lady Abernathy made it clear Dorothea did not exist, directing all conversation only to Martin.

We just need to get through tonight, Martin told himself as the guests arrived. To his surprise, Lady Abernathy's trunks were almost packed, and word been sent to Abernathy House to expect her arrival several days hence. No, he wouldn't believe it until the carriage was on the road, but it did seem she was making good on her threat to depart.

He felt torn, part of him wanting to tell her she did not have to leave the house which had served as her London home these many years. But he also knew his mother would see his efforts at reconciliation as a sign of weakness to be exploited. Faced with a choice of pleasing her or giving Dorothea the chance to take up her responsibilities as his wife, Martin was going to lean in Dorothea's favor. Mother had made her choice.

"Martin!" The word was hissed by Lady Abernathy who stood on his left side, as far as she could stand from Dorothea on Martin's right. "What is That Woman doing here?"

He did not have to look to know the Wilmont party had arrived. "Dorothea invited them, remember?"

"I will not have——"

"You. Will. The Prince Regent will arrive soon, and he graciously agreed to play along and accept Roger back into the fold. His and Cecilia's marriage will be seen as something being celebrated by the family. Will there be talk? Of course there will be. Think how much more talk there will be if you order my wife's aunt forcibly removed."

His tone was quiet, but intense, using the weapon he knew would work best: social embarrassment. Even so, the struggle was visible on her face before she settled back into her formal smile as the next guest appeared to be greeted. "I'm glad you decided to delay your trip," Dorothea said as she and Lady Wilmont exchanged kisses.

"Given all the talk, I wouldn't miss this. I know you're busy, but if you could spare a moment for me at some point this evening, I will be grateful."

Dorothea assured her she would, and Lady Wilmont moved on to greet Martin. "Dorothea's looking happy," she said, as she considered him. "So do you."

"She makes me happy," he said. "But I think you understand how special she is."

He wasn't certain he had ever seen a genuine smile on Lady Wilmont's face, but one graced it now. "Yes, we do."

With that she moved on, as Martin exchanged nods with Lord Wilmont and Alyssa. Out of the corner of his eye, he noted Lady Abernathy and Lady Wilmont greeted one another politely, if coldly. Social duty was done and they were through that at least. Now, all they needed was the prince.

He was, late, not that princes were ever late. But Martin counted themselves lucky the royal carriage arrived a mere forty-five minutes after they had expected him, and after they had begun to circulate among their guests.

The Regent strode into the room as the family gathered to receive him. "Quite the display," he pronounced as Martin made his bow. "Though, I imagine the credit should rightly go to Lady Abernathy, eh?"

He beamed in Dorothea's direction and she responded with a curtsey. "I cannot claim credit, Your Highness. My mother-in-law is responsible for most of the work."

Lady Abernathy looked at Dorothea with a touch of surprise, but recovered to make her own curtsey. "Your Highness is always welcome in our home, and we are most glad for you to join us in celebrating a most auspicious occasion."

With that, she gestured for Cecilia and Roger to step forward. Clearing his throat, Martin announced, "Your Highness, my lords, ladies, gentlemen, it is my pleasure to announce the marriage of my sister Cecilia to Sir Roger Phipps. They were wed twelve days ago, and it is that we celebrate tonight."

An excited murmur ran through the crowd. Announcing a marriage after the fact was not at all unusual, thankfully. More than one eyebrow had to be raised, though, given Lady Abernathy's pursuit of the Duke of Stockwood. Which was why the next few moments were so important.

The prince scowled at Roger. "I heard what you said about me borrowing money, sir."

Roger bowed. "My only excuse is that I was consumed with the costs a wife would bring, Your Highness. I fear I will not be playing the tables for a while."

"Probably good for you. You are forgiven, for who could be angry with a man who married such a lovely bride. I wish you better luck in your marriage than I." He turned to Cecilia. "Well, madam? As this ball is in your honor, would you open the dancing with me?"

Cecilia sank into a deep curtsey, and rose to place her hand in the prince's. "The honor is all mine, Your Highness."

With that, she let him lead her to the center of the floor as the crowd drew back to give them room. The musicians struck a chord and the music of the first minuet began. "Brilliant idea for the prince to open the ball with Cecilia," Martin said.

"That way, your mother can't take offense I usurped her place. Still think she's leaving?"

"We'll see. Did you have a chance to speak with your aunt?"

"Yes. They're scheduled to depart for Bath on Thursday. Lord Tilney plans to depart on Wednesday, most like so he'll be there when Alyssa arrives."

"That's … worrisome."

"It is, except Aunt Honoria's going to cancel the trip Thursday morning. They'll stay in town and he'll be there. I wager it will take him several days to figure out they aren't coming, and then the return trip to London—"

"And hopefully he'll decide Alyssa isn't worth the effort. Did you come up with this?"

"This is all Aunt Honoria, and they haven't said a word to Alyssa so she can't try to get a note to Tilney. I believe this is us."

With the prince and Cecilia having finished the first figure, Martin and Dorothea stepped on the floor to join them, which signaled others could join as well. For the next several minutes, they moved through the stately movements, gracefully weaving in and out. When the dance ended, the prince returned Cecilia to Roger and stopped for a word, the sign to one and all of acceptance. "Look at your mother," Dorothea whispered to Martin.

He glanced over to find Lady Abernathy looking pleased. The family's honor had been saved, even if Cecilia did not marry a title. But he also realized that was not foremost on his mind, and turned back to Dorothea. "Lovely, but I want to dance some more with my wife."

"We'll cause talk," she teased, but didn't object when he led her out to where another set was being formed.

"Let them talk," he said. "I don't care if they find a happy marriage a scandal. I'm where I want to be."

AUTHOR'S NOTE

First, thank you for reading *The Accidental Viscountess*. I hope you enjoyed Martin and Dorothea's story. They have been with me for quite a while and it's a joy to see them released into the world. I'm a sucker for stories where love finds a way despite folks determined to interfere for their own purposes. If you liked this book too, please leave a review.

While our two couples may be happily settled, the season continues on, stretching into June as the Peninsular War continues. It will soon hit close to home for Lord Blair MacDonald, and he finds himself searching for a bride at the insistence of his father, the Marquis of Rutherglen, in order to secure the future of the line. He didn't count on Augusta Eastleigh, daughter of the notorious Lady Eastleigh, interfering with the process. Their story is told in *To Lure a Lord*, coming later in 2020.

If you'd like to know when I have new books arriving, or enjoy the odd history tidbit, along with a helping of knitting and cute cats, please subscribe to my newsletter. You'll also receive a free short story exclusive to my subscribers.

Until next time, stay safe, stay healthy.

ACKNOWLEDGMENTS

Writing is a solitary occupation, but a writer does not create without the help and support of others. To that end, I'd like to thank the members of Los Angeles Romance Authors and From the Heart Romance Writers, who provided emotional support throughout this process — especially when my life and career took an interesting turn in March of 2019. In particular, I'd like to thank Claire Hoffman, Ophelia Bell, Maria Seager, Claire Davon, Debbie Decker, and Alexis-Morgan Roarke for allowing me to vent, cheering me on, providing a kick in the rump when required, and sometimes just giving me the chance to have a good lunch with good conversation with my fellow writers.

Copy editing services were provided by Lynda Ryba of FWS Media, though I take final responsibility for any errors that slipped through. I'd also like to thank Lynda for her friendship and many sessions at our local Starbucks. Sometimes we'd work, sometimes we'd knit, but I got out of the house and a change of scene is always good.

Cover services were provided by Period Images and blurb work done by Kat Sheridan of Blurb Writer. Great folks to work with, and I highly recommend them.

I must, of course, acknowledge the debt I owe to my parents, who always encouraged my writing, and especially my mother, who, when I was growing up, let me read her own efforts as they scrolled out of the typewriter. Still say you should revise the gothic novel with the mutant monkey paw, Mom.

Last, but most certainly not least, I must thank my husband, Fred. When I left the corporate world, he swallowed his panic and agreed I should take the time to devote myself to my writing. Without his support and love, you wouldn't be holding this in your hands.

ALSO BY CARO KINKEAD

<u>Contemporary Romance</u>

Will You? (Kindle Unlimited)

<u>Non-Fiction</u>

Surviving 30 Days of Literary Madness

<u>Historical Romance</u>

To Lure a Lord (Just a Touch of Scandal Book 2)

ABOUT THE AUTHOR

As a child, Caro Kinkead was told Dr. Seuss' job was "writing books," and decided that was her goal when she grew up - along with being a ballerina and an archeologist and about a dozen other things. A fear of snakes signaled the end of her ambition to find the next Tutankamun's tomb, the dancing (and acting) didn't quite pan out, but the love of writing remained, allowing her to enjoy those varied careers and more in her imagination.

Born and raised in Houston, TX, Caro grew up in a family of readers, where she developed a love of science fiction and fantasy thanks to her father, and old movies and the art of costuming from her mother. These days, she and her husband share a home in the Los Angeles area with their cats, a sizable book collection, and more yarn than she'd care to admit to.

Want to know when Caro's next book is coming out? Subscribe to her newsletter or visit her website at CaroKinkead.com